THE LAST WOMAN

THE LAST WOMAN

A Novel

JOHN BEMROSE

MCCLELLAND & STEWART

LIBRARY AND ARCHIVES CANADA CATALOGUING IN PUBLICATION

Bemrose, John, 1947–
    The last woman / John Bemrose.

ISBN 978-0-7710-1114-6

1.Title

PS8553.E47L37 2009   C813'.54   C2009-901615-X

We acknowledge the financial support of the Government of Canada
through the Book Publishing Industry Development Program and that
of the Government of Ontario through the Ontario Media Development
Corporation's Ontario Book Initiative. We further acknowledge the
support of the Canada Council for the Arts and the Ontario Arts Council
for our publishing program.

The Last Woman is a work of fiction. Although certain aspects of the land
claim described in the novel were inspired by various actual claims around
the country, the book's characters, events, and principal settings are
invented. Any resemblance to the lives and characters of any persons
living or dead is coincidental.

Typeset in Scala by M&S, Toronto
Printed and bound in Canada

This book is printed on acid-free paper that is 100% recycled,
ancient-forest friendly (100% post-consumer waste).

McClelland & Stewart Ltd.
75 Sherbourne Street
Toronto, Ontario
M5A 2P9
www.mcclelland.com

1 2 3 4 5   13 12 11 10 09

For my mother,

Jean Bemrose (née Reid)

(1915–2004)

It is difficult to grasp the sheer scale of Ontario's north country. A place of vast, roadless forests intersected by thousands of lakes and rivers, it ranges from the Great Lakes to the arctic seas, and covers an area larger than France and Great Britain combined. Rich in resources, it supplies wood to the province's mills, as well as metals (nickel, gold, copper, silver, uranium ore) to its industries. Its abundant wildlife is a source of furs, as well as a draw to sports hunters and fishermen who come here from all parts of the globe. Not least, its more accessible southern lakes are a favourite holiday destination. Many people in the province own "camps" or "cottages" here – waterside summer homes where they can enjoy swimming, boating or just "taking it easy."

– FROM AN OLD GEOGRAPHY TEXTBOOK

I see men as trees, walking.

– MARK 8:24

The sun suffers through a cloudless sky. Week after week, it pulses from shoreline rock, floods the lake with glare. New reefs have surfaced – sullen herds strewing the channels – while in remote bays, floating carpets of lily and arrowhead have given way to flats of dried mud.

To some cottagers, the drought seems proof of dire change – some critical shift in the climate, discussed over drinks or at the gas pumps in Carton Harbour, with that secret frisson of anticipation that so often accompanies rumours of catastrophe. But others tell stories of summers just as dry – a reassuring thought, finally, for no one wants life on the lake to change. Lake Nigushi is a place where people come to escape change, to enjoy the kind of summers they and their parents knew in their youth. The plunge from the raft. The Monopoly board or mystery novel on somnolent afternoons . . .

She stands at the window with the receiver pressed to her ear: a woman in cut-offs and a sleeveless blouse, hair mussed from dozing on the couch in the dim room behind her, where the ringing of the phone made its way into her dream. She had been swimming underwater with a book in her hand, and then she flew up, lifted by a crane, cables screeching. And now she is at the window, staring into the fierce daylight with scarcely any sense of how she has got here.

Beyond the screen, smooth, fissured rock pours away from the cottage toward the water. On the next island, pines stand in monumental stillness, their long, upswept branches pointing into a brilliant sky. The light has trans-fixed everything: a piece of driftwood, an empty deck chair, a little colony of dry grasses, all motionless in the heat. It seems to her that nothing can move, will ever move again, the afternoon caught in the paralysis of a spell.

The trees draw past to the rhythmic scuff of his boots. Birch. Cedar. Poplar. A massive pine goes by – green, airy boughs afloat against the blue. Behind him, yet another car is approaching. Walking backwards now, he puts out this thumb. Sun floods through the windshield, lighting the face of a woman in dark glasses. She is watching him coolly, but he knows there's no hope – a woman alone – and before she can blow by him, he has turned away.

Hemlock. Pine. Pine. With each step, his canvas bag chafes his leg. His feet hurt and sweat scurries under his damp T-shirt. The road has been paved since he was last this way – an asphalt runway that appears to stop, in the distance, at a wall of greyish trees. But the wall opens;

there is always more road. Maple. Pine. Birch. He is labouring in place. It is the trees that are walking.

Ahead, the sky has plunged to earth. Picking up his pace, he arrives at a lookout where a rusty cable guards the edge of a cliff. Beyond, past sunken treetops and the roofs of the Harbour, Lake Nigushi unfurls its silver. Countless islands, bushy in silhouette, litter the brilliance. A tiny boat is coming in. Its wake flickers behind it, a burning fuse, while the drone of its engine lifts so faintly it might be a solitary bee, afloat in a field of light. It is as he remembers it: the lake with its thousand bays, its smell of rock and water and pine – the smell of life itself. Far out, in mid-sky, an osprey drifts over an island, finds an updraft, and slowly screws itself upward, into the blue.

The main street of the Harbour is a steady fume of cars. Escaping down an alley, he makes his way along the public quay. The lake has shrunk, he sees: a mud ramp slopes to filthy shallows where two ducks paddle through a shoal of debris. Farther out, new docking extends over the bay and there, where an armada of hulls throws back the blinding whiteness of snow, people – more than he can recall even on the busiest of regatta days – bend to tasks or chat over rails.

He passes an old woman asleep in a deck chair. A police car pulled onto the grass of a small park. Meeting a chain-link fence, he stops, wondering, as he hooks his fingers in the mesh: it was not here ten years before, nor was the new hotel on the other side. Under a scattering of umbrellas a few patrons linger. Nearby, a young woman is setting tables in a state of profound absorption that for a time

4

draws him into its depths, held by the movement of her hands as they lay down the plates like so many cards. When she looks up, startled, he sees himself as she must see him: wiry, brown-skinned, no longer young, in jeans and a sweat-darkened T-shirt, peering like an inmate through the mesh.

Detouring around the hotel, he returns to the water. There is no more development here, though a cluster of signs announces its imminent arrival. A rough track meanders among granite outcrops, passes the remains of a shed, climbs among dusty junipers, and brings him, at last, to an inlet where a steel boat has been moored – one of the eighteen-foot runabouts common on the lake. As he watches, the boat swings a little on its rope, bumps a rock, and with futile stubbornness – a mental patient slowly and softly striking his head against a wall – bumps again.

Billy, is that you? Oh my God, Billy!

Her voice is still in him. Held by its echoes, he gazes past the harbour mouth, to where the low cloud of an island has settled on the water. Behind it lie farther islands, hidden in the depths of the afternoon. In his mind's eye, he can see them all, and the channels that wind between them, all the way to the old cottage tucked among its pines, on the island her grandfather had named Inverness.

His wife is sitting on the deck overlooking the channel, her arms laid along the broad arms of a Muskoka chair, her face lifted to the sun. Richard is certain she must hear them – their outboard racketing down the channel – yet it is several seconds before she turns her head, almost lazily, in their direction. He raises his hand, yet the woman in the deep chair simply goes on looking at them, as if the boat gliding toward her were invisible.

It is this that stops him – the long moment when recognition seems to fail. Instinctively, he touches his son's shoulder, where he sits behind the wheel, and at once, with a violence that startles him, Ann twists from her chair and begins to climb swiftly through the pines toward the cottage. Something's happened, Richard thinks. He cannot take his eyes from her. Sun flickers down her back as she hurries under the trees – and disappears around the corner of the porch.

Minutes later, they find her in the kitchen, chopping vegetables. "So I didn't hit the dock that time," Rowan announces as he marches to the fridge.

"Marvellous!" Ann cries, leaning back against the counter. The boy takes out the milk while Richard, a little on his guard, sets down the lunch cooler. "So have you brought me any fish?"

"*No!*" Rowan intones.

"What, no fish? Whatever will we eat?"

"*Mom*, we've got food."

Richard listens to their banter in astonishment. That morning, wrapped in her terry gown, a very different woman had come down to the dock to see them off. Lethargic, distracted – her state for weeks, it has seemed to him – she stood with her hands in her pockets, gazing vaguely over the water while they readied the boat. Moved by her isolation, he had taken her in his arms, but she was so unresponsive he quickly let her go.

And now: laughing at something Rowan says, she sends Richard a look of such unstinted joy, he feels his face heat. When the boy goes off, she turns to him.

"So it was good today?"

"Yes, yes. Apart from the fish. Too hot for fish, really." He can barely meet her gaze. There is something daunting in her elation, the sense of a demand he cannot fulfill.

Opening the fridge, he is rummaging for a beer when her voice stops him.

"So I have some news for you." She is watching him closely, her pale green eyes fixing anxiously on his. "Billy's back."

It's as if she has pricked him with something sharp, so sharp he cannot feel it yet, though he has watched the instrument enter his skin.

"*Our* Billy," he manages, a light, satiric note.

"He called from that booth at the turnoff. I just happened to be in the house. I didn't recognize his voice at first. I thought it was Dad. I mean, for a second – he called me Annie, the way Dad used to." She is flushing herself now, aware, perhaps, of all her face betrays. "His voice was lower – it really knocked me, to hear him out of the blue like that. More than I would have expected. I've wondered often enough if he was – well, if something hadn't happened to him."

"No such luck, I guess," Richard says, cutting her off. For a long moment she looks at him.

"Richard," she says softly, and her worried, beseeching eyes go back and forth between his, as if one of them might yield the response she is looking for. "He was your friend too."

Sitting in his patch of shade, Billy watches the Ford Taurus descend the rock. Loose metal rattles as it slams into a pothole, speeds up a little, and swings toward the water, where it abruptly stops. The door flies open and a heavy young man gets out to walk a straight-backed, gunslinger's walk to the trunk.

Not bothering with socks, Billy pulls on his boots and limps over.

"Tom," he says.

It is some time before Tom Whitehead stops rustling in his groceries and deigns to look at him. "Well, look who the cat," he says. His voice is adenoidal, snuffling, and in his gaze is a message Billy has no trouble reading. Well,

here you are after all these years: the high and mighty
chief, who screwed up good, as we all knew you would –
needing a ride like any poor Indian, and because I don't
think you're worth the dirt on my boots, I'm going to make
you ask for it.

He asks for it. He wades out and takes a seat amidships,
on a slab of stained foam. Behind him, the boat sags as
Tom heaves himself in. Billy sits motionless as Tom rips at
the cord – rips and rips again while the outboard flutters
dryly. On the shore, the little tree where he was resting
looks increasingly forlorn. You dream of coming home,
but you can never dream the details. The taste of metal in
your mouth as the things you have forgotten come back –
the very things, perhaps, that made you leave in the first
place. Ten minutes ago, half an hour ago, he might have
changed his mind. Even now, he might climb out of the
boat and wade ashore. But he goes on sitting, in a kind of
trance, as the engine flutters and the air grows thick with
Tom's fury. Often he has seen a large animal take a small
one and there is always a moment when struggle stops.
The smaller may still be alive – its eyes glisten and even
look around, as if curious – but it lies still in the other's
jaws, or under its talons, almost at peace it seems, immune
to any notion of escape and perhaps even to pain. He has
wondered at this – what it must feel like – and as the motor
catches and they begin their slow troll out of the harbour,
he thinks of it and not for the first time senses that for
all his time away, he has only been circling this moment
of surrender.

Porcupine. Watson. Stoney. The islands go by in the reverse order of when he saw them last. Then, it was fall: he had huddled in his boat, fighting the waves that surged from the open lake, happy in the way of someone denying unhappiness, pounding his boat on the waves. The land claim was lost, and life had become intolerable on Pine Island. His enemies – the ones who had opposed the claim and the ones who blamed him for losing it – had painted messages on the side of his house. Yet it wasn't the threats that bothered him – they had been pretty much standard coin ever since he and Richard Galuta had launched their claim to the band's traditional territory, a chunk of hunting and trapping grounds that as one newspaper had put it was the size of Prince Edward Island. No, it wasn't the threats, it was the knowledge he'd let his people down. He could see it even in the eyes of his supporters – that flash of hurt and embarrassment, that tactful evasion of him, as if he'd messed himself and it was the better part of kindness to look away. He'd put everything into it – worked night and day for years, though it wasn't just exhaustion that finally caught up to him. It was the sense he no longer knew who he was. Before, he was the man, the chief, who for better or worse was pursuing a claim that, if successful – and he was certain it would be – would put Pine Island on track for generations. But when the claim was lost, who was he? He had spells of dizziness; a couple of times he watched himself at a distance, walking along with his head down. The defeat had gutted him, and though he thought of appealing (Richard Galuta with typical blind optimism had

urged him to) he had lost the will to carry on – even sup-
posing that people would still support him (and he was as
sure they wouldn't as he was sure it wouldn't snow in July).
He had resigned as chief, driven his boat to the Harbour,
climbed into his ancient Chrysler, and headed south. His
plan was to stay with friends in Toronto, but approaching
the city, he found himself in the wrong lane, heading west.
It wasn't so much that he decided to keep going as that he
surrendered to the momentum of the car. On he floated,
past Hamilton, Stoney Creek, St. Catharines. On the bridge
to Buffalo he woke from his torpor. Off to his right, Lake
Erie danced and sparkled, and for an instant he divined
the possibility – the wild hope – of burying himself in the
depths of the continent.

Pine Island dock is crowded round with boats – a mass
of silver hulls set clashing and nodding by their bow wave.
Stepping from boat to boat, he reaches the dock and goes
on toward the small houses. He has the queer sense he
has fallen out of time. It is no longer 1986 – or rather not
just '86. It is '76, and '61 – it is all those years and none – a
single inescapable moment in which he has always existed
just here, with the sun on his neck and the coarse sand of
Pine Island beach gritting under his boots and before him,
hunched on the rock, the familiar houses with their glare-
blinded eyes. Some are well kept, flowers sitting out in pots.
Others – more than he recalls – have slipped into neglect.
Roofs patched with garbage bags. A punched-out screen. In
the shade, a bicycle has been set upside down. One wheel
revolves slowly, as if brushed by a passing ghost.

He crosses an area of treeless bedrock. On the far side sits a small blue house half-buried in cedars. A padlock has been affixed to the door and it is as if he has met something that contradicts his idea of reality – an exception to the laws of physics. He stops. He stares at the house. You hear that someone is dead. You weep. You think you know: he's dead. A piece of broken glass to be carried in your chest. Sometimes you forget it's there. Then you move a certain way and, without warning, it cuts again. Putting down his bag, he climbs the steps and takes the cool, heavy lock in his hand. Tugs at the thick hasp. Retreating, he steps through bushes to a window. Inside, sun has lit the end of a table and a few scattered chairs. Down the side of an open cupboard, several postcards have been stuck with pins. They are curling a little, but he can just make out the turquoise sheen of the Caribbean. The white body of a shark. He counts five. *Surely there were more!* Hands cupped to dusty glass, he peers into the shadows of that familiar room, searching for more.

Against the wall of his tent, Rowan's shadow looms, shrinks, writhes – a shape-shifter trapped in a dome of red light. Detouring from the path, Ann stoops before the meshed doorway.

Her son is poised on his knees with his back to her, under the cone of light falling from the suspended flashlight, hands raised like an evangelical receiving a blessing.

"Honey?" She has to speak twice before he turns. "What are you doing?"

"I'm killing mosquitoes."

"Are you feeling all right? Do you think it would help if you –?"

"I don't want one."

Ann hesitates. Perhaps he has no need of a pill. Every summer they take him off the Ritalin. Usually, Inverness supplies all the calm he needs, but today the place has not accomplished its usual magic. It had started at supper – talking a mile a minute while she and Richard made worried eye contact across the table. She suspected their time on the water: too much sun, maybe, and Richard not always as sensitive to the boy's moods as he might be.

"It'd make you feel better."

He lunges at another mosquito. "*Shit!*"

"Rowan!"

"Sorry! I don't want a pill!"

"I'm not saying you *have* to –" For Rowan hates his medicine and she hates fighting Rowan. The boy is frowning up at her now, waiting for his oppressor to leave. She knows he might be up half the night – tomorrow a misery of exhaustion, for all of them. And yet: the tug of her painting is nearly irresistible.

It came to her just minutes ago, at the kitchen sink, a flash in which she saw it whole: not the painting she has been struggling with for weeks, but a new one. It was as if a door had opened and she had glimpsed the drama behind the placid surface of things. A massive, naked figure waded knee-deep through a crowd of smaller figures, in a boiling light: a sense of epic conflict, and at the same time ecstasy – there at the kitchen sink, seeing everything, with a dripping plate in her hands. Giving up the battle with Rowan, she hurries down the path to the boathouse.

Inside, the beam of her flashlight picks out her red canoe, adrift in its bay, finds the screen door to the stairs, and precedes her up the steep well where, with the flick of a switch, her long, multi-windowed studio leaps into existence.

On her painting wall hangs a portrait of a seated woman roughly her own age, in sombre oils, her expression distracted – on the verge of some troubling awareness. Behind her, outside a window, a girl is hanging upside down. Her pigtails droop past her head and her eyes have fixed angrily on the woman in the chair.

This painting, Ann has come to feel, is a failure. She finds its drama unconvincing, and it is layered with so many corrections that the oils have built up into a kind of bas-relief map. "Great texture," Richard has commented, in the same tone he might say "Great bod" of some passing woman. But texture by itself is nothing, she knows; texture's a scam if a painting doesn't live.

Putting it aside, she drags out a much larger canvas, strips away its plastic cover, and stands back to contemplate the white, gessoed blank.

She was asleep when he called – dozing on the leather couch where she had lain down after lunch, "just for ten" as she so often puts it to herself, in the comforting illusion she is free to sleep as little or as much as she likes. Sleep is her frequent companion these days. Sometimes she will go back to bed after breakfast – *just for half an hour* – then wake to the stark light of midday. It is worse in winter, in their Black Falls house, where she feels the pull of hibernation.

She hides her habits from Richard and Rowan, guilty and ashamed for all the time she spends in bed. It's her father's death, she tells herself. She's still working through the grief. She has had him much on her mind these days: his presence so strong at Inverness. His tools in the boat-house. His hat collection – the baseball caps and berets and Stetsons and straws hung on pegs along the hall. Richard has suggested, gently enough, that it might be time to retire the hats, but she hasn't got the heart for it. She suspects that she's still, in some way, waiting for him to come back. And maybe that was why, when Billy called, she thought he was her father. Against all reason, for an electric half-second, Charles had come back.

But no – a moment of confusion, followed by a surge of emotion: Billy.

It had been two years since his last postcard: that picture of the Grand Canyon, addressed to them both. Richard had no time for Billy's cards – he would toss them aside in a fit of angry dismissal, and she learned to keep them to herself. The two men had quarrelled after their defeat – she had guessed that much. But the details remained a mystery to her, for her husband would tell her nothing. As for Billy, she'd never got to ask him, because he had left soon after the decision came down – left without calling her. She would not have expected this, for she felt she and Billy had their own friendship – a corner of tenderness they preserved as their right, a thing as old as their childhoods. Billy had no phone, and when she called Billy's sister, Yvonne told her Billy had gone south for a few days. Three weeks later, hearing nothing, she called again. Billy was in Pittsburgh, Yvonne told her. Why Pittsburgh? What came back was a verbal shrug: "Well, you know Billy." No, Ann did not know *that* Billy, who could turn his back on her like that. "He's all right then?" And Yvonne said, "Seems to be." And fell silent.

Then Billy's first card arrived, followed by others, at intervals of months or even years. His messages were the kind a tourist might write, brief descriptions of sights, of weather, of anything he happened to be looking at. She sensed there was a kind of ironic joke in them, for him: he was masquerading as an ordinary traveller, though at the same time the pictures he chose were suggestive – she did not always know of what. The kitten creeping away from the spilt milk was obvious enough. But what was she to make of the cigar-store Indian with a Hawaiian lei around his neck?

In the long periods between bulletins, she contemplated his absence with a sadness that became habitual – indistinguishable, in many respects, from the lethargy that increasingly gripped her during those years. She might not actually think of him for days at a time. But then, prodded by some chance occurrence – the flash of an obscure channel between islands – he came back with a force that often surprised her. She couldn't imagine the life he was living; at times, she wondered if he was alive. And again she would try to talk with Richard about him, for it seemed – and she knew this was irrational – that it was their quarrel that kept Billy away, and that if she could in some way bridge the distance between them, if she could soften her husband's hostility, or assuage his hurt, if he was hurt, she might effect some change in a situation that threatened, she feared, to become permanent.

What she had lost, what *they* had lost, she believed, was not just a friend but a way of life. For during the years of the claim, when Richard and Billy were close, it seemed to her that something rare had settled on their lives. Triangles were supposed to be unstable, but for those few years when they were in their late twenties it seemed theirs was the exception: a balance of friendship and, yes, she would say it, love, where jealousy and rivalry had little part. She had never painted better than in those years. Never been as free, for so long, from her periodic glooms. As for Richard, he had never seemed more engaged by his work, more eager to embrace new experiences. His friendship with Billy (which at first she had been skeptical of, for what good could come of a liaison between a former lover and her husband?) showed her a side of him she'd never seen: he became more relaxed, more given to outbursts of unguarded exuberance. After Billy had hired Richard as the band's lawyer, he often stayed overnight at Inverness or at their Black Falls house, plotting strategies. She remembered the topographic maps they taped together and spread on floors, the boundaries of the claim sketched out in pencil and finally, Magic Marker; the vista of lakes and rivers bearing coffee and tea rings, pizza crumbs, notes added by Billy in his awkward hand. House and cottage were often full in those days, as visiting scholars and native leaders stopped by in support of the claim. There was a sense of excitement in the air, of energy put to some higher use – for it seemed to her that they were not merely claiming the old hunting and trapping grounds of Pine Island, they were helping right the old, continuing wrongs perpetrated against the country's original inhabitants.

Billy and Richard seemed never to tire. They would talk half the night, and though sometimes they argued, their bond of dedicated bonhomie seemed only to strengthen. The next day, after Richard had left for the office, Billy would rise late, and he and Ann would talk over coffee. They talked about the situation on Pine Island, where Billy had made a number of enemies by pushing for the claim; they talked about Billy's chronically troubled relationships, of which there were more than a few in those days. Listening and offering advice, Ann played therapist with the benign presumptuousness of one who had once been his girlfriend herself. She knew him, she felt: his gifts, his faults, the burden of his moods. Their own affair, started and finished at nineteen – long before Richard came on the scene – rarely came up, but she felt its presence as a ground of intimacy in which their relationship had sunk deep roots.

Sometimes, Billy and his latest, along with Ann and Richard, would eat at Lacy's in Black Falls; or they would fly down to Toronto for a weekend of shopping, a film, a hockey game. Ann could remember walking along Bloor Street beside Billy's current flame, while the two men strode along in front. Richard was a Leafs fan, Billy followed Montreal – and they were arguing over the merits of their respective teams. Richard, at six-four, with a rugby player's build, towered over the slimmer Billy. When they began throwing hip checks at each other, first gently, then with increasing exaggeration, the effect was hilarious. Egged on by the laughter of the women, the men marched down Bloor Street bumping hips.

And then, after the claim failed, after their work of years had gone up in smoke, they had, it appeared, fought in earnest.

"Why won't you tell me what happened between you two?" she cried once to Richard. "I mean, how bad can it have been? So you quarrelled – it was almost to be expected, wasn't it? You were both exhausted, Richard – and then that awful decision came down. People can't go on blaming each other for a few harsh words." As she spoke he shook his head and smiled in that gently superior way he sometimes adopted: she didn't, *couldn't*, understand. "Say something, for God's sake," she pleaded. "Nothing to say," he said, his voice strangulating a little. "Water under the bridge. There was tension between us for months – through a lot of the trial. I never really told you how bad it got. Then we had this blowup. These things happen, Ann. I really would thank you to let it go."

"But if you could –"

"Ann. *No.*" His fierceness shocked her. His ordinary manner was swift, ironic; light. But something else showed now: an anger that reddened his face and seemed to lodge in her chest. She did not ask him about the quarrel again.

Pouring herself a tumbler of white wine Ann goes into the living room and sits, impatiently flipping through a magazine. She can take nothing in but surfaces – the thin, elegantly clothed women fly by like hoardings glimpsed from a speeding car. She is back in her studio still, with the pages she filled with preliminary sketches, with notes, with measurements. Throwing the *Vogue* aside, she sits in a trance. It is some minutes before she notices, through the open front door that leads into the screened porch, her husband working at his table. He sits with head propped on his hand as he writes, his big, sunburned face tilted a little, frowning under his drooping forelock – a hint of the schoolboy, sulking at his lessons. At supper, he had acted with a blithe, faintly wounded nonchalance: Billy's return was nothing to *him*. Swept with affection for him – for whatever burdens he carries in secret – she goes out to him.

"Rich, let's swim."

"We'd be eaten alive," he says mildly, not looking up.

"Not in the water. Come on, Rich, we haven't for ages. I really want to." For suddenly she does: a swim is something they absolutely *must* have. "We're turning into workaholics. Don't you want to swim naked with me?"

"Always," he says. But he goes on filling the margin of a page with his quick, tiny hand. Nearby, his computer makes one of its periodic whines, like a mosquito, and she

can sense the immense pull his work has for him. Often
he will not come home from the office till eight or nine,
and weekends hardly exist for him. She has never quite
got used to this, and though she is convinced she loves
him, she worries they are living their lives in distant par-
allel. Leaning forward, she playfully flips shut his book.

"Honey. This case –"

When she retreats to the kitchen it is not so much with
a sense of rejection as of waste. He doesn't understand
what she's offering: she has joy again, she has energy – no
telling how long it will last! At loose ends, she peers
through the screen toward Rowan's tent, like a giant
boulder in the woods. She scrubs furiously at a stain on
the counter. When Richard appears from the hall, she is
on her hands and knees, struggling to unstick a drawer.

He seems amused by her frazzled state.

"*What?*" she demands.

They go out naked with their towels, through the porch
and down the rock still warm from the day's sun. In the
dark, the path is a little strange, ghostly pines lit by the porch
lights. The deck is nearly invisible and the channel itself is
a blackness off which the faintest hint of coolness rises.
"Well," Richard says, dropping his towel beside her. He
plunges in with a tremendous crash while she stands on the
deck, watching the flashes of water as he swims out into
the dark. Then the noise and flashing stop: he has vanished.

"How is it?" she says.

He does not answer.

"Richard?" Is he playing some game? "Richard!"

"What?" Gasping.

"Nothing. How is it?"

"Beautiful. What's keeping you?"

She does not know. A mosquito brushes her cheek. Idiot, she tells herself: wanting, not wanting. She knows she *will* dive, she *will* join him, but something's holding her back. Off in the dark, past her husband's pale, waiting head, a ripple gleams.

The mortar and pestle stop him, as so many things in the blue house have stopped him. He picks up the little porcelain bowl. Inside, a few dark grains give off a smell of flowers. At once, he sees Matt kneeling in the shade of a tree as he carefully unearths a root. His uncle handled his plants with the no-nonsense tenderness of a good doctor. Sometimes you could hear him murmuring to himself or to the plants, or singing bits of some old song in Ojibway, his lips scarcely moving, so that Billy, watching him as a boy, felt that the song was not coming from him but from far away, from underground, maybe, or from the frail plants themselves. Matt simmered his concoctions on the stove, ground them into powders, put them up in jars:

medicines for his arthritis, for sick people on the Island. Birch for pain. Rosehips for colds. People would come to the door in the night, and Billy, waking, would hear him go off. He'd always intended to learn some of the old lore himself one day. But now: he puts down the pestle. Knowledge, a life's worth, snuffed out by the side of a road.

After their mother drowned, Billy and his sister had come to live in the blue house. Matt was their great-uncle – their grandfather's brother. He and Emma had no children of their own. They were different from his mother, a thing he had trouble getting used to, for he never knew what his mother would spring on him next – a blow from the sky, a rain of kisses. Matt and Emma's steadiness unnerved him. He kept wanting to yell, to hell around, to break things. He didn't trust their goodness. And maybe there was something in him that needed a harsh word or a beating, that craved the justice or injustice of it – it hardly mattered which – just to staunch the craziness that buzzed in him. Yet no matter what he did – and years later, he would cringe to remember – the harsh words and beatings never came.

After his sister moved out, Billy lived on in the blue house with Matt and Emma. In the winters, they ran a trapline from their cabin at Silver Lake; in the summers, he and Matt did building and repair work at cottages around Nigushi. Working with Matt calmed him. The way Matt took his time when he measured a board or the way he pondered where they should hunt – taking days if necessary, while he watched the weather and the plants, and waited for the right thought, the right dream, to guide him. It drove Billy wild at first, though in the end he had managed to take something from it – a deeper patience, an alertness that showed him more detail (that twig where a moose had nibbled) than he had known existed. The calm wasn't permanent though, and it didn't run all the way through. He might be sitting in a bar, a ball game murmuring from its high corner shelf, while before him his third beer offered a forgetful afternoon, and under the table, his foot would be going like sixty. There were things in him he couldn't explain and didn't like. An energy that chased itself. Ideas he couldn't shake. Sometimes he thought he'd been born into the wrong life. He should have been a soldier, a boxer, the man who swung the wrecking ball.

One time in Atlanta, he worked for a painting company that did shoddy work. The foreman was always after his men to hurry up, hurry up, and one day when Billy was angrily slopping paint up a wall the thought of Matt came to him – his patient, careful strokes, the hint of humour in his face, as though he knew it was finally pointless to take so much care with a wall; after all, the paint would peel one day, the wall would fall down; but it was a kind of game with him, and a point of pride, to put up a good job in spite of everything. Disgusted, Billy quit on the spot.

Drifting to Savannah, he went to work in a boatyard, scraping hulls. One night he went to a party in a house on the edge of town. Upstairs, on a bed covered with coats, he dialled Pine Island and heard his sister's voice tell him that Matt was dead. He had hitched into the Falls, she said, to pick up some things at the hardware store. On the way back, his first ride dropped him at the Red Lake turnoff and it was there, while he was walking along the shoulder, that someone had struck him and not stopped.

Billy had made his way outside, into a yard that over-looked the river, under a close, leaden sky torn by the roar of a jet. Half the world had broken off. He could feel the ragged edge running inside him; it was out there too, in the dark over the river, an absence that sucked at whatever was left, a regret so violent he pitched against the fence and vomited. He could not stop thinking that if he had stayed home, Matt would have lived, because he would have given him a ride to town. They had taken the trip together many times: winter, a blaze of snow, Hank Williams on the tape deck, and Matt beside him in his fur hat with the flyaway lugs, eyes shining in his kind, leathery face.

His boat sits upside down on logs beside his house. People – kids, he supposes – have covered it with insults, threats, crude images of monsters, several shitting bums and outsized cocks, a fish drawn with surprising skill – a crowded catalogue of the Island's hates and longings in green, black, pink, and yellow paint. Apparently painting his boat has become a local sport. Working with a scraper, in a couple of hours he manages to clean a quarter of it.

At noon, he looks up to see his sister strolling across the rock – his big, wide-shouldered, older sister, in her purple slacks and sleeveless blouse, skipping with a

sudden girlish lightness over a crevasse. The previous
night he'd sat with her and her husband, Eddie Stokes,
telling stories into the wee hours, while her two little ones,
Brenda and Pascale, slept entangled on the couch. After
ten years away it was strange to be there, at the familiar
table with its blue and yellow specks, under the placid
countenance of the same plaster Mary perched on the top
of the fridge, laughing about Terence MacDonald's piles
as if he'd never been away. Part of him had wished he was
still on the road.

Yvonne has brought him his laundry, the shirts and
jeans still warm from the dryer. He carries two chairs
outside and they sit in the shade of cedars, talking. Her
eyes, so startling in their blueness, keep drifting to the
lake, and when she sighs for the fourth or fifth time, he
sits bolt upright in irritation.

When he asks if he can borrow her boat, she looks at
him as if she can't remember who he is.

"Earth to Yvonne," he says, laughing.

"So where you off to then?"

"Get some groceries." He shrugs, a show of nonchalance. He plans to drive down to Inverness; but he will not
tell Yvonne because she will jibe him about Ann, as she
had last night. When he asked after the Scotts, she'd commented, only a little sarcastically, "So ten years hasn't cured
you?" But she'd told him her news that wasn't really news,
since he had already learned most of it from Ann when he
called her from the turnoff. Ann's father dead. And they
had a son now: Rowan. *They.* In his fantasies, he would go

down to Inverness and find her alone, as he had at nineteen, but they were still together –

Another sigh escapes his sister. "Things aren't so good around here, you know."

"Were they ever good?" he says quickly, grinning. It was how he was with her as a boy: joking away the shadows.

"Up north there, the traplines? It's all clear-cut now. People are sick about it."

He hunkers, determined not to get drawn in. Yet the whole cast of the day has changed. They had laid claim to that land. He had tried for a cash settlement too – some bands were getting millions. They would start their own businesses, build new houses, a new school.

"Some families –" she says.

"I *know*," he says sharply, warning her off. He has seen the broken bottles. The smashed windows. She doesn't have to rub his nose in it.

"Kids are sniffing gas," she says. He looks at her. There had been no gas on Pine Island ten years ago. Booze, yes, the usual weekend binges. But gas! He has seen what gas can do, and anything else with solvents in it: kids slobbering about like sick old men. "Jimmy's doing it," she says. "I tried everything, Billy. He won't listen to me. I was wondering, maybe when you been back a while, if you could speak to him. He always liked you."

"Doesn't Eddy speak to him?"

"You know how Eddy is – old school." Old school: letting the kids learn on their own. If you put your hand in the fire, then you wouldn't do it twice. But there had been no gas in the old days. There hadn't been a good many things.

That afternoon, he puts on a fresh T-shirt and jeans and goes down to the dock. Finding his sister's boat, he starts the motor and backs away until he can head into open water, an unspeakable relief: to feel the cool breeze on his face and know that, behind him, Pine Island is rapidly receding.

The first time he met Ann Scott he was nine. The previous winter, Matt had taken him trapping. For two weeks, during the Christmas holidays, they had lived on Silver Lake, in a cabin so heaped over with snow that only the door and window could be seen, among silent snow-laden trees. Each morning he had woken to the sound of the dogs growling and fighting as his uncle got them ready. Then pancakes and fried meat and tea and porridge and Emma telling him to eat more: it was cold out there. And the morning moon, white as if cut from paper.

He was Billy Johnson, the son of Corrine Johnson and someone else who, he was to realize years later, must have had a different name. It was hard to think about a father you had never met. There were no pictures of him in the house, and his mother did not speak of him except sometimes, when her mood turned (it could happen any time, especially if she'd been drinking); then she might grab him by the ears and tell him that he looked too much like his father. Afterwards, he would stare at his face in the mirror, wondering what parts were like his father. His nose? His stinging ears? He wanted his face to be like his father's, and not, for when his mother was drunk it was hard to tell what was good and what bad. She could flip the world over in an instant, and where a father might have been was nothing.

They were living then – he and Yvonne and their mother – in a small house among the main crowd of houses overlooking the dock. That afternoon he had escaped – run over to Matt and Emma's house, for no particular reason he could recall later, except that he felt safer and happier there than at home. Pushing through the screen door he saw a girl with pale hair cut straight across her forehead. She was sitting at his usual place at the table, watching him almost defiantly, as if she *knew* she had taken his chair and was waiting to see what he would do about it.

The door tapped shut behind him. Someone else was here – a man in a plaid shirt, a string of smoke spindling upright from the top of his head, who turned to regard Billy. Matt was at the table too, at his usual place, while Emma stood by the stove in one of the full white aprons she had made from flour sacks. All of them turned to him in a silence that seemed to spread from the deep shaft of sunlight through which the girl watched him. "You must be Billy," the man said, and Emma, stripping off her apron, said, "Come and have a scone."

Pulling out a chair, Billy sat beside the girl. Across the table, the man in the plaid shirt winked at him, as if sharing a secret, took a pull on his cigarette, and with slitted eyes expelled smoke that floated toward the ceiling and hung there, like the bough of some blue, spreading tree. The girl's hand reached out, took up a scone, and withdrew.

After a while the man – her father? – suggested the two of them go outside and play. The girl got up immediately, and when Billy did not move, she turned at the door and sang back to him, "You coming?" In a trance, he followed. Years later, she would tell him: "You were such an odd boy. You would hardly say a word. I was starting to wonder if you were mental!"

He would tell her he was terrified.

"Of what!" she would say, delighted. More than three decades later, he still does not know, though he can recall the sudden lightness of his body as he followed her into the sun. She wore a pink T-shirt and shorts, and when they stopped by the water, she looked at him with a directness he had never experienced from anyone, as if she had no shame, no fear, no notion of what might happen (what *would* happen?) if you looked at someone too long.

"My father owns a lumberyard," she said, as if setting out an object for his inspection. Her shoes and socks were white; there was a bandage below her knee. "What grade are you in?"

He could scarcely remember what "grade" was.

"Can you talk?"

He nodded.

"So say something."

"I go trapping," he managed, in a voice he hardly recognized – his answer to her comment about her father. Since he did not have a father, what emerged was that *he* went trapping, though it was Matt who handled the traps. But he had helped Matt pull the drowned bodies of the beaver from under the ice, helped rub them with snow, and he had ridden on the sled as the dogs ran panting for home. Trapping – it was the most important and precious fact he could offer her.

She went on studying him, amused, it seemed, by his answer, or by his inability to say more. Then at once, her hands flashed out – he found himself sitting on the ground. She had run off, but she soon turned to contemplate him. "So chase me!" she demanded. "Don't you know *anything?*"

He chased her: along the rock, across a sandy beach, up a narrow trail between boulders to a clearing where lush, flattened grass grew. While he stood hesitating, she flung herself down. The grass, he knew, hid pieces of glass where people had smashed bottles: here and there the shards stuck up like brown knives. "Sit next to me," she told him, patting the ground. Warily, he crossed to her and sat.

On their backs, they watched the high clouds that made their way in from the lake and seemed, directly overhead, to form the banks of a deep white canyon with the blue sky at its bottom. An osprey slowly circled, and in the warm air above their faces a moth went fluttering by. He hardly dared moved. He felt he had arrived in a place that was so precarious it might vanish at any moment, like when the sun made a trembling, golden map on the panelling at the foot of his bed; or when he opened *Adventures of Olden Times* and – moments before his teacher took the book away – found (as he never found again) the picture of

St. George on his horse, tilting his lance as he galloped toward the dragon with its pine-cone scales.

When she gasped, he sat bolt upright, as she had, and stared, as she was staring, at her open hand. A thick red worm was oozing from her palm.

Meeting her terrified gaze, he seemed to see her for the first time. Her lips, pulled taut, revealed a gap between her front teeth. Her tears made glistening snail tracks through her freckles. But it was her eyes that held him. Washed of all confidence, they brimmed with something he would never have expected: a plea for his help.

He led her to the blue house, where Emma took down the box with the bandages and iodine. He knew what had happened was his fault, and the others seemed to feel that way too, for Matt was silent and Emma was mostly silent (she joked a little as she placed a pad and wound the tape) and her father, watching the proceedings through a scrim of smoke, was the most silent of all. The girl would not even look at Billy – she, who had looked too much, was acting as if he wasn't in the room.

Later, slipping outside, he watched their boat grow small across the bay, and when he could no longer see it, he ran out to Gull Point to catch it again. But the channel, dark as blueberries between the islands, was empty.

His mother sat painting her nails, touching the tip of her tongue to her upper lip as she applied the bright red lacquer.

"So I hear you got yourself a girlfriend," she said, pausing to examine her work.

Yvonne, making supper at the counter, said, "You promised not to say anything!"

"I never said nothing – what did I say!" his mother said, smirking. His mother was beautiful – everyone said so. Billy himself thought so. He liked to watch her when she was singing along with the radio, the way she pursed her lips and seemed to blow the words out. She sang as well as Dinah Shore, people said; she sang solos in the church choir. She would sing as she danced slowly by herself through the kitchen, jabbing at the air with her hips. Sometimes Billy danced with her. She would pump their arms as she whirled him around the room. But he had to be careful, because things could change. She might decide she didn't like the way he was dancing. She might think of something somebody said to her last week. But when the change came, mostly he didn't know *what* had caused it. She might suddenly slap him, in a rage: he would go off in tears, saying, "What? *What?*"

The word *girlfriend* shocked him. The boys who hung around the dock had girlfriends: that was the meaning of all that pushing and laughing; the meaning of going off by twos into the bush. His mother had boyfriends. They appeared in the house without warning. They ignored him or demanded to know what he was up to. And his mother might say, "He needs a father. Don't you, Billy?" There was no answer to that; for no man would stay for long, he knew it better than she did.

Now there was a new one: Hooch Robinson. Billy had even less use for Hooch than he did for the others, because of the way Hooch swaggered around the house and poked a sharp finger in Billy's shoulder, demanding to know if he was the real McCoy. A few weeks ago, Billy had ridden in the back seat of Hooch's convertible to his house on the Black Falls highway. Hooch and his mother went inside, leaving him in the car with four baskets of blueberries set out on the hood for sale. He had sat for a long time behind the wheel, pretending to steer, while transports blew past and Hooch's dogs yapped in their pen behind the house. Finally a pickup had driven up, and a man in a black undershirt had got out. Taking two baskets, he drove off without paying. Billy went into the house to tell Hooch, but Hooch and his mother were busy. For some time he stood in the hall, listening to the sounds they made, the chuckling of the bedsprings, the banging of the frame against the wall, then he walked out of the house and down the highway. After a while, Hooch and his mother drove up and his mother got out, her hair all crazy, and demanded to know what he'd done with Hooch's money. Then Hooch got out and kicked him. Then Billy's mother said no one kicked her boy and she kicked Hooch. Then, his tires screeching all over the road, Hooch drove off.

They walked home. His mother stalked ahead of him and when her heel broke, she swore and threw both shoes in the ditch. She told Billy she was going to send him to his aunt in Manitoba because he had just cost her the best man she'd ever had. But when they got to Carton Harbour, his other mother appeared. She bought them cones at Whitbread's store and they sat on a bench watching the boats go by. "I hope you go farther than me," she said. Billy looked up. She seemed to have spoken to a passing sail. "You want to be one of the smart ones," she said. "A doctor, eh? An airline pilot. Not like me. I had to drop out of school when I was sixteen – go to work in the mill. Not like me." She took another lick of her cone. "You don't get far without that piece of paper." Billy wondered what piece of paper that might be. "You listen to me," his mother said. Her voice had taken an edge. "You do your homework. It's important. You got that?" Billy nodded, and for a while they sat in silence. "I always loved books," she said, gazing out at the Harbour. "You got *that* from me at least."

The next day, Hooch called. Soon his mother was singing around the house again – Hooch was back in her life – and now, for Hooch, for the date she had with him that evening, she was painting her nails. And telling him he had a girlfriend.

But he had no girlfriend – not if his mother was a girlfriend, not if the girls at the dock were girlfriends. Whatever he had, whatever had happened to him, was different. There was no word for it; he didn't *want* there to be a word for it; and anyway, what did he *have*? He didn't have anything, at least not anything that anyone including him could see or touch. A feeling in his stomach. The memory of the girl's hand reaching out to take the scone. The memory of the back of her arm brushing his, as they lay beside each other in the grass. As soon as he could, he went back outside. A long red cloud pointed across the sky like a banner. Sitting on a rock, he watched as it shaded to pink, then dark blue, a shadow over the channel where she had driven off with her father.

For days afterwards he felt the lifting of a weight he had become so used to he didn't notice it until it was gone. Now it almost didn't matter whether his mother got drunk or yelled at him. There was a place in him she couldn't touch. He spun until the trees whirled above him. He ran like mad through the bush. Using the jackknife Matt had given him, he gouged a deep mark in a pine; then he gouged another one beside it. The sap made a mess of his knife and his hands, but he felt he had done something that would hold the thing he feared was already slipping away: the feeling that something better than he had ever known was about to happen. *Had* happened. It was fixed there now in the gashes, like two yellow eyes in the dimness of the trees.

Then one day, surprising himself, he swore at his mother. She smacked him and demanded to know what had got into him. When he shouted at her, she smacked him again, and again, and still he came back at her, shouting – shouting for more, really, craving her blows, something hard, definite, for the girl had left him with nothing.

He drifted back to his friends, to the usual swimming and fishing and hanging around the co-op. Still, from time to time, he thought of her. It was hard to remember what she looked like. What came back was a feeling. But it was not the old excitement, the old sense that everything was going to get better. It was the fear he had felt when they first stood together in the sun and he was unable to answer her. For moments at a time, it could stop him completely, as if she was again waiting for him to produce an answer that (if he could only have found it) would have made everything turn out differently.

He travelled around the lake with Matt, who did work for the summer people. They built steps, hauled away rubbish, delivered firewood. He would sit perched up in the bow, watching the cottages draw past. When he saw white kids playing, he always looked for her; but Lake Nigushi with its endless maze of islands and passageways kept her hidden.

One day, they approached a cottage he had not seen before. High on the rock, half-hidden by pines, the old house seemed to be aware of them, almost, to be watching from the deep, shadowy recesses of the screened porch that wrapped it on two sides. On the dock, a red canoe had been overturned.

They were met by the man he had seen at the blue house. As he led them up the path, Billy kept looking at the cottage, but they were soon walking away from it, down another path to an open place where lumber and bags of cement had been stacked.

Later, while Matt was busy measuring boards, Billy crept back to the house, moving stealthily along the screens of the porch until a soft, rhythmic creaking stopped him.

Someone was rocking in a hammock. Then came a thud, and a figure appeared, dimly, behind the screen.

She vanished and a few seconds later came around the corner of the cottage. "Look," she said, thrusting out her hand. In the centre of her palm was a small white scar, like a fishbone. It was like the moment when she had told him her father owned a lumberyard: here was a fact. What was he going to do about it? Leaning forward a little, he peered at the scar. He could not tell whether she was blaming him for it or boasting of it; whether there was something about the scar he couldn't see or understand, something obvious that, if he missed it, would throw him back into the unhappy place of her disapproval. She snapped her hand shut.

She led him down the path to the boathouse, into its dim interior and up a steep flight of stairs to a room brightened by many windows. From a large, green table cut in half by a low net, she picked up a flat thing with a handle.

"Pick up your paddle."

He thought it wasn't much of a paddle. He held it as she was holding hers. Her tongue came out, the paddle flicked, a small white ball came hopping toward him. He watched as it hopped off the table onto the floor.

"You're supposed to hit it back."

Okay, he knew that.

On the floor, digging in a corner, he swept the little ball toward her. But it bounced off a table leg. He scurried on all fours, scraping it frantically between her legs. Then he stood up, grinning, his face hot.

"That's not the way! Do you know that's not the way?"

In a flood of shame, he crossed his eyes, twirled on the spot, and fell down: dead.

She squealed and picked up his foot. Laughing, she dragged him across the floor until finally she dropped his leg and stood looking down on him with her hands on her hips. "Want to draw?"

On a low table below the windows were stacks of paper and cardboard, cans of crayons and coloured pencils, a huge tray of watercolours. They sat side by side on two stools, making pictures. He loved art, his favourite class at school. He loved it when Miss Kilkenny handed out the big, white, stiff pieces of paper on which he might make anything, anything.

"What's that?" she asked him, after a while. He had drawn a tall, wide-shouldered man emerging from a tree stump – stepping out of it with a grin.

"Nanabush."

"Looks like a man to me. Not somebody's Nana."

"He is a man," he said. "He changes himself into things." He pointed. "He changed himself into a stump so he could catch some ducks."

"Why is he red?"

Red had seemed right. Now he wondered if it was wrong.

He came back the next day with Matt, and again they painted. She made a picture of a girl in a multicoloured dress facing a line of mountains with her hands up. Her skill astonished him – he could not draw so well himself – but the detail that absorbed him most, that made him look up at her, as she frowned at her work, was that the girl's skin – her arms and legs and the backs of her hands – were bright red.

They went into the cottage. The rooms were dim, cool; she sat on a couch of green leather, patting it to indicate he should sit beside her. "This is our living room," she told him. She pointed at the tall shelves. "My father's books. A lot of them belonged to Grandpa and Nana. Grandpa's dead. Nana can't come up here any more. She's in a nursing home." He looked around at the shelves, the pictures, the red and blue regatta ribbons pinned on a wall, the newspapers heaped on a low table, the patterns in the worn rugs, the stone fireplace where under the mantel three dark stones made a kind of face. The place was still and cool; the ceilings were far away. A smell of pine wafted from the wood box. He had never been in such a house before – its spreading rooms – rooms behind rooms where the daylight glowed mysteriously. And all this was her.

In a room off the hall, he saw a big bed with posts, a rumple of sheets. "My parent's bedroom," she announced. She flipped a switch and overhead the blades of a fan began to turn, wafting a breeze onto their lifted faces. He laughed for no particular reason – for delight, for relief, for amazement that the world contained such things. "You're funny," she said. She was beaming at him with pleasure; he wondered if he should try falling down again. Her eyes, he saw, were the same colour as birch leaves when they first came out.

For the rest of that summer, while Matt was building the new guest cabin, the only days that counted were the ones he spent with her. She had not told him her name, though hearing her father call her Annie, he knew what it was. She called him Billy, or Billy-Billy, or some such nickname she made up on the spot, delighting them both. But he did not call her anything. And yet, when he was alone, he spoke her name. On Pine Island, he breathed it south, over the water, in the direction of her cottage. Her name had a power.

Sometimes, on the days he didn't go to her cottage, he feared she had forgotten him. Yet each time when he arrived with Matt, she was there to greet him, prettier and odder than he remembered – the oddness centred in her eyes, which held, for all their playfulness, some suggestion of sleep.

Through July and August, the new guest cabin rose among the trees. Sometimes, they sat and watched Matt work, or did simple jobs. As she bent to pick up a board, her pale hair, almost as pale as the wood that opened under Matt's saw, swung down. When she rolled down the edge of her shorts to examine a mosquito bite, the whiteness of the untanned skin astonished him: it almost didn't look normal.

One day she took him up to a room on the second floor. Piles of books, a bed, a birdcage with paper birds inside, a Hula Hoop, a pair of skis, a photo of a woman in a tiny skirt, poised on tiptoe, a huge blue bear with one eye missing – fragments of her wondrous life, its entirety too large to see. She threw herself back on the bed, just as she had thrown herself on the grass that day, and bounced, legs loose and flying, in a solitude of pleasure.

One day he found a fisherman's plastic float that had washed up – a little red-and-white ball. Teasing, he refused to give it to her and they ended up wrestling on the ground. Grabbing her wrists, he overpowered her.

"Okay," she said, lying still.

He let her go. He did not get up right away but continued to straddle her, and for a little while, out of breath, they looked into each other's faces. Later in the summer, when the guest cabin was finished and he no longer went down to Inverness, this is what he would remember: how she had looked at him in perfect stillness, perfect seriousness – all her mischief disappeared – in the green stillness of the afternoon.

As he idles along the shore of Inverness, it glides above his boat – the deck that had not existed a decade before, with its deep wooden armchairs and low table where someone has left an overturned paperback, a glass containing a slice of lime. Up the slope of rock, the old cottage rotates behind its pines. The dark veils of its porches, the needle-drifted roof, a little window tucked high under an eave, all turning to fix him, placidly, as he swings around the point and, his engine burbling on a lower note, approaches the boathouse. No one seems to be around, though their boat is at the dock. He is just tying up behind it when, up at the cottage, the back door opens and Ann emerges onto the steps. For a long moment they simply regard each other, across the little bay where a few lily pads rock in the aftermath of his wake. Then she starts down the path toward the boathouse.

Behind her, the door opens again and a copper-haired boy appears, with Richard towering behind him. They, too, take Billy in, until – Richard tapping the boy on the shoulder – they set off after Ann.

Her gaze as she strides out the dock meets his directly. There are dark places under her eyes. His memory of her, he realizes, has faded, as the worn photo in his wallet had faded – the photo-booth picture they took at nineteen, her face under its level bangs confronting the camera without expression. At once she is restored – not the Ann of nineteen, or even of ten years ago, but a woman of strange familiarity. "You!" she cries, mock-scolding. "You were supposed to give us some warning." Then she is in his arms: the brief shiver of hair along his cheek, her body against his. Pulling back, he sees she is tearful. "You've gotten so skinny. I thought those southern women knew how to feed a man."

Too soon, the others are there. "Look who I've found," she says to the big, sunburned moon of Richard's face. As he takes Richard's hand, Billy is surprised by a rush of affection – a sense they had had some good times, done some good things, after all. But the grasp of the large hand is brief: Richard steps away. "And this is our Rowan," Ann says, bringing the boy forward. Richard's big bones, but Ann's eyes, peering shyly from a round face. Rowan also takes Billy's hand, pumping it with an exaggerated earnestness.

They go up the path together. Ahead of him, Ann's calves flex as she treads the carpet of pine needles – past the cottage and down through trees toward the new deck. "My father built it two years ago," she sings back to him.

"Just before his stroke," Richard adds from behind. "I guess Ann told you he passed away."

By the time they reach the deck, Rowan is no longer with them. Billy and Richard sit while Ann picks up the glass and book from the little table, then stands before them, taking orders for drinks: radiant, he thinks. Her gestures – that way she throws out her hand, as if presenting some entertainment, a bit ironically – are the Ann he knows. That nearly invisible mole over her mouth –

Both men watch her go off, uneasy at being left.

"So," Richard says. He is wearing shorts that reveal his thick legs; his big arms rest along the arms of his chair, and he gives off an air of worried seriousness Billy cannot remember. "I want to ask what you've been up to, but that's an impossible question – impossible. We'll get it out of you as the night goes on – you're staying for supper, no arguments. Put some weight on you there."

"I don't know," Billy counters, glancing at Richard's stomach. "This seems a dangerous place for a man."

"Occupational hazard," Richard says, patting his modest paunch. "Too much fast food in the office. No, I can't blame this on Ann: she's always rationing me on lettuce and tofu. Make a rabbit of me."

"So you're prospering," Billy says.

"Everyone needs lawyers, it seems. 'Kill all the lawyers,' Shakespeare says, but I take it as significant that no one has. We had to move out of that house downtown – we're out at the Plaza now. Great spot. My office overlooks the old fields. You can see *deer* sometimes," Richard says, raising his eyebrows as if this revelation might interest Billy especially.

Billy has to make an effort not to look at the cottage. "Too bad about Ann's dad –"

"Yes! Yes." Richard's eyes close. "It's been pretty hard on her – you know how she was about him. But cancer – it was a mercy, really." Their conversation keeps breaking off; their old fluency is gone, broken by silences that are increasingly awkward. Richard keeps frowning distractedly over the water, as if more important business were awaiting his attention. A boat goes by. Both men look up, and as it swings into a gap between two islands, Richard launches into a story about a woman on the lake. It seems a non sequitur – told for no reason Billy can see except that Richard tells it well. He listens to the tale of love gone wrong, the woman's cottage burned down by a rejected lover. Now and then Richard pauses, with a suggestive, penetrating glint of his small eyes: Billy's cue to laugh. He can barely smile. At the conclusion, Richard chuckles himself and, after a well-timed pause, delivers the denouement: "The moral being that justice comes in unexpected ways."

Billy plucks at the leg of his jeans. The remark cuts too close to home. Is that what Richard intends? Surely after all this time, they can put the claim behind them. Another boat is approaching. Again, they both look. "That the Schonfelts?" Billy says, as it plows off. Frowning in his grave way, Richard tells him no. "So many strangers on the lake now. We've sort of been discovered." They both fall silent again, as the wake from the new boat smashes on the rocks.

It is a relief when Ann appears with her tray. She has put on a dress of some light material, her shoulders bare under thin straps. As she stoops over the low table to pour their wine, the tops of her breasts are momentarily visible. Flushing, Billy looks away.

Sitting in another of the deep chairs, she leans toward him. "All right now, tell us *everything*. That last postcard? You were on the Caribbean –"

He gives them his best story, about the time he went snorkelling: the striped fish, the yellow fish, shimmering past in clouds; the great eels drifting out from their lairs, with their heads like dogs. He had been fascinated by the barracudas – silver torpedoes hovering motionless, then pivoting on the spot like compass needles. "I had this urge to go over and touch one. Wanted to stroke it."

"You *would!*" Ann cries. "He was *always* wanting to touch things," she tells Richard.

"Indeed," Richard says. "So what were you working at?" A flash of shrewdness, as if he has guessed what Billy has avoided telling them – that, for the most part, he was working at bad jobs for poor pay, when he was working at all. The job that took him to the Caribbean had been an exception. He had crewed on a millionaire's boat, and he spins out anecdotes of the rich man's eccentricities: the way he liked Billy to take him out in the Zodiac to feed the dolphins. The late-night confessions at the ship's rail. Increasingly, he talks with a heartiness he does not feel. For what, after all, does he have to show for his time away? A roll of twenties in his pocket. A few stories.

Richard grills steaks on the gas barbeque behind the cottage. In the kitchen, Ann chops vegetables. Billy drifts between them, trying to make a show of evenhandedness, but with Richard the conversation still goes haltingly. Escaping to the kitchen, he plants himself beside Ann. She tells him about her father's time in the hospital, and when she becomes weepy, he reaches out and squeezes her bare shoulder. "Look at me," she says. "Here I am going on about Dad – but Matt! We were *so* upset. We put flowers by the road. There were lots of others. I went up to the Island for the funeral. Richard wanted to but he had to be in Toronto that week." She tells him about the ceremony in the packed little church. The hymn-singing – so moving – and old Betty Clearsky moaning in her pew. And the new priest who kept mispronouncing the Indian names. "He spoke pretty well, considering. But it was odd – so much history in that room, and of course he didn't know any of it."

He watches her knife making pennies of a carrot, adrift with thoughts of Matt.

"He always taught me to kill cleanly," he says, apropos of nothing. His throat is hard and he has to pause for a moment. "Better to pass up on a shot than make a bad one."

She is looking directly at him – holding his thought, perhaps expecting more. But something in her attention daunts him; he feels he has nothing more to offer her, nothing commensurate with his experience of Matt, or with what she deserves, and on the pretence of hunting for the wine bottle, he turns away.

They eat on the screened porch where the sun casts a flickering archipelago on the inner wall and makes of Rowan's face a living mask. Beside the boy, Ann's arms and chest quaver in the light. She is telling Billy about their trip to Paris, and is more than a little drunk, Richard thinks. "The Louvre!" she exults and lifts her glass. A bit of wine slops. She was entranced by the late-medieval work: the saints and Christs and gold skies that to Richard seemed two-dimensional, almost primitive. They had inched down the high, endless corridors, from room to stuffy room, from frame to frame, from saint to saint: Richard soon bored but glad he had given her a gift she valued. He had taken her to Paris to cheer her up; and for

that week, she seemed years younger, keen to walk everywhere and see everything, keen for a student's lunch of
bread and wine on the islands, keen to prowl Père Lachaise
and the Luxembourg. But back home, after an initial burst
of work, she had been waylaid by her old fatigue, her old
sad drift, and had applied her usual remedies: wine and the
swearing off of wine, jogging and therapy and meditation.
The spark lit by the Louvre had seemed well quenched, but
now he hears for the first time what their trip meant to her:
"I love how they ignore perspective, time – I mean, Jesus on
the cross, and over his head, *in the same painting,* a window
showing his birth in Bethlehem, or the Annunciation. They
felt free to put in anything – make the mind jump around.
I want to try something like that."

Beside her, Billy has leaned back and placed his hand on
the back of Ann's chair, with what seems to Richard a show
of casual possessiveness. Still smitten, Richard observes. As
for Ann, she seems oblivious to everyone but Billy; she
laughs excessively at his stories and keeps pouring him
more wine.

"So what's your next move?" Richard asks dryly, in a
lull. "You thinking of guiding again –?"

"Thought I'd try at the Blue Osprey," Billy says, removing
his arm from Ann's chair. Suddenly he seems tired, wary.

"Well, it's a different world there now," Richard says.
"Golf course, tennis courts, high-end customers. Very
impressive, actually. Gerald's work – Jack died about five
years ago. Not sure if they're still in the hunting and
fishing line –"

"I think they *are*," Ann says. She turns to Billy. "I'm not sure you'd *want* to work there. The place looks like Disneyland."

"The lodge was on its way down," Richard persists. "Gerald's really turned it around. He's got a lot of out-side money behind him, big development firm from Toronto."

"Mafia," Ann murmurs darkly.

"Well, Italian," Richard says, with a grain-of-salt glance to Billy. "They've laid out a beautiful course."

"He *golfs* now," Ann announces.

"She refuses to believe we're actually members of the middle class. So what's the matter with golf?" Richard says. He is smiling, though in fact he is irritated by her jab. It is an old thing of hers, behind which he recognizes a heartfelt criticism: that he is *so* bourgeois, while she is – artistic, he supposes.

Reaching for the wine bottle, Ann does not answer. Billy has fixed unhappily on his plate while Rowan, lost in his own world, tortures a bean with his fork. Richard surveys the failing party with grim satisfaction: he had not expected better. "Hey, Row," he says to his son. "Tell Billy about our fishing trip."

"We didn't catch anything."

"We drove over to Pointer's," Richard tells Billy. "That shoal between the islands – it's all dry land now. But I thought some of the deeper water looked good."

"Huh," Billy says.

"It's the drought –"

"It's that golf course," Ann says, coming out of her

reverie. "They've got these monster sprinklers," she explains to Billy. "They're pumping out millions of gallons."

"Not millions, not every day," Richard says. "In normal circumstances –"

"Well, these aren't normal circumstances, are they?"

Richard shrugs as if indifferent to the point while she goes on about the drought, mainly to Billy, in a tone that makes him feel uncomfortable: as if she were holding him responsible for the state of the lake. Billy, too, seems uneasy. He barely murmurs in response, and soon afterwards announces he'll be shoving off.

They walk him to the dock. A flat-sided moon has turned the channel to foil. Richard watches as his wife and Billy embrace. Then Billy sets off, his wake sparkling behind him as his boat carries him down the channel and out of sight.

Later they do dishes together. Conversation has failed, and the only sound is the splashing and clunking of dishes as she scrubs.

"It was good to see you and Billy talking again," she says after a while. "I thought the evening went very well –"

"Hardly surprising you would think that –"

"What do you mean?"

"If you can't see it, Ann."

"You're upset," she says, straightening at the sink.

Turning to put up a glass, he struggles to suppress his anger. Under the weak overhead light, the kitchen suddenly seems a poor, depressing place, with its worn floor and battered counters. He wills himself to icy calm. "Look. I'm not questioning your right to friendship, I never have. But you *know* we've been estranged. It was hard to sit there and watch you *dote* on him like some kind of –" Stopping just in time, he takes a dish from the rack. "And maybe you had a wee bit too much wine?"

"Ridiculous," she says sharply. "So you'd rather I cold-shouldered him? You've never even deigned to tell me what really happened between you two."

"You know that's not what I'm talking about."

"What are you talking about then?"

She turns to him, eyes blazing. The fierceness she can summon astonishes him: a force that seems to come from outside the Ann he knows, from outside the recognized bounds of their marriage.

"Maybe just a little moderation?" he says. As soon as he can, he escapes to the porch and resumes work. Some minutes later Ann goes by. He does not look up, but when she passes out the porch door, he glances through the screens just in time to see her descend the steps. She is wearing nothing but a towel slung over one shoulder. Dimly, he feels her nakedness is directed at him – a pale weapon in the night. Seconds later comes the crash of water as she dives in. Flicking over a page, he tries to go on working. But his concentration is gone. He can hear her swimming briskly into the channel, then silence – silence that stretches on for several seconds, broken only by the distant lap of water. He peers out. His wife is a strong swimmer, but still –

After a while, the faint chop of her stroke resumes as she swims off.

Rounding the corner of a house on Pine Island, Billy finds Fred Plante standing in a blue hospital gown, smoking. Fred had not been old when Billy left; now the man's hair is white – as if old age has come upon him in a single night, like plague out of the bible. His hand trembles with the cigarette he lifts to his mouth.

Billy stops, respectful. This man knows as much as anyone on the Island: bush lore and stories and family history. It was said that long ago he killed a man. "Killed his man," as people put it, as if for every man another man was reserved for just that purpose.

"You escape from the hospital, Fred?"

"Rather die out here," says the rasping voice. "Ten minutes out here worth a year in there."

They stand without speaking. Billy feels no particular discomfort: on Pine Island silence is as much a form of communication as words. Billy has nothing to say, and perhaps Fred doesn't either, but how will they know unless they wait for a while? As if prompted by the same thought, they both turn toward the lake, where, far off, a few gulls are circling. "My grandfather had a dream," Fred says, and pauses to take another drag. There are ordinary dreams, and there are dreams that float up from the heart of things – dreams told to few and handed down like heirlooms. For a while Fred squints toward the lake. "When all the trees are gone, the people will be gone too."

Fred tosses away his butt and for a few seconds watches it fume beside a rock. "But then what did those old farts know anyways, eh?" He shuffles away, leaving Billy with the sense the remark was aimed at him. By launching the claim, he had ignored the advice of several elders. Others, includ-ing Matt, had supported him. The divisions had spread until a kind of civil war had infected the Island. Friends had stopped speaking to each other. Old feuds took on fresh momentum. Apparently, it isn't over yet. He watches the old man go off. In the open back of his gown chevrons of fat, spotted with bedsores, quiver with each step.

———

As the days go by, Billy has the deepening sense that something's coming unstrung. The sun isn't just hot, it bites. The lake doesn't *look* right. Passages between islands have turned into pastures of dried mud. There are new animals in the bush, new birds in the sky: the old folk talk of it constantly. Several times he's woken to the cries of people drinking and fighting; once to the stertorous roar of a chainsaw – no good sign at four a.m. And in the morning, blood on a rock, licked by a dog.

Yes, something's unravelling, something so old, so basic, so taken for granted, so beyond the power of ordinary words to describe, that now it's coming apart, people can only feel angry and confused.

And yet, the limpid evenings come as always. Out on Nigushi, the islands drift in purple and mauve. He thinks of Ann Scott often. In the kitchen, as she wept for her father, he had touched her shoulder: he can still feel the coolness of her skin. She had told him they were going to Black Falls the next day. Rowan was starting hockey camp. Richard had his usual appointments. He thinks about Richard – this new, substantial Richard, pompously aloof one minute, genial the next. Over dessert, Billy had caught him gazing at him, those small bearlike eyes bright with some unreadable emotion. Richard had looked quickly away.

Yvonne throws a barbeque to welcome him home. People sit around the yard on chairs while the smell of burgers floats from the grill. Billy sits chatting with friends, pleased to discover he still has a few on Pine Island. His niece, Brenda, wants to play catch with a beach ball. The little girl laughs when he lets it bounce off his face and runs off to twine herself around her father's legs.

On the high porch overhead, the kitchen door opens and slaps shut.

"Jimmy!" Yvonne calls. "Come down and see your uncle."

Billy's nephew was three or four when he left. Now, looking up, Billy sees a long-haired teenager peering over the rail. A good-looking, smooth-skinned face. Widely set eyes – Johnson eyes. As the boy comes down the stairs, Billy gets to his feet, galvanized by a sudden sense of youth, family.

For a while they make hesitant small talk. After a few minutes Jimmy collects a handful of sandwiches and drifts off to an empty chair. His nephew wants to be an underwater engineer, Yvonne has told Billy. "There were some divers working on the lake last year – something to do with one of the wrecks. I guess he got talking to them."

Billy watches the boy as he eats – the way he keeps drawing back his hair, with an almost girlish fastidiousness; the way he stops chewing and stares, abstracted, into space. After a while, Billy moves to a chair beside him. "So what the heck is an underwater engineer?"

At first, Jimmy does not respond. Then a foggy adolescent's voice sounds. "Like if they're building a bridge, the underwater engineer designs the parts that are underwater. Or if they're going to blow up a bridge, he has to go down and look at the underwater parts – tell them where to put the dynamite."

"So it involves diving?"

"I did some last summer."

Billy waits for more, and when it does not come, he tells his nephew a little about his own diving experiences: the red fish, the blue fish, the barracudas pivoting like compass needles. The boy appears to be listening, but after a few seconds, his attention sinks away. "So you have to take training, I guess." Blinking, Jimmy looks at him. "To get your diving papers – you have to take a course or what?"

"Lots of courses."

"You need high school or –" Yvonne has mentioned that Jimmy talks all the time about dropping out.

"I guess. Yeah."

Another silence falls. His nephew's isolation seems deeper than a normal fourteen-year-old's. There is something stunned in him, Billy thinks. Remote from life. He has the boy on his mind the next day as he works on his boat. When Yvonne drops by, he asks, "You sure he's doing gas?"

"Sometimes he gets these sores around his mouth. Or you can smell it on him." Minnows of light flicker over the hull. "There's a whole gang of them. A year ago they were all good kids. Then something happened. I date it from Ross Shewaybick."

He has heard about Ross, the boy who hanged himself.

"Why do you think Ross –"

She shakes her head. "It was Jimmy who found him. Up there at Pepper Point. I don't think he's ever got over it. He won't talk about it – just gets mad." The minnows go on swarming. "Sometimes I think there's something they see, these boys. Something they can hear, you know, calling to them. You can't argue them out of it. They don't hear you."

He knows what it is: the dark place. He knew it when he was young, even before his mother drowned. He knew it worse afterwards – the thrill of coming close to it, without letting it take you. In some moods you felt you could play the game and never be caught; in others, you didn't care.

The next day, driving his boat onto the lake, he heads for the Blue Osprey. He has never liked crossing the open lake – Nigushi six miles wide at this point, hundreds of feet deep – but it's the shortest way to the lodge. Around him a vast silken calm spreads toward the crayon stroke of the far shore.

Off to his left, a gull flaps up. Its beak is open, and though his outboard muffles all sounds, he seems to hear it cry out.

The December afternoon before his mother drowned, she had danced him around their tiny living room. "Tonight's my night," she told him. "I got a feeling in my bones." He had witnessed these eruptions of optimism before and knew they came to nothing. When she said that tonight was her night, she did not mean finding a man: finding a man was no trick at all for a beautiful woman. She meant finding a man who stayed, a man she *wanted* to stay: a good man, in other words, not like Donny Pace, who had broken her arm, or Hooch Robinson, whom she'd caught stealing from her purse, but a man with some kind of steadiness: a man you could count on to do the ordinary things with you like eating or shopping without turning them into some test of his power or a chance to put you down.

She had caught a ride into Black Falls with Bart and Mary Simmons, who ran the post office in Carton Harbour. They had dropped her at the Rendezvous – so he discovered many years later when he read the police report. By then, he was familiar with the Rendezvous, with its bolted-down chairs and metal mirrors – a windowless, low-ceilinged place where you never knew what time of day it was and the golden pitchers of beer rose and fell like the pistons of some slow-motion destruction machine. She socialized in other places as well, better places, and why that night, given her mood, she had chosen the Rendezvous was one of the many questions he would never answer. Others had noticed her there – "Intoxicated. Danced with several partners" – but according to the report, no one had seen her leave. The report picked her up again at the Harbour, where someone happened to see her trudging by through a light snowfall. By then, she had already walked, the report surmised, from the turnoff – a distance of six miles; and she had eight more miles to go, by the shortest route, over the ice. He could barely bring himself to think about the next part of her journey, for she was on her way back to him and Yvonne. They had gone to bed expecting they would wake to her, or at least to a phone call, as they had so often in the past. While they were sleeping, their mother drowned.

He could see her trudging over the ice that had little snow cover yet, though there must have been enough to disguise the hole that was waiting for her. The night was mostly overcast. Perhaps a few stars had shone inter-mittently, and in the snow's glow she must have made out the dark thin reefs of bush along the larger islands, the gleam of light from a cabin. She was wearing boots and carried her dancing shoes in her purse. But she must have been cold in her skimpy coat, the wind cutting, and perhaps it was this and not alcohol that had disoriented her, the cold settling too deeply. Perhaps she was singing to herself to buoy her spirits. What he could not bear was seeing her, in his mind's eye, progress toward the faintly steaming slit in the snow, while he was unable to cry a warning.

They had not found her until spring. He was not allowed to see her, though her white coffin was set at the front of the church, with a bunch of evergreen on its lid. The priest, old Father Donahue, spoke of her at some length: he had known Corrine Johnson his whole life, he said, he could remember the hot summer night she was born. His kind, rough voice went on, describing the time she was chosen to play Mary in the Christmas pageant – and what a fine Mary she was, he said. Listening to him, Billy glimpsed a mother he didn't know, who'd had another life as a child, as a young woman who one day, kicking off her shoes, had plunged into icy water to save little Peter Squance. Who was this person?

Afterwards, he followed her (what they *said* was her) in her white coffin along the trail to the graves. It had snowed a little that day, idle flakes disappearing on the coffin lid, among the crosses and spirit houses, among the gloomy pines, with the choir singing in their red robes. Standing between Matt and Emma, he and his sister watched her go down into the ground. But he had not seen her and did not entirely believe it was her, and so for a long time afterwards, in certain moods, he would watch the lake, remembering how she had told him that one day she would find a good man; and she might go off with him for a while – this man who owned a nice house, who would buy her nice clothes. And then (he could depend on it), she would send for him.

The Blue Osprey sits at the end of a long bay – a rambling log structure overlooking a lawn where twin poles fly the flags of the United States and Canada, drooping in the windless air. He walks up a brick path and passes through the front doors into coolness, the lustre of distant skylights. Others are here, but they are not the fishermen and hunters he remembers from the old days, in their plaid shirts and assorted caps, with their gun cases and tackle boxes and cartons of Molson Ex. These patrons wear tennis whites and golf clothes. They hurry through the lobby with their racquets, or drift out of the dining room where the checked cloths have been replaced by white, and the stuffed head of the moose has disappeared from above the stone fireplace, and the waitresses bustle through a setting of white and cream, of tinkling water and tropical leaves, bathed in music so soft it is possibly an illusion.

A young woman clutching a handful of menus hurries toward him. Baring her teeth, she flicks a glance down his body to the boots he blacked that morning with a burnt stick.

"I'm here to see Gerald Spicer."

"I'm not sure he's in right now. Perhaps you could come back later?"

"Why not check," he says quietly. "Gerald and me go way back."

He enjoys her hesitation, enjoys the defiant flicking of her ass as she hurries upstairs. As he waits, a middle-aged couple stops outside the entrance to the dining room.

"Just go on in," he tells them. He meets the woman's startled glance with a smile.

In a few minutes the hostess is back. She directs Billy to the second floor, where an open door leads into Gerald's office.

"Billy Johnson!" Gerald cries, rising behind his desk. Jack's son: the remote young man grown into this crisply authoritative fellow in dress shirt and striped tie. Behind him, a picture window, like some glowing aquarium, reveals the green, sunstruck expanses of a golf course.

Gerald's hand is damp, his smile brief, rabbity, under his trim moustache. Offering Billy a chair, he returns behind his desk. On the wall beyond him, where Jack's photos of hunt camps and fishing trips used to hang, is a large colour shot of racing cars, herding through a bend under an orange sun.

"So what do you think of it?"

"Ah . . ."

"All the changes!"

"Impressive," Billy says.

"Totally changed the name of the game here, whole new type of clientele. I loved the old lodge, but it just wasn't cutting it any more. We decided the time was right to go upscale, really put some money into the place. People still want to think they're getting wilderness, but they don't want to put themselves out too much – go figure. So we sell what we call the northern experience – great food, luxury accommodation, golf, tennis – all in the same great surroundings. Of course a few still want to go fishing and so on. We take care of them too. How you doing, Billy?"

"Good."

"Good. Excellent. You've been away for some time. What, a couple of years now?"

"'Bout that."

"How are things at home? It's been some time since I've been to the Island. How's your big sister?"

He tells him everything's great.

"Good!" Gerry's hands are rapidly fiddling with a bit of paper, twisting it up and pulling it apart. Billy misses Jack's old, dim office; he misses Jack's stories, spun out to the accompanying clink of bottle on glass. Jack's way of doing things had been so relaxed and off-hand, he hardly seemed to be working.

"Say, sorry about your uncle!" Gerry says, looking up suddenly. "Sorry – I forget –"

"Matt."

"Yes, Matt. Tragic, really. My dad was very fond of him, you know. One of the best guides we ever had – really something, I guess. So – what can I do for you, Billy?"

"Was wondering if you had anything in the guiding line."

It is all he can do to say it. He feels *that* close to walking out. Now he watches Gerald's face change, its surface animation gone smooth, blank, as he fixes on the paper in his hands. The other man has gone away to where he keeps his true accounting; and in that place, there is no room for Billy Johnson. There is something shameful about this, for both of them. For a few seconds they can no longer even pretend they are connected. Glancing at him, Gerald tosses aside the paper and says in a more serious voice, "You have to realize, Billy, that the emphasis here is different. We're not really wilderness any more, whole area's changed. I'm not saying we don't take people out, but hunters and fishermen are getting to be a rare species, around Lake Nigushi, anyway. All the changes – the clear-cuts – well, I'm sure you're well aware. Now – we still keep a few guides on call. It's not steady work, of course, but we'll certainly keep you in mind."

Murmuring a vague response, Billy stands, relieved to be finished. His face is hot, and as he heads for the door, he doesn't realize, at first, that Gerald is still speaking to him: "I'd really like to show you the place." As they go down the stairs into the lobby, Gerald points out the teak front doors ("dropped five thousand bucks on them"). Outside, he insists Billy see the course. Boarding a golf cart, they hum down an asphalt path toward the green glow of the fairways. "This is a Phil Waits course," Gerald tells him as they draw up on a knoll. Before them, as far as they can see, sprinklers fling long, shuddering plumes over the grass. Billy does not know who Phil Waits is, but he catches the pride in Gerald's voice as he explains how he and Phil worked on the design together. He keeps glancing at Billy, eager for his approval, it seems, and though Billy responds with an occasional nod or grunt, there's such an air of unreality about it all, such a feeling of bleakness, that he has trouble staying focused. And the sun beats down on the emerald fairways; and the sprinklers go on shushing and jiggering; and the sweat is prickling inside his shirt.

An hour later, arriving at the Harbour, he walks to Whitbread's store. A new cement-block extension runs into a field, but the old country storefront persists, its tall show-windows plastered with the week's specials. Taking a cart, he heads toward the produce section. *When the trees are all gone, the people will be gone.* For some time he stands without moving, as other shoppers push past: Fred Plante's words opening a vast space, invisible to the eye, but felt – a chill fleeing over it like a breeze shivering the surface of a lake.

A minute later, he sees Ann Scott at the pharmacy counter. She is talking to a clerk and at first doesn't notice him approach.

"Well!" she says, colouring.

"Thought you'd gone back to the Falls."

"I've got a painting going – couldn't leave it." She goes on watching him, as if trying to make out exactly what or who he is; after her warmth at Inverness, he is taken aback.

He waits while she makes her purchase, then they go outside, into the sun, and walk to Lola's restaurant, where they take a table on the empty deck. She has put on sunglasses with outsized frames, which give her the look of some exotic insect. He asks about her painting.

"Here's Lola," Ann says, and for a couple of minutes they deal with Lola.

"How's your painting?" he persists, after the woman goes off.

"It's so fragile at this point. I can't really say much about it." For a moment she is silent, then the huge dark eyes fix on him. "It was good to see you and Richard talking again." She pauses, and when he doesn't respond, she tries again: "I know things weren't good between you when you left –" He shakes his head. He does not want to talk about Richard or the land claim. He does not want to revisit the past. He wants to reach out and remove her glasses.

"You know, he's never really told me what happened –"

"I may have said a few things," he allows, shrugging. "We were both pretty angry. Upset." He feels cornered, resentful. For some time they sit in silence, drinking the coffee Lola brings in thick china cups.

"You haven't been happy, have you –"

He shifts in irritation. Happiness: people are always going on about it, about their right to it and their search for it. As long as you're happy. Makes him sick, really.

"Why did you stay away for so long? Was it the claim, or –"

"I don't know, Ann. Why do we do anything? You go into a city, you get a job or you don't get a job, but somehow, you live. The sun shines the same as here. It didn't seem to matter where I was."

"Sounds like depression," she says. Another of those words, the opposite of happiness, a place with neatly defined borders, to be escaped at all costs. "I've come to know something about that."

"Didn't realize you'd missed me that much," he says.

"Things go flat," she says, ignoring his joke. "Nothing means anything. There were times when the only reasonable thing – well."

He looks up, alerted.

"But then it goes," she says with a faint smile, sweeping past the shadows she has evoked. "It's gone now. I don't ask why – I just – go back to painting."

They fall silent again. Out in the Harbour, boats sit motionless in the sun-blackened noon. Stirring her cup, Ann starts to talk again about Richard. She's worried about him, she says. He's got thick with the upper crust in Black Falls, he's involved in local politics. In fact, he's thinking about running for the legislature. But he has no real friends in that world, she says. "Nothing like the two of you. He's alone, really. All he does is work."

He watches her intently as she talks: the way she touches one finger, thoughtfully, to the handle of her cup; the way she brushes a hair from her cheek. He doesn't want just an hour with her. "Could you take off those glasses?"

For a long moment she stares at him and then, with both hands, removes them. Her glance is pained, elusive.

Taking her free hand, he draws it toward him.

"Billy –" she warns, but he is beyond warnings now: he no longer cares. Her hand is cool, surprisingly cool, and remains open to the stroking of his fingers.

He finds the little white scar. It is fainter than he recalls: a fading scimitar. "I see a lot of confusion here."

"Oh, tell me something I don't know."

"There's a man who's very close to you. This man loves you –"

"Billy," she scolds softly, pulling her hand away.

They walk along the quay without speaking. At her boat, he unties her lines for her.

"When can I see you?"

She is standing behind the wheel looking up at him: the sunglasses again. He feels he is oppressing her.

"You make everything impossible, Billy." Below her dark mask, her lips tighten in an expression he can't read.

———

Later that week, he drives to Mad Jack's, an uninhabited island a mile from Inverness. The approach to the island is more difficult than it used to be – heaps of boulders denying him passage. Finally, he leaves his boat and wades ashore, clambering up a hill of pink rock. Standing with his back to the sun, he finds the little hollow shaded by the low, spreading branch of a pine. Twenty years of dropped needles have made the depression shallower, but all around, the island looks remarkably the same: the same long swells of rock, rolling away under a blazing sky; the same mobs of white pine, their dark, ragged branches streaming toward the southeast. Mad Jack's burns still under the summer sun, as sharply defined and fresh as ever. Yet what happened here has left no trace: it is a kind of mockery.

She knelt a little to one side, so that the red canoe heeled over slightly while her blade cut the water with slow, lingering strokes. He had never seen anyone paddle with such effortless economy: the hull progressing as if drawn by a magnet down the brimming channel. She was wearing a white sunhat with its brim rolled up, and sunglasses, so that at first he did not recognize her, though he was primed to, had been primed all morning, ever since he and Matt had pulled into the familiar island to work on the dock.

And now: the knock of her paddle on the gunnel, the sudden pivoting of the hull. He was standing in the water where the dock met the boathouse, hammer in hand. He had turned nineteen that summer.

She paused to talk with Matt before paddling along the side of the dock. A few feet away she stopped and began to unload. "I won't be in your way a second," she told him. Walking by with a pack and a woven basket, she disappeared into the boathouse and returned seconds later to haul up the dripping canoe and overturn it on the dock. Again she went past. Her voice was lower, but her face – she had removed her sunglasses – yes, it was Ann Scott. He had not seen her since the summer he'd first met her.

Some time later, she returned. "Dad wondered if you and Matt would like to stay for supper. I'm Ann, by the way," she said, looking down from the dock.

"I know," he said, shading his eyes.

"You know?" A hint of playful remonstrance. "So, and what's *your* name?"

When he told her, he could sense something stop, behind her eyes.

He helped her carry plates to the porch, setting them out on the table where purple and white asters poked from a glass. He drank her in: her broad hands cutting cheese; the faint, blonde hairs lacing her forearms; the strong-looking full-ness of her compressed mouth. She was the same and yet not; and the change seemed to have come upon her in an instant, like in one of the old stories Matt told, when a woman was changed to a bear, or a girl into a star.

Her parents had divorced, she told him, fussing at a napkin. She had gone to live with her mother in Montreal.

"For a long time I hardly came here at all. I used to go to my mom's cottage in Quebec. I guess that's why I never saw you." She paused to regard him. "So tell me what *you've* been doing for the last ten years."

He grinned at the impossibility of this, but what he saw was fire: a torrent of flame pouring through the canopy of a spruce forest with the roaring speed of a train, while he and the other firefighters turned to run for their lives. It had happened the previous summer, when he'd signed on with a crew near the Manitoba border. Two men had been killed in that incident and he had helped carry out their charred bodies. But he did not tell her about that, there seemed no way to begin, no *place* for it here, among the plates and folded napkins. "Nothing much. Helped Matt around the lake." He shrugged.

At the table, her father described a hunting trip he had taken in the Rockies. The smoke from his cigarette floated upward, forming the cliffs and peaks where the ram he had stalked for three days eluded him yet again. Matt smoked too – Charles lighting his cigarettes for him – and to Billy's surprise talked more than he usually did in the presence of whites, telling them of a storm he had survived on his trapline twenty years before: all night long, trees had blown down around him. "I kept trying to boil tea, to keep from freezing. But that old wind, she kept blowing my fire out."

Listening with her head propped on one hand, Ann Scott was rapt. Billy felt it too: the excitement of life stretching before them. Because it was a wonderful thing to sit

there with the old folk talking, and to be young: to feel the
adventure of life laid out by their stories, and to know you
would go there yourself one day – into the country of your
life. He did not realize he was there already.

When she said she wanted to draw him, he followed her
out to the boathouse and up the stairs to the room she called
her studio. The ping-pong table, now pushed to a wall, bore
jars of pencils, brushes, cans of turpentine, stacks of paper,
stones. There were drawings stuck to the wall with masking
tape, painted canvases propped on the floor: a wind-tortured
tree, a green face with one eye.

He sat on a chair while she leaned over the board she
balanced on one knee. She studied him, then looked
down, her pencil moving. He had never posed before,
found it uncomfortable, would have laughed had it not
been her sitting a few feet away, studying him with a
gravity that commanded him. Still, it was odd having her
look at him as if he were a thing. Her eyes flicked to his
hair. His nose. She was taking him apart.

She was just starting to do oils, she told him, talking as
she worked; but she still loved to draw, drawing was the
basis of everything. She spoke of line and texture and reality
versus imagination while he listened alertly, aware of his
own ignorance. He had dropped out of school at fifteen.

The next Saturday he sat for her again. He did not
recognize himself in the drawing she made: the deep
shadings of charcoal evoking a face more handsome, more
resolute, than his own. "I think I've got you there," she
said, touching the area around the mouth. "And your hair.

You've got beautiful hair." She said it matter-of-factly, holding out the paper to study it.

He'd had lots of girlfriends – it had been three years since he'd gone all the way with Barb Hammer on the leaky air mattress they'd dragged into the trees behind Guppy Bay. But with Ann Scott, his experience seemed to count for nothing. He remembered that from before – the sense of being a bit lost around her, a constraining nervousness.

When she finished sketching, they went for a swim and afterwards lay on towels on the rock. He told her stories he didn't know he knew, for he had never spoken them before. He told her how he had shot his first moose when he was thirteen; how he had followed its tracks in a skim of snow; and when he finally found it, how it had not run away but simply looked at him. He did not tell her how he had grieved afterwards; how, butchering the moose with Matt, he had secretly whispered to it that he was sorry; how, even when they had tied a little packet of bones in a tree, to placate the moose's spirit, he could not stop seeing how the moose went down on its knees with a queer, grunting sound as if it were grieving too. He would never admit to this feeling because it was a sign of weakness; it was not how things were supposed to be between a hunter and the animal who had given itself to him. He had killed many moose since, and while he never had so strong a reaction of sadness again – he loved hunting – each time he felled an animal he would touch its warm flank, partly to thank it, but also with the slightest hint of regret.

Nor did he tell her about getting drunk at the Rendezvous, or about how he and Gary Sweshikin had escaped the police one night in a stolen car, or about his mother and her troubles. In his happiness with Ann Scott, he lived partly in hiding, and close to shame.

She told him, in turn, of a trip she'd taken the previous fall to Europe, of paintings and cities and ruins, of walking in a cave under Paris among stacks of bones, and of the time she and a friend had hiked up a mountain and then, coming down, had got lost in a mist and nearly walked headlong over a cliff. She spoke again of her parents' divorce. "I was mad at my father – he wasn't treating my mom very well – that's why I went to live with her. But really, it was harder. We always rubbed each other the wrong way. I used to think sometimes, Well, I know why he went off. I'd leave too if I had to live with *her*. But then I couldn't stand his girlfriend. I could never forgive her for taking Mom's place. It wasn't her fault, but –" She was sitting on the rock with her elbows on her knees, her head down, despondent. Reaching out, he touched her wet hair. Her eyes, filled with a level seriousness, met his. Slipping his arm across her back, he kissed her. Her mouth was barely responsive, and when he pulled back, she was still watching him, as if she were weighing the kiss against the person who had given it.

One afternoon when her father was away, she took him up to her bedroom on the second floor. It was not much changed from how he remembered it: a large, rather stuffy room, with two screen windows opening toward the channel, under a sloping ceiling. There were the same bookcases crammed with books, the same bedspread with the giant yellow flowers, even the same blue bear, staring from its one remaining eye. "You go over there." He stood where she indicated, on the opposite side of her bed, while she removed her clothes with a confident briskness, standing at last in her panties and bra. When she discovered him watching, she blushed and covered her chest with her arms. Stripping to his shorts, he slid under the sheet beside her.

"I bet you're pretty experienced at this," she said.

"A bit."

"Let's do it then."

Afterwards, she wept between bouts of laughter. On the sheet was a bloodstain shaped like a pear. He stroked and held her. She pushed him on his back and examined him between his legs: something electric and fierce in her look now, something at once fascinated and repelled as she lifted his penis between her fingers and studied the wrinkled sac beneath.

In the following weeks, when she met his boat, he could sense her impatience. Usually they went up to her bedroom, though if her father was home they would trek off to a cove at the back of the island where she had cached an old sleeping bag. Her appetite astonished him: it outran his own, or at least her capabilities did. Once, when a boat was idling through the marsh, she insisted they keep going – though they could hear voices, and though his back must have been intermittently visible above the rock.

Another day, in her room, hearing her father arrive, they hardly had time to get into their clothes. When they came downstairs, Mr. Scott looked up from a map he had spread out on a table. "Just showing Billy some books," Ann sang with forced casualness. Billy liked Charles Scott and had assumed he liked him, but at that moment, meeting the gaze of the figure hulking straight-armed over the map, he experienced a chill, and he recalled faces that had looked at him that way in the Falls, faces pent with unspoken disapproval and even, in some cases, rage, as though his very existence was an affront. And something connected to this look must have happened between Ann and her father, for the next time Billy saw her, she told him she couldn't see him for a while. She was having company at Inverness – an old girlfriend – and she had to finish some drawings for her portfolio. She seemed flustered: smiling and reddening as they stood together on the boat-house path, casting down her eyes, as if embarrassed not just at what she'd told him but at something she could *not* say. He was certain it was over. For things ended; he knew it beyond doubt. There was nothing you could do about it. Turning, he walked away.

She pleaded for him to stop, and when he kept going, she grabbed his arm. "Billy. Billy, listen." He turned and saw the anxiety in her face. "Do you know Mad Jack's Island –"

The next afternoon he arrived first, in his boat, and some time later, waiting on a granite slope, saw her approach from the south in her red canoe. She had brought the old sleeping bag they had used on Inverness. They spread it in a little hollow beneath a pine whose low, floating bough dropped a flickering net of light over the plaid lining. From their shelter, they could survey the passages, the unoccupied islands – the whole archipelago stretching north and south. But where they were, they were snug, hidden.

Through July and into August, when the air filled with the clacking of grasshoppers' wings, they met under the pine. It seemed to him that everything spoke of their state – the islands baking in heat; the cool dark water where they swam without suits; the great, smooth waves of rock, bearing away their mobs of pine. He had often felt that the trees were aware of him – that they could hear him and were attuned, even, to his thoughts – and that he in turn could tell, sometimes, what they were saying – but with her this intensified. The pine that shaded them made a third.

And yet: there was something in her he could not reach, and so his joy was never complete. At times she seemed alone in her pleasure, watching him with a bored, pleased indolence as if she were in some way larger or older than he. Her body was a mystery to him – the way it kept renewing itself, perpetually and without effort, to his wonder. He explored it as closely as she would allow: the cleft in her collarbone, filled with her scent; the gill-like flesh between her parted legs. She had a power and seemed conscious of its sway, for there was something almost triumphant about the way she sat gazing over the channel. What was she thinking? When he asked, she told him, "Happy people don't think." He did not believe her.

Sometimes, when she went off out of sight, padding away for a pee or to explore the island with her sketchbook, he experienced stabs of panic: old, familiar stabs that he had not felt in years, for he had schooled himself to hardness. But it seemed – he half-knew this was crazy – that when she disappeared from his sight, her white sunhat sinking below a ridge, that she had left for good.

Of course, she always came back. And he pretended that nothing was wrong. Yet a day came when he could not contain himself and on the slimmest of pretexts started a fight. He knew he was wrecking everything – that the result of his ranting would be to make her disappear for real. But he expected this anyway; better he reject her first.

She fought back, tearfully, while he was cold-hearted, exulting. She paddled off, the red canoe disappearing (as it seemed) into a granite hill. At first he gloated. Then he found himself alone.

He started running – along a ledge, through junipers, onto a cliff. He saw her an instant before he jumped – the interior of the canoe far below him, and she kneeling under the white blob of her hat. But already, he was airborne, aware (too late!) of the ledge thrusting into the dark blue water below. He missed it by inches, plunging into layers of deepening cold. He was nothing now. He was cold water and darkness and struggling limbs: the chain of bubbles that pulled him up toward the light. He popped up by her gunnel. "I'm wrong," he told her. He meant he was all wrong; he meant the mistake of himself.

They went back to Mad Jack's. And kept going back for the rest of the summer. But their meetings had changed. Aware of their power to hurt, they grew tender. At first this was exhilarating, but gradually the restraint wore at them. They became self-conscious. Where before they had glided by instinct, now they fumbled among misunderstandings. He was not touching her the way she liked! He sulked. She broke a favourite glass. Silence deepened beside silence. He stole glances at her: the way her lower jaw stuck out a little – why had he never noticed that before? It seemed not so much a flaw as yet more evidence of her secret life. For no matter what she told him, no matter how intimate they were, he felt the presence of things withheld. Around them, the summer was changing. Colour had come into the poplars, and in the skies ducks and geese beat back and forth, as if trying to decide whether to come or go.

Occasionally, she spoke of going away to art college, in a casual tone that seemed to take his understanding for granted. He guessed she was preparing him for her departure. Brooding on this, he withdrew; she cajoled him to come back to her. They finished a bottle of wine and danced drunkenly on the rock. But their jollity had shallow roots now; they ended by quarrelling. Holding her, he sensed the truth: she was already leaving.

One afternoon kneeling to her pack, she looked off over the island and spoke to the rolling waves of granite: "So you know. I'm going to England next month."

He thought of that pink island on the map of the world. His grade three teacher had told him, *Now point to England, Billy.* Rapping it with the pointer, he'd made a cloud of chalk dust rise behind the map – good for a laugh. The Queen lived in England. The Beatles came from England. It had never been a real place to him; she might have announced she was going to the moon.

He looked off to the maze of islands with their tortured pines. The future contained these places where things you saw every day ceased to exist. It astonished him that anyone could speak of the future casually.

She had gone on rummaging in her pack. Pulling out her sketchbook, she flipped it open and, turning toward him, began to sketch. But in a moment, she tossed the book aside.

"Don't you care!" she snapped.

He looked at her: one astonishing statement after another.

"What?" he said.

"That I'm going away. That we won't come here any more."

"I care."

"I never know what you're thinking."

He frowned: was she supposed to?

They went for a walk over the high granite and down into the hollows filled with bushes, following a faint trail. She took the initiative, marching briskly out ahead of him, while he followed miserably behind her, hitting at the bushes with a stick.

She stopped outside the clutch of poplars where Mad Jack had had his cabin. Mad Jack had been a soldier in the war, so people said. For a few years afterwards he had lived here, though all that had survived were a few rotting logs and some relics they had found: a washbasin with the bottom eaten out, an axe-head frowsy with rust.

"Do you love me?" she said.

He had never told her he did. The word meant nothing. The girls on Pine Island: *I love Ronnie Blake. You love Ernie.* Tomorrow they would love someone else. His mother had loved a different man every month.

What he felt for Ann Scott had no name. For an answer he might point to the blazing islands, the skies strewn with pebbled clouds – the great word of the world that was forever speaking itself. But even that would not be enough.

When he saw she was weeping, he held her. She lifted her wet face: "Because I love *you*, you know."

And he did tell her he loved her. The words rasped from his constricted throat. He was weeping himself now. Like a boy.

They entered their last phase on Mad Jack's. She was cheerful. She brought lunches. He said little. She was frenzied in love-making, while he grew cooler. Stones still had weight, and fell when you dropped them. The sun still crossed the sky. The laws of life still held. They could choose what to do. One day he asked her why she had to go. "Why not stay here?"

She looked at him as if he had suggested flying.

"On this island?" She spoke almost with scorn. "I've been accepted. This is my chance to work with Armand Perry." She had talked of him before: a well-known artist. A "genius."

"I could come with you," he said. Days and weeks of thinking were behind this simple statement. Yet it took all his courage to offer it. "I could get a job and save up enough by Christmas. I could come over."

"Oh, Billy," she said. He could not tell if she meant yes or no.

The sun no longer settled over Credit Island, but over Dooney's Point, farther south. The rock of Mad Jack's was no longer too hot to walk on, but warm, like someone's flesh. What he knew of loss was what his mother had taught him with her death. It was absolute. But her death had come without warning, and what he faced now was proceeding by slow, relentless steps. She must have felt it too, this creeping advance. This slow torture. At times, making love, it seemed to him they were intent on hurting each other, each blaming the other for not finding a solution, each trying to wring an alternative from the clash of mouths and limbs, from the small pale cries of love: each trying to burrow into safety. At times, they seemed to have found it. Momentarily at peace (but as much exhausted), they lay motionless under the pine.

One day, she did not show up. He waited from early afternoon until after dark. He slept, then woke to the sun in a new place, throwing the streaked light of morning across the rock. For all he had thought about this moment, and tried in his way to prepare for it, he found himself unable to believe it was actually happening. He waited for another day until, late in the afternoon, he got in his own boat and drove to Inverness. No one was home. The Scotts' launch was gone. Driving to Carton Harbour, he found it tied at the public dock, its rain cover snugly fastened.

Using a soft pencil, Ann has blocked out her painting on the canvas. A naked woman, rather larger than life-sized, stands with her knees a little bent, her feet widely planted. Her face, so far, is vague – a statue's corroded by the elements. Already, there is something massy about the woman Ann likes, a suggestion of endurance in her thick thighs and wide hips, a sense of explosive strength as if she were leaning braced against a load.

In an open notebook propped on her painting table, Ann has made working sketches of the figure in different poses. In one of the drawings, the woman is surrounded by many small figures. Several of these diminutive people have propped a ladder against her leg; others are tugging on cables attached to her wrists. In other drawings, more miniature elements appear. A cannon. A flag. A church steeple. A factory modelled on the paper mill in Black Falls.

She's lost the thread that was leading her forward – the sense of what to do next. She turns to the window. Down through the screen, the channel sparkles along a bank of pink rock. The heat and dazzling light have a hypnotic effect, and for some time she simply drifts. *You had no right to touch me like that! To speak to me like that!* He had broken a trust, she feels – the unspoken understanding that they were close, that they had a relationship in which a look, a tone of voice, could suggest a bond, an intimacy. But there were limits. *You must have understood that!*

Outside, the shadow of a branch trembles on the rock. She throws down her notebook.

Wading into the water, she pauses, fingers brushing the placid surface. On the next island, not sixty feet away, a thin, dark shadow slips from the rock – as if oil had poured from a crack. For a moment, she does not understand what she is seeing. A black, glistening *something* is pouring endlessly into the water.

"Oh," she breathes.

As a girl, she was terrified of watersnakes. Once, canoe-ing with her father, they had found one sliding through the reeds. Water snakes didn't bite unless cornered, he told her, speaking in a low voice from the stern. But what safety he gave in one moment, he took away in the next when he told her they had dirty mouths and jaws that only worked one way. If one bit you, it would hang on until it was cut off, and by then your wound was probably infected. *Your* wound, as if she carried it already.

It is swimming below the rocks – nearly invisible now, a ripple among ripples. Then it lifts its head: a low, flat arrowish thing, weaving its way toward the marsh. "You beauty," she says, while her fingers touch ice along her breastbone.

She swims in the opposite direction, out through the narrows into the main channel. By the buoy she stops and treads water, gazing back down the channel to where it bends, a little ominously, out of sight. A short distance off, their deck overhangs the water: she could climb out there. But she makes herself go back the same way, around the point and into the side-channel. Beside the boathouse, her robe lies crumpled on the rock. Ahead, the marsh glints among its reeds. Breast-stroking now, she swims toward it.

Treading water, she surveys the oil-blue passages. She *knows* the snake is here. That sloping boulder, that ripple along a half-sunk log – all him, or signs of him – messengers from his underwater kingdom. *Come on. Let's see you then.* But except for the flutter of a small bird, changing its perch, there is no movement.

The wet dabbing and stroking of her brush; the short, dry, fibrous note of the bristles, pecking at her canvas or leaving a silent path of cadmium orange while the sun goes from window to window, laying translucent carpets on the hardwood. Mixing paint in aluminum pie plates, sipping or forgetting to sip at her cooling coffee, she is once again magnetized by her canvas. Sometimes she looks away, not really seeing the sunlit channel hazing through the screen – then back again to her painting, hoping to surprise it. To have it surprise her – to announce to her where and how it must evolve next. And who knows where they come from: these tiny spurts of growth. Not solely from her effort, but from some gap between possibility and discovery.

The smell of oils. The pecking of her brush. As the sun tracks over the roof of the boathouse and the room grows hotter, her efforts meet a rising resistance. The painting tells her less. She might go off to the bathroom, or to the kitchen to wolf something down (she scarcely knows what). Then almost without noticing, she is back. As her brush moves the thick, glistening oils around the canvas, her headache no longer matters, her mental fog is swept away, and again she finds a way forward, until, nearly sick with her efforts, she reaches the end of her painting day. Cleaning her brushes, she keeps glancing at what she has done. Then, having left the boathouse, she sits stunned on the deck with a glass of wine.

One evening the phone rings. The sound startles her – a violation of her solitude. She fears it might be Billy, but picks up. Richard. He is robustly cordial.

"Rowan's doing really well at hockey camp."

"Good, good!" she manages. It takes an effort to re-enter her other life.

"So how's the work going?"

She tells him she's had a breakthrough. Her own voice sounds odd to her, a desert-island voice, speaking after years of silence. Really, she does not want to talk about her painting, and after a few words she trails off. A silence falls. To her, it seems filled with pressure, as if he were demanding more. It is something she is familiar with: it's there in the shrewdness of his small eyes, with their prodding insistence, as if he were saying, *That's all? Surely you must have more for me than that?*

"Hey, I miss you," he tells her.

"Miss you too," she says, though in truth she has hardly thought of him.

He phones the next night as well. He has asked Reg Benoit and his wife to Inverness for the weekend after next, he tells her.

"That's when the Gotliebs are coming, Richard."

"We'll have to put them off."

"But they can't come any other –"

"Annie, you know how important this is to me. The nomination is toast without Reg's support. I think he's leaning my way. The signs are good. He was very enthusiastic about coming to Inverness. He's a tennis buff – excited to know we have a court. That's their only free weekend this summer."

"So you've definitely decided to run? I thought we were going to talk about it." She feels herself bristling as she

imagines the arrogant Reg Benoit and his wife. At least he
could have asked me.

"We'll talk. But please, let's reschedule the Gotliebs."

"Why couldn't the six of us have dinner?"

"There's history between Larry and Reg. It wouldn't
work, trust me. Just do this one thing, will you?"

When Ann doesn't respond, he puts Rowan on the line.
The boy's clear voice pierces her.

"Dad says you're having a good time at the camp."

"Yup."

"So, you've scored some goals?"

"Mom, you don't go to hockey camp to score goals. It's
like – drills."

"Oh, sorry. Rowan – Rowan?" She can hear the televi-
sion going: he's distracted.

"Oh wow! There's a crocodile attacking a gazelle.
They're crossing a river and the crocodiles are waiting for
them, mostly they get through but one's – he's like
attached to his neck. Oh God, he's got him by the neck.
He's only a little one!"

She asks him to put his father back on.

"Are you sure this program's all right? He sounds
awfully speedy."

"He's fine, Ann. It's really quite incredible footage."

She is reminded of the snake but does not mention it:
her snake can't compete with their current excitement; and
anyway, the snake is hers.

———

One evening she takes out her canoe. It is over sixty years old, her father's as a boy, bought for him by *his* father from the factory in Peterborough. Inside the hull, its varnished ribs are a deep gold, its seats are made of woven gut. Kneeling on a life jacket, she paddles north, intending to circle Inverness.

With each stroke, her paddle sends a tiny whirlpool spinning away across the surface; when it emerges, it casts a swishing patter of drops. She passes the deck and soon afterwards the guest cabin; then the tennis court with its sagging net. Near Cigarette Point a gap between islands reveals the open lake. Nigushi is calm, under a low sun, the air so still she is lured into stillness herself. For a while she drifts, her paddle laid across the gunnels. Thirty years ago, she had paddled with her father on just such an evening. The same rocks. The same pines. The same light, suffusing Nigushi's glass. In another moment, she will hear his voice.

Standing over his hospital bed, she had silently urged him to die. Shrunken. Rasping under his oxygen mask. She could not bear it, not after what he had been. Two nurses came in to "help him get comfortable." One heaved him up while the other rearranged his pillows. Upright, he opened his eyes and stared – his blue eyes suddenly vivid through the room as if he had suddenly seen or understood something of absolute importance: some idea that had eluded him his whole life. At the same time a kind of deep, unearthly belch erupted from his mouth (the mask had slipped). The nurses laid him back down. "You'll feel better now," one of them said, repositioning the mask. They left. Under half-fallen lids, her father's eyes seemed frozen. Ann hurried after the nurses, but even before they came back with the stethoscope, she knew what she had seen.

She sat for a long time with him. Held his cooling hands. Tugged away the sheet and pulled up his gown. Seeing her father naked: that was what finally tipped her out of the state of numb competence she had occupied for weeks. Seeing not just the untidy clump of his genitals, shrunken under their grey bush of hair, but all of him, laid out for the first time to her eyes: the thin shanks; the dimpled, raw-looking knees turned outward; his head with its misshapen mouth. In a rage of grief, she wept for him, for herself, for the bitter joke of human life. She re-covered him and, sitting on the edge of the bed, smoothed back his hair. But it was no longer him.

She has reached the marsh at the back of Inverness. The light floods from behind her now, washing the reeds that bow away on either side as the hull pushes through. In a patch of open water, she drifts, until, bestirring herself, she takes a notebook from her basket and begins to sketch.

The sound of the outboard infiltrates so gradually she only looks up a moment before it breaks off. Someone has arrived on the far side of the island. She thinks little of it – people are always stopping to fish. After a while, roaring back to life, the boat drives away.

Later, she opens the fridge and discovers the fillets. Two creamy white slabs on a blue plate. For a second, it is as if she has put them there herself and forgotten. A thickness of incomprehension, and then – remembering the boat, the motor – she understands.

For some time, she doesn't move. Then she shuts the door.

After a while, she throws together a small salad, boils some new potatoes, fries one of the fillets in olive oil, and carries her meal to the porch, where she sits at a small table by the screens. The pickerel is sweet, dense, perfectly cooked. Putting down her wine, she falls into reverie, oblivious to her surroundings. When a splash sounds from the channel, she is not quick enough to see what made it. But she peers intently.

He sits on his front step cleaning his rifle. Taking care not to scratch the barrel, he works the cleaning rod through the breach until its flannel-wrapped tip protrudes from the muzzle. Handling the gun is second nature to him, its weight a comfort, the duties he owes to it, a pleasure. Sometimes, when he can't sleep, he imagines carrying it in the bush above Nigushi: the willow flats west of Coke, good moose country; or the high, piney ridges above Charlton; or the blueberry hills along Silver where he shot that bear with the tag. Come August or September, he'll go up there again and stay at Matt's cabin (his cabin now), a thought that lifts his spirits and sets him working vigorously. A few

seconds later, he remembers a cliff on the Fife River. Matt
had taken him there on one of their first hunting trips –
eased their boat under the wall of rock that, swelling overhead, almost cut off the sky. Matt shut off the motor, and
in the ensuing calm, as water lapped against the hull, Billy
had looked up the rockface. They had arrived somewhere,
he felt it instantly, a place with its own atmosphere, its own
privacy, like when you step into a church, and in the dim
coolness other kinds of thoughts are possible. The rock,
he thought, seemed aware of them.

The first image was so faint he nearly missed it: two stick
men, drawn in red. Then he saw the others. The canoe with
its three paddlers. The tiny thunderbird. The open hand.

He had heard of this place, where the shamans of old
painted their dreams in red ochre. Across the dun rock,
the figures were engaged in mysterious actions. They were
motionless, but he sensed this stillness was an illusion. In
their world, they were busy at important work. The canoe
was always making its way up the rock; the stick men were
always releasing their arrows; and the moose under its
great rack – he had not seen it at first – was always stepping toward the crevasse where a stain of water gleamed.

Reaching out, Matt deposited something on a ledge
above the waterline. "For the little ones," he said.

Years later he would leave tobacco there himself. For
the little ones – *Mememguisiuk*, the old folk called them –
mischievous helpers whom few people had seen, though
everyone was familiar with their handiwork. A coffee pot

overturned. A favourable wind arriving out of nowhere. Once Matt had heard them singing, out of the rock.

His behaviour at Lola's had taken him by surprise. It was as if some thin strand that had held him back for years had quietly let go. But Ann had not reacted well, and he wondered if he had spoiled something permanently between them. Then the idea of bringing her a fish occurred: a peace offering, an apology, an excuse to see her again. He stood in his boat, casting into the green-shadowed pool under Ferguson's Rock. The pickerel struck almost immediately, as if it had been waiting for him. Playing the fish in, he had scooped it in his net, cleaned it on shore, and placed the wrapped fillets in his cooler: everything intensely pleasurable, because it was done for her. But later, driving to Inverness, he wondered if he was pushing too hard. *You make everything impossible, Billy.* Noticing her canoe was gone, he took it as a sign: he would leave the fish and slip off.

He had just closed the fridge door when he paused to gaze down the hall toward the front of the house. The late sun, infiltrating through the porch, cast quivering shards along the hardwood and walls. He had always loved the old cottage, and this evening it seemed alive, beckoning him down the hall to the open doorway of her first-floor bedroom. From a bedpost hung some silky, lilac-coloured thing: the sort of garment a woman would put on for a man. Nearby, on the floor, lay one of Richard's enormous running shoes. He could sense their marriage in the room – a density in the atmosphere, as if years of conversation and argument and love-making had left a permanent trace. Her life included so much more than herself. What right did he have to disrupt it? What could he offer in return? There were books piled on the bedside table. A drawer half-open below a mirror. Years ago, when he'd confided his feelings to Yvonne, she had commented, "If you lived with her, you'd get as bored as with all the others." But as his gaze settled on the unmade bed, he knew he did not believe her.

Most days he visits Yvonne, who has a phone, to see if Ann has called, or the lodge with news of a job. Often he finds the house full of the children Yvonne looks after while their parents are at work or are in no shape to look after them themselves. Crayons underfoot. The TV blasting. Kids sprawled on the floor or spooning up soup ladled from the pot she keeps going on the back of the stove. "Union Station," she calls her place with the pride he senses behind her complaints. His sister is the most competent person he knows. He has seen her walk into camp with a hundred pounds of moose meat on her back, from a kill she made herself. A wide-shouldered woman with a powerful laugh – though the grimness can show too, when she's tired or fed up, like bedrock. He thinks she had too much responsibility too young. When their mother was in bad shape, it was Yvonne who held things together –

cooked and cleaned up and made sure he got to school, though she was hardly more than a girl herself. He can remember waiting outside their house, afraid to go in because their mother was on a tear. Then Yvonne appeared beside him. "Come on then, let's get warm." Somehow his sister knew how to calm their mother, and before long she would be sitting at the kitchen table weeping over a cup of tea and telling them how much she loved them.

One afternoon he goes with Yvonne and a few of the children to pick berries. Yvonne carries her baby, Pascale, in a Snugly, while Brenda and the others totter along the dusty road with their pails. On the way, they pass the old fastball diamond. Half the rusted backstop has fallen down. Hip-deep weeds cover everything, all the way to the collapsing outfield fence.

"Look at that," his sister announces. "What a pity, you know?"

Yvonne has the irritating habit of asking him if he knows. You have to give her an answer, because she'll say it again until you do. She says it again. He says he knows.

In the bright sun, a couple of the little ones squint up at him. "People don't care any more," Yvonne is saying. "We used to mow this every week. Now the kids hardly know what a ball is." Where second base used to be, a bush stands like a stranded runner. "You should try for council," she says suddenly, turning toward him. "Why not? There's elections next fall."

"Sure," he says. "Climb back up on the cross. Just once more, for old time's sake."

"You were never Jesus," she says.

"Somebody should have told *them* that," he says, gesturing toward the houses.

"All kinds of people would vote for you," she says. "We really could use you, you know. Your experience. The new chief –" She explains that the new chief, Margo Mackay, can't get anything done. "Her ideas are good, but the old guard don't want to try anything new."

"I think I did my bit," he says, turning away.

"You gave it more than a hundred," she says, plodding after him. "But, hey, you had ten years off. That's a good rest by anyone's standards."

They leave the road and wade into some low bushes. The strawberries are warm and small, with a flavour unlike store berries: little essences of summer. But he can't enjoy them. *Ten years off.* Did she think he was on some kind of holiday? Already, his time away – the jobs, the people he called his friends, the cities he lived – seems no more distinct than last night's dream. He never stayed in one place for long. He would be lying on some cardboard flat behind a factory, or beside some woman he hardly knew, and again the land claim would start happening to him. You said. He said. Arguments running in his head like a rat in a wheel. He couldn't stop them, not even at the bottom of his eighth or ninth beer. So one morning he'd climb on a bus, if he had the money, or stand beside the highway with his thumb out, and again the continent would come to his rescue – the skies, the retreating horizons, filling him with the conviction that down the road things would be different.

The next morning, he's sitting with Yvonne at her kitchen table when Jimmy comes in. Ignoring their greetings, the boy cuts himself a piece of pie and sits to eat it, to all intents and purposes alone.

"So I stopped by Whitbread's," Yvonne says to him. "A job," she explains to Billy. "Deliveries to the cottagers. He'd be out in a boat all day." And back to Jimmy. "Perfect for you. Those running shoes you want, they don't grow on trees."

"They're racist over there," Jimmy says after a while, in a muffled voice.

"Come on," she cajoles, darting a look at Billy. "You think they're racist everywhere. If John Whitbread's racist, so am I."

The click of Jimmy's fork.

"He won't hold it open for you forever," Yvonne says. "I told him you'd come in tomorrow."

"Could have asked me first."

"I did ask you."

"I don't think so."

Sighing, Yvonne sends another glance to Billy, who lowers his eyes. He has some experience of what it's like to be badgered by Yvonne Johnson. When the washing machine falls silent in the basement, she goes off to attend to it.

As before, Billy feels drawn to his nephew, yet he can't think of anything to say. On an impulse, he sets a lead sinker (he's been rolling it between his fingers) on the table. It wobbles away and comes to rest against the ketchup bottle. "One fish in three days," Billy says, as Jimmy looks up. "Been away too long. Fish aren't where they used to be. How're you finding it?"

"Okay, I guess."

"I tried the black boulders there, where Watcher's Creek comes in. One good pickerel – all I managed all week. Where do you go? Or is that a trade secret?"

"We use a mask," Jimmy says. "Old diving mask. When you look through it, you can see the fish."

"And lay the hook right on their noses. Pretty smart."

"Don't fish much any more."

"No? How come?" It is out before he can think. Briefly, the boy's gaze flashes with anger – not at him, but into the deep solitary space where, Billy imagines, Ross Shewaybick's lifeless body hangs. For some time neither of them speak.

"Thought I'd go out tonight," Billy says at last. "Always got room for one more."

Jimmy glances up and for a second looks much younger than he is.

After supper, Billy carries his tackle box and two poles down to the dock. A slight breeze has come up, setting the boats rustling, bringing a touch of coolness. He feels exhilarated by the change, and by the prospect of fishing with his nephew. But Jimmy doesn't show. Finally Billy drives off alone and anchors in the lea of a nearby island. But he has little heart for fishing now, and after a while he starts his motor and heads back toward the lights.

The next afternoon, in a dull mood, he goes for a walk. His way takes him along the shore path toward northern parts of the Island where no one lives. In some bays, the shrinking lake has exposed acres of bottom. He treks over mud flats among a scattering of large and small boulders. It is like a desert here – the sun fierce, the powdered mud rising in clouds around his boots. In places, animal tracks pepper the flats: moose, weasel, racoon, dog, fox. The heat is oppressive, and he's glad to return to the path that keeps, for the most part, under trees.

Big pines ascend a slope. The atmosphere has changed – the trees drawing him into the still, sun-pierced understory. He climbs among giant pines where the air is cooler and shadows stripe the rust-coloured duff: a deeply private place, holy to his mind, where he has often felt close to those no longer here.

Many of the trees are browned by drought. Digging with his heel, he finds the soil like powder. Climbing higher, he comes to a plateau where the pines stand farther apart and the space between is littered with wind-felled trees. The fuller light is harsh, settling a relentless pressure on the brain. Balancing along a trunk, he catches a flash of white – patches of brilliant white, as if snow had persisted by some miracle in the July woods.

Plastic bags: scores of bags, caught in bushes, strewn along the ground. Revulsed, he is about to turn back when a cry comes. It sounds only once, muffled and far away, a cry from the piney depths of the afternoon, so faint that he stands quite still, wondering if he has imagined it. There is something terrible in its brevity, as if human life had risen in an instant and as quickly vanished, sinking away forever into the heat and mosquito-plagued shadows of the bush.

Creeping forward, he comes across several boys sitting or lying about in a clearing. In their hands are more of the plastic bags, which they keep lifting to their faces, as if peering inside. Their movements are slow, languorous – they are more like old men than boys, enclosed in a sickroom atmosphere, from which drifts, now, the over-powering stench of gasoline.

A boy leans over and vomits, to the jeers of others. Another boy lies face down on the ground. One foot and then the other lifts and falls back, desultorily, kicking up puffs of dust, as if he is trying to walk straight down, into the earth.

Before Billy can think, he is in their midst, their stupe-fied faces staring up at him.

"Good work, good work," he hears himself say, his voice breaking. "Killing yourselves up here. Good work!"

It is as if they do not speak his language. Some fool is shouting. Nothing to do with *them*.

"*Well?*" he demands. Already he can sense his help-
lessness here. He snatches up a tin. It contains a couple of
inches of gas, as clear as apple juice, which he flings on
the ground.

"Great move, buddy," a voice says.

The boy is standing with his back to a tree. A rangy,
good-looking kid of thirteen or fourteen whose blue eyes
fix Billy with hostility.

"Who are you?"

"Who am I?" the boy echoes, his drugged, insolent gaze
swinging to the others, as if to be asked for his name was
something absurd.

A few of the boys croon with slow laughter. The boy
looks back to him now, with such victorious contempt that
Billy has to resist striking him. The boy is beyond his power
and he knows it. They are all beyond his power. Still, he
must go about ripping bags from hands, knocking over
tins. Most of the boys watch indifferently. One surrenders
his bag with a worried look, like a student handing in an
exam. Still leaning against his tree, their leader sends out
his sarcastic commentary. *Great move. Wow. Sign that guy
up.* Billy's only consolation is that his nephew is not here.

A shrill falsetto pulses from the deeper bush. Following
the sound, Billy finds a boy kicking viciously at another.
The victim, who lies on the ground, is doing nothing to
protect himself. But with every kick he shouts like some
great bird: *Hak! Hak!* The blows land with sickening force
on his chest, his legs, his head. *Hak! Hak!* When Billy
grabs the kicker and starts to pull him away, he struggles

to go on kicking. And he's weeping, Billy sees – his face burning with fury and grief, as if *he* were the aggrieved party – as if he were battering himself senseless on a door that will not open. Breaking finally from Billy's grip, the boy staggers off.

The other boy lies quietly now, with his head on his arm. A bubble of spit and blood glistens at the corner of his mouth. He lets Billy help him up, but as soon as he's on his feet, he runs off, after his oppressor.

Numbed, drenched by his own exertions, Billy listens to the boy's cries that get smaller until the woods are quiet. Returning to the clearing, he finds it empty. Around him, the ground is littered with plastic bags, pop tins and candy bar wrappers, pieces of abandoned clothing, and the charred remains of a fire. Picking up a running shoe, he stares at it for a moment, then tosses it aside.

At the base of a large pine, a little boy, not more than five or six, lies with his knees pulled up. His face is filthy, his chin slimy with drool. When Billy rouses him, he opens his eyes and smiles in a vague, trusting way. He's too stoned to walk, so Billy lifts and carries him.

He goes back the way he came, down through the pines. Here and there the sun, sloping on a shallower angle, bands the huge trunks with orange. On his shoulder, the little boy murmurs incoherently as he clutches at Billy's T-shirt. He smells of gas, but his hair gives off a faint scent of soap: someone has cared for him.

By the lake, he props the boy against a rock and fetches water in his hands. Sucking noisily, the boy drinks, and when he's had enough, Billy soaks a corner of his own shirt and dabs at the small face.

"So what's your name, guy?"

"Ants," the boy says.

"Ants? Ants in your pants?"

The boy giggles, and Billy tousles his hair.

He hears footsteps on the path behind him. Turning, Billy sees his nephew emerge from the trees. Jimmy takes in Billy, the boy; he glances up the slope.

"Your friends have left," Billy tells him sharply, turning back to his work. In the deepening silence he senses shame. "Do you know who this is?"

"Lance," Jimmy says, scarcely audible.

"That would be Lance –?"

Jimmy sniffs and lifts his head; he will not look at Billy. "Cormier."

"Well then, let's take Lance Cormier home."

They trek in and out of bays, beside the brilliant lake. Billy carries Lance Cormier on his shoulders. Behind, the slopping of Jimmy's running shoes fades, comes on, fades: over mud flats, over tongues of baking rock, down troughed paths where their footsteps are nearly silent.

Leaving the shade of the woods, they start across a sand flat. About halfway over, tracks appear in the greenish, scummy sand. Billy waits for Jimmy to catch up.

"Beaver," Billy tells him. "Really big –"

Jimmy tosses his long hair, apparently indifferent.

"So, look," Billy says to his nephew. "I'm not going to tell your mother where you were headed. She knows about the gas anyways. I guess you know that. But this gas –"

"What business is it of yours?"

Jimmy's eyes are fixed in some deep, burning space. It's as if someone else has spoken; but his anger arrives like a blow. Billy turns away. As a boy, he would not have dreamed of saying such a thing to an adult. *What business is it of yours?* It seems a new kind of question, impossible in the old world. You didn't have to be someone's father or mother to care. You didn't have to be someone's child to listen. They don't believe us any more, he thinks. They're like those boys in that book, wrecked on an island. They don't believe anybody. They're going to eat us alive.

They go on, through birches, through pines, through a field of weeds. They are close to the houses now. He can hear someone's chainsaw stuttering in the heat. But he can no longer hear Jimmy; looking back, he finds the trail empty.

He is awake for half the night. The next afternoon he finds his sister sitting on her back porch in the shade, Pascale asleep at her feet.

"I been thinking," he says. "Maybe this winter, in the holidays, Jimmy and I could go up to Silver Lake for a while. Check the cabin out. Maybe do a bit of trapping. Could help."

His sister turns her handsome face impassively. She daunts him, his sister; in her eyes he glimpses considerations that elude him.

"There's no trapping up there any more. I told you that."

She has told him that north of the lake, where most people have their trapping grounds, clear-cuts have broken up the lines. But he refuses to believe things are as bad as she says. His sister is a great doomsayer.

"I haven't seen the cuts myself," she tells him. "Debbie Roy went up with her dad. She says it's terrible. She says she cried for a week. There's nothing left, Billy."

That night, he dreams of a three-legged bear. It has a queer, hopping walk, and keeps pausing to nose at its stump, which resembles a twist of melted plastic. In the fur on its back, a tiny roll of white cloth has been tied up with red ribbon: a medicine bundle? Then the bear turns into a woman with one eye, and the little bundle is tucked behind her ear, like a cigarette.

He wakes soaked in sweat. When he goes outside, everything looks the same – the woodpile under its mouldering tarp, the view through birches to water – yet he senses that something has changed. For several minutes he stands motionless. In the north, over the tree-tops, the sky seems false, hollow: blue paint smeared on a board.

Ann Scott's failure to meet him at Mad Jack's Island was not the end of their summer, not quite. Two days later, Billy was sitting on the steps of the blue house with Emma, helping her shell peas, when Ann walked up the path. She was wearing a sleeveless blouse and those short-ish pants she called pedal-pushers. She was moving quickly, her head down, entirely self-absorbed, but when she looked up and their eyes met, he stood up abruptly, oblivious to the scattering peas.

She appeared as if she hadn't slept for days. There were deep circles under her eyes, their gaze now evading his as she knelt to help him pick up the peas. When Emma went back in the house, they stood in silence.

"I'm sorry I didn't come to Mad Jack's," she said finally, to the ground.

He asked her what had happened.

"Oh, what happens?" she sang, on a reckless note, as if an answer were impossible. "My father is insane, you know." She daggered him an accusing look, as if *he* were her father, and pointed suddenly. "Let's go over there."

He followed her toward the lake. It was a calm, grey day. Every sound – the knock of an oar, the distant plaint of a motor – distinct. She was quiet now, and as they made their way over the uneven bedrock of a peninsula, she seemed alone, scarcely conscious of him. Once or twice she glanced at him, then stood looking at him directly for a long time, her mouth a little open, her gaze lit with emotion. Heaving a great sigh – he thought she was about to cry – she walked away.

When he caught up to her, at the farthest point of land, her cheeks were wet. "There's something I should tell you –" she said, almost inaudibly.

"What?"

"What's that?" she said, and she clambered down the rock to pick something up – a fishing float carved in wood, painted red and white, shaped like a little top. "Funny!" she said. "Do you want it?" He shook his head. She threw it in the lake. "A float that floats," she said vacantly.

"Come on, Ann, tell me."

"Just hold me." Her body shook in his arms; she wept into his shoulder as she struggled not to weep. He doubted she had changed her mind about England; yet part of him, in the face of her odd behaviour, clung to that hope.

"You don't have to go," he told her.

"Go where?"

"To England. You don't have to go."

She went still in his arms, as if considering, as if this was a novel thought. He stroked her head until, abruptly, she pulled back to regard him. "I'm going tomorrow, Billy." The tenderness in her voice hurt him more than what she had said. She flushed and averted her eyes. "I better get back to my boat." They said nothing to each other as they went down among the houses and crossed the beach to the dock. Just before she drove off, her face lifted with a look of misery; again she seemed to be struggling with herself, on the verge of saying something she could not say.

The next day, he hitched into Black Falls, determined to get an answer to the question she had avoided: *What was it you wanted to tell me?*

In a phone booth, he leafed through the directory and found two Scotts. One of the addresses led him to a small, poor house by the paper mill: it was clearly not hers. The other belonged to a big frame place among a group of similar houses, held in a bend of the Old Woman River. There was a yellowing maple on the lawn and a deep, vine-shaded porch where a black-and-white cat sat watching him. The driveway, like the garage it led to, was empty. Certain it was her house (though he had no proof other than this certainty), he climbed the steps to the front door and banged the heavy knocker. Peering with cupped hands through a window, he saw magazines lying in disarray, a gleam of fireplace implements. Everything he saw spoke of her – of some facet of her, too new to be anything but mysterious – and of her disappearance: details of experiences with her he would never have.

She finds herself entranced by her moored canoe, adrift on the deep, trembling flag of itself. By a rock with the face of a Roman emperor. And by the mornings and evenings, banding the shores with a new geology of rosy light; and the ragged dark flames of the junipers; and the cedars huddling like bishops over the rock. Ecstasy: but melancholy at the core. She knows she will never live long enough or paint well enough to capture more than a sliver of it.

Her giantess stalks into a rich, late-day light. Unscrewing a full-length mirror in the cottage, Ann lugs it to her studio and props it beside her canvas. Stripping off her clothes, she studies herself in the glass: her own body has become another object, a bit alien in its animal strangeness: what pale, erect, alert-eyed creature is this? Her brush dabs at the canvas. But no, she isn't seeing clearly! She studies her reflection more closely. That branching vein. That mole.

Up by seven each morning, she takes her coffee on the deck. Everything, these days, has the clarity of first sight. The soft clunk of her dark blue mug on the table. The light's slow guillotine down a rock. A merganser floating on green water, as still as jade. In her studio, every brush is alive. Filbert. Fitch. Round. Hake. She feels she's re-discovered why she became a painter. She has the old exuberance again. She could be eight years old, sitting before a sheet of blank paper: a new world.

One evening, pouring herself a second glass of pinot, she puts a Joni Mitchell tape on the boom box and dances around the living room. She is far, far in another place, as she moves slowly, at ease in her swaying body, singing around the living room and out onto the porch, past the hammock and the old table and the screens where the pines press close, just beginning to stir in a rising wind. When the phone rings, she tries to ignore it. Finally, she stops and stares at the black, ugly thing trilling on its wicker table until it stops. In another life, Joni leaves Africa behind, skating away down a prairie river. Moving abruptly, she runs the tape back to the beginning of "Carrie" and starts again. But she can't get back, the garden's closed, and when the phone starts again, she goes to it almost angrily.

Richard sounds impatient. "Where were you?"

"What's up?"

"Everything okay?"

"Fine," she says, immediately regretting the sharpness of her tone. "Great, actually."

"So have you called the Gotliebs yet?"

"Richard, I said I would and I will." The music is still blaring and she excuses herself to turn it down. She feels flushed, off balance: tensed against Richard for nagging her and annoyed with herself for forgetting to call. When she picks up the phone, he says, "Hey, I love you, you know." A pause falls and she feels he is waiting for her to echo his phrase, but she can't, not at the moment; the feeling isn't there. "Thank you," she says quietly, while the silence at her ear grows hard.

She calls the Gotliebs and, for the sake of kindness, lies. "We've got our wires crossed. Richard has the minister of natural resources coming out that weekend – some other political types – party stuff, been on the calendar for months. I just didn't notice." She can sense Pamela's withdrawal – a note of suspicion behind her cheerful acceptance – and suddenly Ann is sick of the small lies and soiled shortcuts of friendship, sick of herself. Later, outside, the sight of her deck chair floods her with sadness: the empty chair, a magazine dropped beside it, like a glimpse of a life she hasn't lived.

Her painting starts to go badly. Not all at once, but she is distracted now – by what she cannot say. She loses patience, curses at her mistakes, throws pencils and brushes around the room. She does some yoga to compose herself and, not entirely composed, tries again. By the next afternoon it is clear: the holy ghost has up and left. She knows it *will* do that, it has done it before; but how long it will be absent for – a day, weeks, *years again*? She struggles on, but a sense of panic grows in her as the painting no longer tells her what to do. Was that *it* then? Was that her rebirth as a painter – a two-week wonder?

On Saturday morning, she picks up Richard and Rowan at the Harbour. With her work failing – the old desolation threatening – she turns to them gladly, with a hint of desperation. She fusses over Rowan and tells her story of the snake. She wants to be close to Richard. At supper that evening she tells him she's rescheduled the Gotliebs.

"Good," he says distractedly and turns away to Rowan.

As usual, he has brought his work. For the rest of the weekend, she hears him tapping on his computer or chatting on the phone. *It might seem unfair, but you have to consider it from the point of view of the law.* And: *Uhuh, Uhuh. Uhuh.* Speaking with a quick impatience she knows so well: he understands what you're saying before it's out of your mouth. She brings him snacks. Coaxing and cheerful, she tries unsuccessfully to draw him out.

She turns to Rowan, who now and then will still allow her to hug him or stroke his hair. He wants her to play a video game that hooks up to their TV. You shoot at gremlins with a toy gun. The thing grates on her and she wonders how he can be so excited by the identical little

figures chugging along to their inane music, falling off
cliffs, climbing walls, coming on and on like insects in a
nightmare. "I can't do this!" she cries at one point, throwing the gun aside. At the look on Rowan's face, she takes
it up again. And outside: the bright day wasting.

Later, they paddle into the marsh to search for the
snake. The hull brushes through the dry weeds, and for a
while they are stuck in a shallow patch, until she gets out
and heaves them free. And the sun is hot, and the gunnels
are tacky, and among the reeds, nothing moves but themselves. Rowan is wearing a hat; but still she worries about
his getting sunstroke. Her son seems to her to exist perpetually on the edge of dangers he is not aware of, so she
must be doubly vigilant. *Give the boy some space*, Richard
keeps telling her, and she knows he's right. She loves her
son too much, she thinks: or not well enough.

They beach the canoe to explore an island. While she
detours into the bushes for a pee, Rowan goes on ahead,
and when she finally catches up to him, he's stopped on
a flat rock beach on the other side of the island, facing a
seagull standing thirty or forty feet away. The white bird is
watching him closely. Rowan seems to be trying to engage
it: he has hunched himself up, like the bird, and is holding
out his arms like wings, slowly moving them up and down,
with more patience and grace than Ann would have thought
possible. The bird itself seems unsure. It ruffles its feathers
and, throwing back its head, emits a cry. Rowan answers
with a softer cry. Now the bird stretches out its wings as if
about to take flight but then, apparently thinking better of

it, folds them again and tucks up one leg while balancing on the other.

Rowan, too, tucks up a leg. And so the two regard each other, boy and bird, balancing on one leg, while Ann watches them both. At last the gull flaps off. As Rowan turns to follow it, he finds Ann and, to her delight, calls to her eagerly.

"I was talking to a bird!"

"Yes, I saw!" she cries back.

They go back toward the canoe together, climbing up and down over the hills of rock. He is talking about the bird, but not maniacally, not out of control, not in the least. He is calm, and keeps pausing in consideration. Ann stays as close to him as she can on the rock, among the prickly junipers: listening intently as his face floods with animation, reaching out to brush his damp hair.

That evening, Pamela and Larry Gotlieb come by with their boys to pick up Rowan: he is staying overnight at their cottage. When they leave, Richard goes back to work. At a loss after Rowan's departure, she washes the dishes and cleans the stove, thinking the whole time she should paint. But she cannot make herself go up the stairs. There is a kind of repugnance in her. Because what if her painting's no good? What if she's been fooling herself? So much work and worry and stress – for some colours smeared on canvas! It seems madness to go back to that, and she wants it more than anything. But she cannot make herself go up the stairs.

Later, she keeps herself awake by reading in the living room. Now and then the whine of Richard's computer sounds in the porch. At last, he turns it off and comes in to her, sitting on the couch with a pronounced sigh.

"Hard go?" she says, smiling. She has been waiting for him.

"No harder than usual. I have to say, the law has lost some of its allure."

Something in her comes awake at his confession. He rarely allows her these glimpses.

"You think politics would be better?"

"More variety," he says. "Worse money. It's not really about the money."

"A chance to help?"

He shifts uncomfortably. "The law, the kind I do, it's beginning to seem all the same. I never really cared for the law."

He has never admitted this, though she has half-guessed it – that he has chosen the law not out of love, but for more practical reasons; perhaps he never really chose it at all. Dragging his hands over his face, he falls silent. Concerned he will slip away again, she says, "You've been a wonderful lawyer though."

"There are better."

She can sense his disappointment in himself – a vulnerability that moves her. "If you want to run, I'll be behind you. I can't promise I'll play the political wife, at least not like some play it, but – I want it for you, Rich. If that's what you want."

Still he remains silent.

"I just hope we don't drift away from each other. It's hard enough as it is. People have to make time for each other –"

"Isn't that what we're doing now?" he says, a bit peevishly.

"Yes! Yes!" Whenever they talk like this – and the times are rare – she comes up against his resistance; and behind the resistance, what? Fear? Anger? She thinks of his father, who tyrannized their little house with his rages. And his mother, the last word in interfering women. When Ann first met Richard, Doris was still buying his underwear.

"I'm afraid for us sometimes," she says. It comes out before she can think. "I don't mean that to be as ominous as it sounds, but we have to be more than a business partnership who keep our sides of this – enterprise – going. We've become kind of dry, don't you think?"

"Well," he says, heaving one leg over the other. She knows he has taken her remark as a criticism.

"You know I love you," she says, reaching toward him. It has come upon her in an instant: a swift intuiting of his need, of all they have been through together. She grips his hand where it rests on the broad arm of his chair. Fumbling a bit, it turns and squeezes hers.

That night they make love, and the next day a kind of melancholy fills the cottage. From the moment she gets out of bed, she feels like weeping. Just before noon, the Gotliebs bring Rowan back – they are on their way to lunch at the Harbour. After they leave, Ann talks Richard and Rowan into going out in the canoe.

The afternoon is hot, the rocky shores with their juniper bushes go by with the drugged pulse of her headache. She does most of the talking – she can hear her cheerful voice willing them all into a holiday mood. Behind her, Richard scarcely responds, while his paddle takes sharp bites of the water. From her seat amidships, she compliments Rowan on his bow work, and he tells her, testily, he *knows* he's a good bowsman. Feeling slighted, she falls silent.

At last they beach the canoe on an island and carry their cooler to the shade. Immediately, Rowan wants to go swimming. "Not too long," she calls after him. "We don't want the food going bad," and Richard says, in his patient-impatient cajoling way, as if she really should consider relaxing some time, "It'll be *fine*, Ann."

She perches up on the rock while Rowan shows off for her, crying "Okay, watch this one!" He runs tearing off a small cliff to cannonball into the water. After each splash, he climbs out to see how far the drops have flown. "You try it, Dad."

She watches her husband climb the rock. His big pale body has grown a paunch he seems half-proud of. When she met him, she had not been particularly attracted to him, physically. In bed they proved not to be the best of matches, but her more sexually compatible lovers had seemed deficient in other ways. Not that pleasure wasn't important – at times in her life it had been all-consuming – but the men she knew between Billy and Richard had been, in some critical sense, deficient. Lovely in their way, intelligent, original, sensitive, but there had been too much of the boy about them. They all had big dreams but nothing ever seemed to come of them. Richard was different. She had sensed it right away. There was purpose in him, and a calm, steady pursuit of it. He would get somewhere that mattered and he would do so by his own hard work, his own merits. He was three years older than she, and there *was* something more mature in him, mixed with a kindness that in those days seemed without ulterior motive. The naïveté of his devotion moved her; he seemed not to see her faults, or at least not to care about them, and she found herself trying to be the finer person he imagined. Combined with his ability to set and stay a course, this quality made him extremely attractive. She could sense in him the possibilities of a life for herself – a solid place where she could give her attention to her work and, some day, to having a child.

She had painted well in those days – the early days of her marriage. She had received good reviews, she had been named one of the country's best under-thirty artists. And after Billy came back into her life, into their life, her surge of work had continued. She painted *The Chronicle of Childhood* then, which was bought by a public gallery outside Toronto. It was only later, after the land claim failed, that the greyness set in – not all at once, but in patches of lethargy, of lost directions, of paintings she could only half-complete. She did finish some – darker works that sold poorly. But there were too many days, far too many days, when her senses seemed blunted and the world outside her unreal.

Her husband crashes into the water and when he pops up some distance away, he looks over at her, as Rowan did earlier.

She claps her hands and grins.

That evening she drives Rowan and Richard to Carton Harbour: they are returning to Black Falls for the week. In the parking lot, Richard asks her to call Elaine Shewaybick to help with the dinner for the Benoits the following weekend. "Make sure she understands she can stay the night. Don't want her driving back in the dark." Ann questions whether they really need Elaine, but Richard insists. "I don't want you stuck away in the kitchen. The Benoits will want to see you." Back at Inverness, Ann sits for a long time in her chair overlooking the channel. All energy, all purpose, seemed to have drained away. Making herself get up, she goes in and calls Elaine's place, on Pine Island; but it seems her phone has been disconnected; she will have to drive up to the Island in the morning.

The next day, she wakes feeling a little better. She *could* work, but she's still loath to climb to her studio. Avoiding it, she swims, changes into fresh clothes, and sets out in the motorboat for Pine Island.

The floating dock, as usual, is crowded with boats, and she has to tie up on their perimeter, stepping from boat to boat until she reaches the dock. A little girl sits in a boat by herself. Ann speaks to her, but she goes on staring straight ahead, her hands clasped in her lap.

Crossing the beach, Ann is climbing toward the houses when a movement startles her. A dog has got up – one of the big, half-wild dogs of the Island. Shaking itself off – releasing a cloud of dust and straw – it begins to edge toward her, growling as it slowly places one foot, then another.

She stops. Up the treeless lanes, no one is in sight. Behind her, at the dock, the little girl sits with her back to her, intent on her solitary journey.

"Go on! Shoo!"

People have been attacked by these dogs, she knows; a child was nearly killed. Beyond, the houses go on simmering under the sun, indifferent. She feels she has met a kind of truth. *Nothing cares for me here.* When the animal charges, she cries out in fear, but the dog veers off the path and promptly collapses, panting as if laughing at its little joke.

She goes on up the lanes. She's completely off balance now and sweating heavily. *Why did I ever wear jeans?* (*Because you don't like your legs,* answers a small voice.) Rounding the corner of Elaine's house, she finds half a dozen women sitting about in lawn chairs. On the ground, in the shade cast by the house, are scattered sewing baskets, rolls of tanned hide, swaths of coloured cloth. Elaine isn't here.

"I hope I'm not interrupting," she smiles, coming forward. As one, the women have fallen silent, like birds in a bush. "I just ran into one of those awful logs. I mean, dogs. Really, I was sure he was going to eat me."

Making herself the butt of her own story, she succeeds in provoking a few smiles. She knows most of the women here and expects to feel at home. But today, she finds them impassive. "I just need to speak to Elaine." Someone says that Elaine will be out in a minute and the silence continues. Normally, such reticence does not bother her on Pine Island, where chatter for politeness' sake is not the style. But today her response is to talk more – though she senses this is only making things worse.

Nearby, a woman with heavy arms is sitting with her sewing in her lap.

"Oh beautiful, Deirdre!" Ann says. "I hope you'll sell that pair to me." The big suede mitts *are* beautiful. Deirdre has covered the cuffs with wine-coloured felt, and on this she is beading a flower design.

After a pause, Deirdre says, "Well, maybe Ross'll sell them to you."

"Oh, they're for your husband!" Ann knows she has made a gaffe, assuming Deirdre was making the gloves to sell in the co-op, assuming that the offer of money would be welcome. For a moment she sees herself through their eyes: the white woman who comes to buy things. It is a relief when Elaine appears and she can go off and talk with her.

In the end she leaves feeling as she used to in school, when she was rejected by the reigning clique of girls. Near a clutch of dusty poplars, she stops. The path to her right leads to Billy's house and for some time she looks at it, past an abandoned bicycle toward a clump of birch that she knows lies within sight of his windows.

Halfway to the trees, she is struck with the sense she has done this before, walked toward the blue house in a state of anxious uncertainty, with a feeling that her life, somehow, hangs in the balance – and that what is happening to her is not entirely within her power. So the afternoon of grey calm, all those years ago, comes back. It had happened. That slipped condom, in all probability. Her doctor had broken confidence and told her father; her father had phoned her mother in Montreal and in no time her "predicament" had become the atmosphere they breathed. There was an assumption that "it" had to be taken care of; in one way, she was grateful. But her parents were so quick to take over that she felt completely ignored. Her vague, neurasthenic mother had become steely and organized. Since Ann was going to London, and since London was far away, Bernice took advantage of a family connection and made "arrangements." Her father's contributions were less helpful. One day he threw a china figurine at the wall. He shouted at her that she must not see Billy again. Of course he had already told her this once, to no avail. *This time* – but he could not complete his threat. She pitied him, in his exasperation. He seemed diminished; while she experienced a sudden access of power. She was in some way unassailable. Everyone was terrified of what was inside her. With utter calm, she looked back at him. He left the room. At the base of the wall lay the headless figurine.

Driving the boat to Pine Island, she felt she was fleeing a communal madness, toward a place of safety. Her

mother had said, *Do not tell Billy. He does not need to know.*
She had agreed, but racing through the islands, any sense
of a fixed plan had evaporated.

When he stood up in surprise, scattering the bowl of
peas on the ground, she saw for the first time how young
he was. Those wide-set, eager eyes meeting hers: he was a
boy, really. She saw herself living with him in some poor
house in the Falls, tending a squalling child, while he
dragged himself off each day to work in her father's lumberyard. Her freedom gone, her hopes for her art gone.
No, she would spare them both.

But a few minutes later, walking with him over the
rocks, breathing the scents of the lake, all her terror of
spoiling her life lifted, and it seemed the most natural
thing in the world to have a baby with him. What was she
so afraid of? She started to weep, and she could not stop.
Surely there was room on their voyage for an extra pas-
senger. For half a minute, the thought seduced her. But
then she saw, again, how impossible it all was. She
couldn't have a baby and she couldn't tell him about it:
because he would want her to have it. And in any case, no
matter what he said, she was going away. How could she
tell him about her pregnancy and her decision to end it,
and then disappear, leaving him alone with such knowledge? So she kept her secret, and the whole way back to
her boat, walking beside him, she seemed to feel a tiny life
fluttering in panic inside her.

———

She finds him sitting on a chair near his woodpile, working on an outboard motor he has fixed on a board between two trees. He looks around as she approaches and she experiences a plunging excitement, a kind of dread, which she covers by adopting a jocular tone. "One of your lovely dogs came after me," she tells him. "You're a savage people, aren't you, keeping such *beasts!*" She speaks with ironic emphasis: the sort of thing her English friends might say, that she might have said herself while living in England.

His eyes, she notices, are pouched with fatigue. He is watching her closely and still hasn't spoken, which only increases her nervousness.

"I came up to ask Elaine to help us out. So, what are you up to there?"

He looks back to the engine. "Oh. She's been acting up on me."

"Well, they'll do that, won't they, these females? No end of trouble."

She tells him more about the dog. She can't seem to drop her joking, slightly arch manner, though she is perfectly conscious of it – her voice running on too loudly, while underneath she wants to weep. He tells her a little story about the same dog, while she stands listening, relieved that he has connected with her. Following him into the house, she drifts about, chatting with him while he makes sandwiches. His homemade shelves are stacked with paperbacks: biographies, history, thrillers, popular science. The sight of his books moves her, has always moved her: he never completed high school.

Carrying two kitchen chairs outside, they sit in the shade with their plates balanced in their laps. He seems reticent, burdened, and she tells him about a recent trip to Toronto, a month before – hoping to engage him, to signal that she's put the strains of Lola's behind her.

Some distance away, two boys are making their way across the rock. Noticing Billy watching them, Ann breaks off. One of the boys is stomping on a beer can. The other picks up a stone and fires it toward a house where it rattles on the roof and drops to the ground. There is anger there, and a kind of loose despair, as if at any moment they might throw themselves off a cliff.

Billy's intense focus alerts her. She asks who they are.

"Oh," he says, seeming ill at ease, "the tall one's Randy Kennedy. The other, I think he's Kelly Laverne's brother." They watch until the boys are out of sight.

When he begins to talk, it is slowly, hesitantly, as if each detail were painful to recall. He was out for a walk, he tells her, when he came across some boys sniffing gas. She hears about a boy kicking another boy, about a little boy curled up, stoned, under a tree. The story appalls her.

"That's awful," she breathes, after he has been silent for a while, and feels the futility of her words.

She asks what can be done.

He shakes his head slowly, and she thinks this is his answer: nothing. "Oh," he says, looking off to the lake. "If their fathers had jobs. If they *had* fathers, some of them. If all booze vanished from the face of the earth. If people would go back to the bush . . . We've been saying the same things for years. But maybe it's not that at all . . ."

He is still for a while, then with a shrug he looks up at her, and in his eyes is a faint smile as if everything he's described is a bitter joke: the fatalism that forever marks the gulf between her world and his.

Some time later, when she says she should be getting back, neither of them moves.

"By the way, your pickerel was delicious. Thank you."

He nods in acknowledgement.

She gets up and starts to leave, then stops. "Do you ever think about the old days with Richard? The three of us?" She can feel herself redden, sensing the topic is unwelcome. "Anyway. Maybe come down some time when he's there."

Billy gives a nearly imperceptible nod and goes on watching her with a tender, unguarded openness. Heart slamming, she turns and walks away.

In his office in the Sherwood Plaza, on the outskirts of Black Falls, Richard hovers by his secretary's desk.

"If Reg Benoit calls –"

"Yes, I'll put him through."

"Or his secretary. Or an aide – whoever – I'll talk."

"Yes. I know." A twitch in Marg Corelli's cheek, the merest hint of impatience that momentarily reveals what she is probably thinking: that he has told her this before and that after twelve years of pretty much faultless service, she might reasonably be trusted to get it right. Annoyed with himself, Richard drifts to a filing cabinet, ruffles through some papers to no particular end, and finally – no help for it – returns to his office. The doorway gives a view of his littered desk and, behind it, through a picture window, the long-abandoned farm behind the mall. Humps of bedrock. Clusters of cedars. Bleached, leaning fenceposts. The saddled remains of a barn – all that has survived of some family's struggle to wring a living from land that should never have been cleared. He was elated to move out here to the Plaza, after the cramped old house where Doug Parsons had first set up his practice. In the right mood, he can take delighted notice of maples turning red, or a deer venturing from the bush that throws a dark streak across the horizon. But on this summer's day, as he turns past the end of his desk, the sun-whitened pasture oppresses him.

"All right, where were we?"

The woman perched on the edge of a wing chair smiles tepidly. Not long ago, a friend had appeared at her house to tell her that her husband was having an affair with a local businesswoman. "The cottage," she says, in a weak voice. She is pretty in a faux-blonde, cookie-cutter way; Richard finds her tiny mouth intriguing – a sea creature's mouth, a valve. "It's mostly paid off."

Richard makes a mark on his pad. "Whose name is it in?" His pen makes two idle loops, and he looks up. "Gail? Whose name?"

Her eyes brim with water: as if she were drowning from inside. When he indicates the tissue box beside her, she takes no notice. Rounding his desk, he plucks up a few tissues and tucks them into her hand. While she wipes at her cheeks and examines the wad of tissue, Richard waits.

He swivels in his chair, pulls the cap of his pen, replaces it. Through the wall, he can just make out the high, happy tenor of Doug Parsons in full flight. He can see his partner, tilting back with his feet crossed on his desk, the phone coddled at his ear, his fingers tearing a bit of paper to shreds, his eyes still lit, after decades of lawyering, with the joy of the chase. He has to admit that he's never had Doug's fire. He chose the law because he wanted to make good money, because business didn't interest him, because he had to do *something*. Something to launch him as far as possible from the tiny Scarborough bungalow where no room was far enough away from the rest, no door thick enough to keep out what he did not want to hear. Yes, one day he would have a peaceful, ordinary life. After long persistence, he has achieved what he wanted, more than he ever imagined; and he is proud of this, proud of his family, his status, his living, proud of the tenacity around which his sense of himself, of his power and ability, has coalesced – this thing in him that can forge ahead, no matter what. It had been a boon in law school, a necessary boon, for he had to override his distaste every time he opened a law book and met those sentences modelled, it seemed, on the Gordian knot; sentences strewn with absurd repetitions, distinctions so fine they made the old theological question of how many angels could dance on a pinhead sound almost sensible.

Confessing his weariness to Ann the other night had been difficult: to his surprise, he had experienced shame. For he does not think of himself as either emotional or a quitter. Talking with her, he felt he was both. *But you've been a wonderful lawyer.* He wanted to weep at that, he hardly knew why.

Politics: his first love. He's done backroom work for his party, he's gone door to door, he's been a delegate to policy conferences, he's gone cap in hand to local businesses: he's paid his dues, and when, at a barbeque at Reg Benoit's Random Lake house the previous year, Reg remarked in the presence of several senior party people that he'd make a first-rate candidate, Richard felt his time was arriving at last. He knew in his bones that politics would never turn into the dry-as-dust duty law had become, for he's already savoured one of its principle pleasures: the sound of his name on other people's lips. Since word has gone round that Reg has singled him out, people act differently toward him. They approach him to ask if they can work for him; to see if he could have a word with the minister. They assume he has a power he does not have, at least not yet, and though he does his best to disabuse them, he can see (and takes secret pleasure in the fact) that they do not believe him. His name has been in the papers. He was interviewed on a local TV channel on the subject of garbage disposal. He has discovered he thrives on the sense of being at the centre of things, someone who can make a difference.

But Reg has not yet given him his clear blessing, and since Reg – who holds the seat next to Nigushi – is not only the minister of natural resources, but the party's northern Ontario boss, this is critical. Richard is not sure whether he should ask Reg outright or wait for him to act on his own. Meanwhile, he has heard that two or three others are circling the nomination: a fact that has deprived him of sleep – sent him to the bottle of lorazepam he hides from Ann in his golf bag.

He has left his door ajar so he can overhear Marg. *Parsons, Honderich, and Galuta. Yes? Yes? No, I don't think so. No, he's busy right now.* Across his desk, a woman with inky blotches under her eyes is staring at him. For a second, he cannot remember why she is there.

The interior of his BMW is stifling. He punches up the air conditioning and, as he swings into the traffic, slips Wynton Marsalis into the tape deck. This moment is usually his best of the day: a pocket of freedom where the gods of possibility can regroup.

But today, he has a headache, and the traffic is slow. A young woman in a hard hat and fluorescent bib stands beside the road, working a Stop sign in a cloud of shimmering dust while behind her enormous machines back and run, back and run. At the next light, he beats his fingers on the wheel (no longer in time) as his gaze strays over the hazed city toward the distant cube of the paper mill. On the bridge, there's another holdup. Below, on the sun-smitten rock, a gull stands with its head back, its neck and chest convulsing in a silent scream.

All day, for no particular reason, he's been aware of his father – as if Sully were loitering nearby, just out of sight – an old, familiar feeling of oppression. His father had not been like other fathers. His friends had fathers with names like Bob Stone or Jack Boileau: self-contained men, who held impressively aloof, and who went to jobs indoors, in offices and mills. But his father was Sully Galuta, Polish immigrant, garbage collector in the city of Scarborough, self-styled expert on every subject under the sun, butcher of the English language. One day Richard's best friend referred to Sully as "a big know-nothing." They had fought – more or less to a draw – and when Richard went home with a torn shirt and filthy face, Sully upbraided him. What did he mean by wrecking a good shirt? Did he think money grew on the leaves? People would think he was no better than some goddamn wop. And Richard, who had just been defending his father's honour, found himself hating the man who loomed over him in his undershirt. Too proud and angry to explain himself, Richard had turned away and received for his audacity a smack across the ear that made his head ring.

Yet he had loved his father, at least in the early days: his rough affection could make the sun come out. Sully led him into the local ravine to collect mushrooms; or they drove out of the city to watch the hawks on their annual migrations – times alone, when Sully's more embarrassing excesses could not be witnessed by anyone. Life with his father was a kind of secret, known only to him and his mother. Doris waited tables in a greasy spoon – a thin, energetic woman who walked with a slight tilt, as if advancing into a strong headwind. Richard sensed she was constantly managing her husband: steering him toward cheerfulness if he was down, or trying to moderate him if he got too high. Sometimes the two of them danced around the tiny living room to Lawrence Welk. His father would pump and twirl through the polka, surprisingly light on his big feet; and his mother, who was slight in comparison, would put her head back and laugh – on a note that to Richard sounded false, and touched him with a faint, inexplicable fear. He felt collusive with his mother: very early on, he learned that his father was deficient, even pitiable. It was important not to take your eye off him.

Occasionally his mother appeared with a bruise around her eye or on her cheek; she might, one morning, limp out the door to work. At such times, she was more determinedly cheerful than ever, frantically insistent they were no different than anyone else and, even more importantly, no different from the people they believed themselves to be.

Once, the two of them had gone camping, father and son. And Sully was happy as he so often was in the woods. Through the trees of the provincial park, other tents were visible. "Like this," Sully told him, as he dug a trench to carry off the rainwater. He chopped down saplings to make a frame for the tent. He chopped firewood. As their perogies sizzled in the pan, a ranger arrived to tell his father he had broken several laws: he would have to pay a fine. Spittle flying, Sully had raged about how no one in this country knew how to camp the right way, and how he was going to speak to the mayor of Scarborough, who was a personal friend of his, while the man in the uniform went on calmly writing. Afterwards, Sully tore their camp apart, flinging the illegal tent poles in the lake, kicking dirt into his illegal trench, and they started the long drive home. In the car, the monologue continued, while Richard silently vowed that when he grew up he would not be like his father. It was a defining moment of his life: all his reasonableness and self-control flowed from it; his hatred of strong emotion; his ability to float above the fray, unflappably sanguine, with a hint of pity or contempt for those who could not control themselves.

Sully dropped dead of an embolism when Richard was eighteen. He can recall, still, his father's head laid on its satin pillow in the funeral home. The few strands combed back over his bald head; his mouth too big, as if it had been stretched; and the hands, the huge, nicked hands clasped over his one good suit, the beaded loop of his rosary draped across his fingers. The numbness of those days lasted for a long time, as if Sully had gone out with a final, enormous explosion, stunning Richard and his mother both.

Escaping the traffic at last, he turns into the neighbourhood of Cartier Point: an enclave of big, 1920s-era houses held in a bend of the river. Fifteen years ago, they bought a two-storey, stuccoed house with a tower he considers pretentious, a stone's throw from where Ann grew up. When recently he suggested they move to a new subdivision on the edge of town, Ann wouldn't hear of it: she didn't want one of those new houses, she said, with their oversized garages that made the whole street look like an industrial park. She was adamant, as she often was; her ferocity, her deep certainty about some things, were qualities he both respected and feared. He had a sense sometimes of putting his own opinions on, like a style in coats; and while he had his convictions too, he thought that at times she was excessive in the way she clung to hers. She *knew* those houses on the new estates were bad. They were wrong. They were an excrescence in taste and social living. And when he said, modestly, "Well for *you* they are. Lots of people, me for instance, actually like them," his relativism left her unimpressed. He felt superior to her in these matters: more reasonable, more generous. And yet at the same time, he envied her her passions – the natural authority they gave her. There was something primitive in his wife, he had thought more than once. Something capable of striking at random, out of an obscure depth.

Their neighbourhood is in decline. Some of the bigger houses have been broken into apartments; many lawns and gardens are no longer well kept: he can't imagine Reg being impressed. They had compromised with an addition – family room and expanded kitchen below; a studio for Ann above, its huge windows overlooking the long backyard, the maple tree, the crumbling brick of the enormous outdoor grill built by an earlier owner, the dyke that protects the neighbourhood from the river. He slides past the overgrown hedge, its tiny leaves crisping in the drought, stopping just short of the open garage where her Honda sits. He misses his wife. Her decision, weeks ago, to stay at Inverness took him off guard. Billy had shown up and stayed for supper. Later, she had been getting ready for bed when she announced that she couldn't leave her new painting – it was simply going too well. She intended to remain at the cottage on her own. He picked up something in her voice – a nervous eagerness to gain his favour, as if she were afraid he might not grant it (when had he ever stood in the way of her painting?) – a certain thickening of her words, as if she were holding something back. He thought immediately of Billy – a crude reaction, he decided, and unworthy of her, of them both. Yet waking in the night, he finds himself returning to Billy obsessively – to the Toronto hotel room where they confronted each other ten years before, after hearing they'd lost the claim. Billy sitting on the edge of his bed while he paced the fading carpet, arguing that they should appeal. Billy hadn't seemed to be listening, but sat in silence, rigid as wood, and it was only some minutes after Richard finished that he began to speak. He had attacked Richard's handling of the case, accusing him of going maverick, of ignoring their agreed-upon tactics. But he had said worse, much worse. Richard can't shake it from his thoughts. He finds himself back in that tawdry room, compulsively speaking the words he was unable to speak at the time: piling up his arguments, point by unassailable point. But it is never enough.

It galls him that Billy and Ann are both at Nigushi. It's true that Pine Island and Inverness are miles apart. But seen from the vantage point of Black Falls, a ninety-minute drive to the southwest, that distance shrinks to almost nothing.

In the kitchen, Mrs. Paisley sits behind the glass-topped kitchen table, with her thick shanks braced under the lap of her patterned dress and the pages of the *Black Falls Sentinel* spread before her. Richard makes dutiful small talk while she waits to be picked up by her husband. No, Ann hasn't phoned, she tells him. He pours a Scotch and calls hello into the family room, where Rowan is watching TV. He'd rather join his son, but Mrs. Paisley is tapping her finger on the paper.

Someone from Pine Island has been convicted of a stabbing in a downtown bar, apparently. "So *terrible*," she croons. "These people."

"Well." Richard swirls his Scotch. He knows it's pointless to argue with her. "It's only a chance that he's native."

For a second or two she stares at him from behind her bifocals.

"I'm afraid to go shopping. I've got nothing against them. But we can't have them just lying around."

"I really don't think they're any danger to you," Richard murmurs, glancing at the clock.

At last he can sprawl beside Rowan. It is a good moment – the best of the day – to lounge beside his son with his

Scotch as two guys with sticks wearing white pyjamas whack the hell out of each other.

"So how'd it go today?"

"Fine."

"How's the backwards skating?"

For a long moment Rowan simply looks at him. There is a sweetness in his face, a wondering openness that recalls his mother's more reflective moods. Reaching out, Richard squeezes the boy's knee in its faded jeans.

The white pyjamas continue their battling. It's a collage of footage from various matches, held together with the dubious bonding agent of disco music.

"When is Mom coming home?"

"Well, like I said, after this weekend – we've got a big dinner this weekend. I don't know if she'll come back on Monday with me or stay up for a few more days. She's got a painting going."

"I don't want to go to the Ducettes'."

"You wanted to before," Richard says, smiling encouragingly.

"I *said* I don't want to."

"Rowan, listen –"

"Really, I don't!"

Rowan's tears astonish him. They seem to astonish Rowan too. He sniffs and turns back abruptly to the TV. "Let's turn this thing down," Richard says. Finding the remote, he kills the sound. "Now, are you listening? You know you had a good time at the Ducettes' before. We had trouble getting you away."

"I want to be with you and Mom."

"It's just two nights, Row. We have people coming, for my business. It'll be boring, I can guarantee," Richard says, speaking as calmly as he can. "Remember, you *asked* to go to the Ducettes'. They're making special plans. You're going to the water slides." Rowan is watching the screen with his jaw thrust out – that, too, like his mother. "You *love* the water slides. Rowan, buddy, look at me –"

On the smooth rock shores of a bay not far from his house, their gold-brown bodies stand in the late-afternoon sun or cannonball into water crosshatched by their play. He listens to their cries, their watery explosions, as he works around the house. Their existence seems to him provisional, like the light that glows on their skin and gives the lake its steely sheen. When a day goes by without their appearing, he worries they have returned to the clearing. Yet the light keeps coming back. And the boys come back to the rock.

Since he surprised them that afternoon, they have avoided him: stepping off the path at his approach, falling silent as he goes by, unresponsive to his greetings. It is clear they remember how he had laid into them. He half-regrets it now. He should put them out of his mind. What good can he do? But he wakes thinking of them in the morning. At night, sitting out on his step, he listens to them laughing as they chase each other in the dark, and for a time all seems normal, and the hope rises that they have turned their backs on the gas.

But he cannot tell for certain. He can only see what he can see. That cut over George Shewaybick's eye, glimpsed across a pile of boxes in the co-op – where did that come from? What are those boys carrying in that rolled blanket? Yvonne has given him names, bits of information, and soon he can fit each boy into the web of Island families, reading their parents and grandparents in the turn of a mouth, the darting of a glance. For they are aware of him, no doubt of that. At a distance, a few of them stand watching him across the rock, as a group of animals will watch in the stillness before flight.

Sometimes he sees girls among them – a promising sign, for he believes the girls are a good influence. In some ways, they have it worse – they have us to deal with – and yet (he's noticed it at Yvonne's) they have more maturity, more calm.

Among the boys, only Lance Cormier acknowledges him openly. He will sit on Billy's step and drink chocolate milk: a bright, eager little fellow with a ready laugh, perhaps a bit too ready.

Linda Cormier had been in her nightgown when Billy arrived with her son. Holes in the interior walls – the

wallboard punched right through – a stench of shit and
Linda, smelling of booze, chastising the boy for upsetting
her. Lance had clung to him, and in the end, with his own
past waking, Billy had brought him to Yvonne's.

Despite what Yvonne said about the clear-cuts, he keeps
thinking of taking Jimmy to the cabin on Silver Lake. Just
being in the bush can put a person right. He has seen it
many times.

One night he's at his sister's when Jimmy appears.
"Come and sit down!" his mother says. "We're hearing about
Mardi Gras." The boy has stopped inside the door. "Go on,"
Yvonne urges Billy. "The girl in the cat suit!" Brenda is
there too, playing on the floor; and Eddie, sitting across the
table with sawdust in his hair from his job in Black Falls.
Billy goes on with his New Orleans story: the party, the girl
in the cat suit, the men in the room upstairs. He does not
look at Jimmy again, but his attention tends toward the door
where the boy hovers. The story is for his nephew now.

Yvonne laughs. Eddie smiles. Brenda bangs a plastic
baseball bat on the floor. And still, by the door, the boy
waits with his head down, hair hanging past his face, as if
he were more interested in his shoes.

Billy has never put so much into a story. The girl in the
cat suit. The men in the room upstairs. The man with
the gun. Yvonne is roaring. By the door (he only dares look
once), Jimmy is frowning into space, his eye, the only one
visible past the wing of his hair, fiercely bright.

Sometimes Billy has coaxed a chickadee to take food from his hand. The crimp of its claws; the thrill of its tiny, pulsing life. Jimmy's presence is like that: a wrong move, or even the thought of one, and he will vanish.

Finishing his story, he begins another. His sister is soon laughing again – calling him her bad little brother. With exaggerated casualness, almost like someone asleep, Jimmy comes to the table, draws out a chair, and sits.

Yvonne tells stories from their childhood – the good ones involving a joke, or a piece of luck so outrageous you had to suspect the little people. The talk drifts to more distant times. That famine spring. The year the lakes were overrun with beaver. Now and then they fall silent, as the spaciousness of the country enters the room; the silences of winters past.

Billy tells a story of ice-fishing up at Silver Lake. He forgets even Jimmy as he talks – even though he is telling it for him: to show him another life. When he rediscovers the boy, he has pushed back his hair behind both ears and is watching him.

Two days later, he is outside his house working on his motor when Jimmy shows up. Alert, Billy goes on fiddling.

"This gas feed," he says, after a while. "Dead worm's got more appetite."

The boy watches intently. Sometimes with both eyes, sometimes only with one, as his hair falls back down. "Been thinking," Billy says, and has the sense of approaching a precipice. "Maybe you'd like to go up to Silver some time: see the cabin. Might be in rough shape, but . . ."

Jimmy says nothing. Billy works at a nut with a wrench; at last Jimmy's foggy adolescent's voice comes. "Mom says it's wrecked."

"Well." He twists the nut. "We could fix her up, if she needs it." He grasps the nut with his fingers. "Anyways, we could take a tent. Do some fishing. Maybe get us a moose."

More silence. He is pretending now, pretending an ongoing interest in the motor, pretending he's relaxed.

The boy's voice comes again: "What do you think happens, like – when we die?"

The question chills him. Yet in a way he is not surprised. *Ross Shewaybick*, he thinks. The boy's stiffened body, head on one side, spindling slowly under a tree.

"You mean, where do we go?"

"Like, do you think we exist still. Is there anything – like, after?"

"I guess that's the sixty-dollar question." Billy taps his wrench at a bolt: what does he know? "After my mother died, I felt she was still around. After a while, years really, I didn't feel that any more. She'd done what she had to here, I guess, then she set out on her three-day journey."

"You believe that stuff? The three-day journey?"

It was said the spirit travelled for three days to a good place, a better place – not the Christian heaven, he likes to think, but a place of bush and lakes: a place like this, without the pain.

But he does not know if it is true. Sometimes he thinks life's a crock. You live, without ever having asked for it, life drums on you (and maybe just a little you drum on it) and then it's over: and it means nothing. But you could not tell a boy that.

He wishes it was an earlier time, when he was a boy. People believed then, without even knowing they did. Not church belief, but the belief they drew in with their breath. You could sense it all around you – the way a man cut open a hanging carcass; the way a woman stitched up a rabbit-skin blanket – belief flowed in the sureness of their movements, in the shape of their lives.

But now most people ran from one thing to another, or did nothing at all, because belief was seeping away.

But you could not tell a boy that.

You believe that? The three-day journey? There is as much hope as skepticism in his nephew's voice, and he can prolong no longer. "I think so," he says, pausing in his discomfort. "Yup, think so."

When he gets his motor back on his boat, he lets Jimmy test-drive it, sitting amidships while his nephew steers. Jimmy handles the boat well, but as they come back, the motor splutters and dies. Stepping through the hull, Billy loses his balance, and for a moment has to steady himself by planting his hand on his nephew's head. It is the first time since Jimmy was little that he's touched him.

That night he dreams he is walking on a bridge that arches through the sky, over a vast expanse of water. On the other side is a land of such beauty he cannot hold back his tears. It resembles the earth – a place of rivers and forests and light, though the colours are more intense. A circle of men is there, sitting on the ground. At their invitation, he joins them and speaks about his life in the world he has left: how his deepest joy was to be on the land, amid the trees and the light. To hunt, to walk, simply to breathe: no joy to compare to that joy, no gift so great. The others nod knowingly. There are feathers in their hair. They are warriors and hunters and shamans; and though he does not recognize any of them, he feels completely at home. As he talks, he is overwhelmed with emotion and has to pause from time to time to collect himself.

Now a man who is as grey as ash walks up to the group. He reaches out and touches a finger to Billy's left cheek and makes a mark there. At first, he is frightened: who is this man, this ghost warrior? But the others do not seem alarmed. Reassured, he goes on talking.

The next day, he wakes in a buoyant mood, as if a screen between him and life has been removed. Everything is fresh, radiant.

He walks to his sister's. He wants to tell Jimmy that the three-day journey is true. Isn't that the meaning of his dream? That there is another world beyond this one? But Jimmy has not come home, Yvonne tells him. She hasn't seen him since yesterday. She's short with Billy, distracted by her children, and more upset, he senses, than she's letting on.

In the summer kids will sometimes stay out all night – probably Jimmy is fine. But after looking around the community and not finding him, he walks to the clearing. To his relief he finds it empty.

On the way home, he runs into the boy who had refused to give him his name that day in the clearing. Dwayne Turnbull. Yvonne has told him she doesn't like Jimmy hanging around with him: he's trouble, she says.

But he has his own opinion of Dwayne Turnbull. One time at the swimming place, when two boys were arguing, Dwayne, squatting higher on the rock, had observed silently until they started to push at each other, then he had come down the rock and separated them.

And now he is approaching, striding along with that cocky air. Dwayne looks up and Billy catches the openness of surprise. Then the face shuts down.

"Dwayne," Billy says. The boy barely mutters in response. He clearly intends to push on past, but Billy has blocked his way. He stops, his eyes full of suspicion and hostility. "I'm Billy Johnson. Jimmy's uncle."

"The great chief."

Billy ignores the mockery. "Yup, I was chief for a while. 'Bout ten years back."

"I heard you were gonna get us our land back."

"That's right."

"I guess it didn't work out."

"I was looking for Jimmy," Billy says. "You seen him?" The boy does not respond but stares in a neutral direction, off the path; Billy has a sense of angry dismissal. But there is something else here too: a kind of patient endurance, terribly familiar. It's as if all his people are here, waiting as they have always waited.

"No," Dwayne says finally and prods at the ground with his boot.

"Look, about the land claim," Billy says. He has a sudden urge to make the kid see how it was, all those years ago. "We put up a tremendous fight. But the thing was, we were before our time. The courts didn't even recognize we had a *right* to our land back then. So it was uphill all the way. We made some mistakes too. We were learning as we went along. But, Dwayne, we were in the right."

The boy sniffs. He has scarcely moved.

"It isn't over, you know. Someday we'll try again. Maybe when you're chief."

Dwayne shoots him a look of outrage and alarm.

"Why not?" Billy says. "You could do it. I know you could."

The boy's head goes down. He is breathing hard, as if caught in a sudden ambush not knowing which way to run. He seems on the verge of tears.

"Fuck you," he mumbles finally and pushes past Billy, nearly falling over a rock as he makes his escape. Billy watches the white T-shirt until it disappears down the path.

Trudging home, he is weighed down by a sadness that gives to the houses a cruel, sharp look in the bright sun. He remembers the ghost warrior – the cold brush of his finger – and the fear that something has happened to Jimmy settles more deeply with each step.

On the dock, several kids are shouting to one another as they jump from boat to boat. Maggie Roundhead. Wayne

McAllister. That boy with the shaved head – Ernie Squance. Giles Mackay's granddaughter. Balancing for a moment on the end of the dock, she rises a little on her toes and, quick as a kingfisher, knifes into the water.

Jimmy is not among them. Still, Billy climbs onto the dock. He does not know what he is doing now – simply moving forward because his momentum has carried him that way. All around him, the kids go on with their play, balancing on the moored boats or sitting on the edge of the dock as he plods through their midst. When he can go no farther, he stands looking over the bay, as pale as milk in the lowering sun. Below him floats the wet, dark head of Giles Mackay's granddaughter.

After a while he turns back and sees Jimmy. The boy is lying in a canoe almost hidden behind another boat. He has wormed his way under the thwarts, and is lying on his back with his open hands crossed over his chest, staring at the sky.

Before he can be noticed, Billy slips away.

The phone rings and it's Gerald Spicer's secretary; they have a job for him at the lodge. Gerald's partners are arriving in two days and would like to go fishing. Could Billy come over the night before and get the boat ready?

When the time comes, he walks to the little bay where he parks his boat in fine weather. Half a dozen boys are ranged along the shore, throwing stones at a floating log. Jimmy is there, and Dwayne – his head visible above the others. Billy's first instinct is to retreat. He doesn't want to put either them or himself through the usual awkwardness. But he has to get to his boat.

It sits in their midst, its motor drawn up, its bow pointed up the sand. No avoiding it, he thinks, and walks toward the boat. A couple of the boys, turning to pick up stones, notice him and fall still. "Hey, guys," he says in acknowledgement. Almost instantly the stone-throwing stops. Tossing his jacket in the boat, he is about to push it out when Lance Cormier says, "Billy! Watch this!" The little boy proceeds to wind up in elaborate imitation of some big-league pitcher – provoking a stir of amusement among the others – and fires his stone a mile wide of the log. Another boy scoffs, but Billy says, "Great form, Lance. You just have to work on the direction."

"Like this!" one of the other boys says, and he flings out a stone that drops close to the target.

"Good one!" Billy says and sees the stone lying beside his boat – a perfect throwing stone, a little flat, about the size of a plum, white granite streaked with grey.

He can feel their eyes on him as he picks it up and takes aim. He hasn't thrown for ages, and though he wasn't a bad ballplayer in his time, he knows he's rusty, that he might let the stone go a fraction too soon, or hold on to it too long and embarrass himself. But he's lucky, the stone arcs out, curving a little, and drops: a white blossom erupts beside the log.

"Anyone beat that!"

Pausing to push back his hair, Jimmy throws.

Another stone answers. And another. Soon everyone is throwing, the air is thick with stones, and over the western islands, the sun is a great yellow stone falling slowly.

He stands in their midst, throwing and encouraging them, laughing with pleasure. At the end of the line of boys, ten yards to his right, Dwayne, too, is throwing – though his manner is sullen and restrained.

Billy begins to throw alongside him, timing his shots to answer to Dwayne's. Soon they're engaged in a silent competition. He can feel the boy's anger in the snap of his arm, his eagerness to beat him. So he throws a little wide intentionally, and when one of Dwayne's shots bounces off the log, says, "You've got a damned fine arm. Ever play ball?"

Dwayne turns away to find another stone.

"You remind me of Pete Roundhead," Billy says, persisting. "Played third for us the year we went to the championships. Had a cannon for an arm. Accurate too. Norval Tooke hardly had to move his trapper."

Dwayne frowns as if he were examining each detail warily. Another boy asks, "You went to the championships?"

So he tells them. "Every game, that park over there would be full of people. We had this hitter, Bob Lavoie, came from the Falls – one home run, he drove that sucker so far into the bush we never found her till spring." They laugh at that, all except Dwayne. Yet Billy senses he's listening. "You guys'd make good ballplayers," Billy says. "Sure, you got good arms. We could give it a try some time – play a bit of ball." The boys stir a little, but none of them speak. Soon afterwards he shoves out his boat and starts the engine. As he pulls away, he looks back. The boys have not moved. They stand along the shore with the sun on their faces, watching him.

He sits in the same low chair as before while Gerald leans back against his desk in tennis whites, his arms folded, his face drawn. In the window behind him, the golf course refracts the glow of the evening through its emerald depths; a shaft of gold light falls across the carpet and burnishes the photo of the racing cars on the opposite wall. "This party I want you to take out – they're my biggest backers – it's important they have a good time. Between you and me, Billy, I'm not sure they really get what we do here.

"Frank Carpino – he's the main guy – puts up half the new buildings in Toronto. This place is really peanuts to him, more of a hobby, you might say. It would be a very good thing, Billy, if you could find him some fish. Maybe take them to the west there, some of the more remote bays. No portages, though – don't want him to have a heart attack – he's already had a couple. And don't go too far north, especially if there's a wind coming from that direction. Don't want them to hear the logging."

He spends the twilight hour readying the boat: a big new launch with a futuristic hull of white plastic, seats sheathed in red leather, a mini-bar, a fish finder, two powerful outboards. He checks the rods, the tackle, the live bait, and as darkness falls he retires to the cabin they've reserved for him. The swaybacked mattresses of Jack's era are gone: he reclines on a firm bed with half a dozen fragrant pillows behind him, flicking through the satellite channels.

On the wall by the bathroom, half-hidden by a lamp, hangs a black and white photograph taken, he guesses, about forty years before. A group of fishermen pose with their arms around each other's shoulders, grinning in tipsy, exaggerated camaraderie. Recognizing the guide squatting before them, he cries out. Matt looks younger than Billy is now; and it is partly this that moves him, to see him in his prime: barrel-chested, his black hair combed straight back. He thinks he knows how it was in that camp, at that moment. Matt would not have wanted to appear in the photo, but the men would have insisted. *Matt, Matt, you get in here*: raising him to equality with them – as they saw it – and enjoying their own generosity.

Matt might like the men or he might not; from his face it was impossible to tell. Unlike them, he would not have been drinking – his work would not allow it. Already, he would have set up the camp, cleaned their catch, set supper going. Entering the photo was just another task. His uncle's gaze, unlike the others, does not meet the camera. It was as if he were only nominally present in the little camp at the edge of the lake, his reality hidden, elsewhere.

By six the next morning, Billy is back at the dock. At six-thirty a sleepy young woman appears, pushing a trolley that bears a large, old-fashioned picnic hamper and a Styrofoam cooler. "Gerry wanted you to have this, 'case the fish aren't biting."

After she leaves, he goes back to planning the day. To Red Rock? No, too little water. Over to the reefs by Snake Island? He has done this often enough in the past: stared over the lake, balancing the weather with his long experience of Nigushi, until an answer pops up. Somehow, he just *knows* where the fish are hiding. But this morning Sealey Bay has an alien look, the light striking off the water with a harsh, tropical directness, and by the time his guests come tramping out the dock, half an hour late, he still has no idea where to take them.

Frank Carpino is well groomed, about seventy. He is wearing a khaki outfit and a wide-brimmed hat he holds in place with one hand as they run out of Sealey Bay. In the seats behind them sit Frank's son, Giorgio – thick-set, thirtyish – and Jim Patelli, an older man with a jovial, nervously deferential manner. As they drum around the great buttress of the Garden Peninsula, a stippling of the surface indicates the presence of shoals and he slows the boat to a crawl.

Giorgio leans forward from the back seat: "How fast will this thing go?"

Billy tells him he has never driven the boat before.

"Gerry says you're our most experienced guide."

"Been away," Billy shouts over his shoulder.

"Let's find out then," Giorgio shouts back. "Open her up."

"Problem is," Billy tells him. "There's reefs around here – a lot closer to the surface than they used to be: could tear the bottom out."

"Looks all right now," Giorgio shouts. "Just give us a blast."

Reluctantly, Billy opens the throttle; the bow lifts a little.

"Hey, don't be an old lady. Show us what she can do."

Ahead, he glimpses the slight shift in colouration that indicates another shallows. Ignoring Giorgio, he slows.

"What are you doing?" Giorgio shouts. "What's the guy doing?"

"I'm sure he knows his job," Jim Patelli says with a diplomatic laugh.

They cross open water and enter another straits. Rocks he has never seen before rise like the mottled skulls of giants beneath the surface. Whole islands have been joined by the emerging bottom, making larger islands. He finds himself in a dead end. The way ahead, clear a decade before, is a saddle of yellow rock on which he makes out the dark, mounded shape of something dead – possibly a deer. Vultures are waddling around it. At their approach, the huge birds run hopping into the air and beat away across the treetops.

He works the boat around slowly, reversing and creeping forward. He still doesn't know where he's going, feels he's only acting the role of the competent guide. Then the thought of the Vermillion occurs. The river is farther north than Gerald wants him to go, but it has always yielded fish. In forty minutes they are there.

The mouth of the Vermillion is a rock garden, more extensive than he has seen even in the worst of droughts. But the water still flickers around giant boulders, spreading into a diminished pool. And there are fish – blips of white light that hover in the screen of the fish finder. Soon everyone has a line in. The boat tugs on its anchor. The surface dimples with the flow. Through the heat comes the smell of pines.

"This place is no good," Giorgio announces after a while.

"Patience, Giorgio," his father says wearily. Billy understands that Giorgio's father does not need fish to make it a good day. But Giorgio exudes a roiling, angry energy. Men in such a state never catch fish, Billy knows. The fish will have nothing to do with them.

The others have some success: a small pickerel for Frank, two bass for Jim. Giorgio casts in a desultory way, and winds in sullenly, his impatience stilled by the hammer of continual disappointment. It's he who rummages through the containers until he finds the beer.

Billy suggests they break for lunch, and they ease into a landing spot where the rock drops off as abruptly as a dock. He sets out the lunch things in the clearing above, where a kind of rude table had been made by nailing some boards between cedar trees. They sit in the shade, on folding chairs, eating and drinking and gazing toward the river as it slips around rocks with a steady, soothing hush. The older men talk, but Giorgio sits on the edge of his chair concentrating on his pastrami and cheese sandwich, scowling at a bit he removes from his mouth.

"So you used to be chief," he says to Billy suddenly. "You know, I don't get this land claim business. You laid claim to all this, right?"

"That's right."

Giorgio shakes his head and goes on chewing. Billy hopes he'll drop the subject, but after another swig of beer, he adds, "So, like" – he is grinning collusively at the others – "are we supposed to give the whole country back to you?"

"That would be a start," Billy says.

Giorgio frowns at his joke. The others are listening with a stillness that suggests they are embarrassed, their heads down.

"At least we're doing something with it. You weren't doing that much with it, seems to me."

"Well, we were living off it," Billy says quietly and at that moment hears the machines. It is as if a door has just opened and the faint clanking of caterpillar treads has entered the place where they sit. Then the door closes and the sound stops. Billy glances around; he can't believe the others haven't heard.

"Yah, yah, back to the land and all that," Giorgio is saying. "But the returns weren't much, were they, the way you used to live? You got cars now, houses. It's not right you should want your land back too. You made your trade. If you'd stuck to teepees, maybe I could see it."

Frank sighs. "Giorgio. This is too nice a day for arguments."

"Just making conversation, Papa. I think you guys

should concentrate on getting your act together. All your problems. I mean, we give you billions and nothing changes. Welfare corrupts – and I'm not saying just Indians, *anybody*. My father came to this country with nothing and he didn't ask for a thing. He just got to work."

"*Giorgio.*"

"Well, you did. You started with nothing. Now you're a big man. I'm just saying, it's possible."

"That's good to know," Billy says, getting up; his appetite is gone. He goes back to the boat, pulls up the chain of fish, and begins to clean them on a board. After a while, Frank Carpino arrives to stand nearby. He lights a cigarillo.

"You smoke these things?"

"No, thanks." He's sliding his knife along a ribcage, his fingers coated in the watery, slippery blood.

"My son is a bit of a hothead."

"Well," Billy says, as his knife emerges near the tail, "I guess it's the privilege of the young."

"He's not as young as he looks. Or acts sometimes."

Billy understands he is being offered an apology. For a while, they are silent. Billy slips the fillet onto some waxed paper. Then the door opens again and the grumble of heavy machinery slips through. Overhead, in a drift of blue smoke, Frank, apparently oblivious, is saying, "You know, I've built things all my life. Condos, apartment buildings, malls, houses – God, the houses – I've covered whole counties with houses. We do them on a theme, you know, we give them pretty names, as if they were real places." Frank takes a long drag on his cigarillo, blows smoke as he looks around vacantly. The door has closed: the only sound now is the hush of the rapids. "Where I come from, there are houses everywhere. Houses piled on houses. You couldn't talk in your own kitchen without the neighbours hearing you. In Europe, everywhere you turn there are houses, people – somebody behind every bush – not like this."

The old man walks off and stands for a while urinating at the base of a cedar, his cigarillo clenched in his teeth, his stream pattering fitfully. Returning, he gazes over the water. "Just to stand here and know it's wilderness all the way to the north pole – you sort of start to breathe again."

The next day, Billy sets out for the clear-cuts. Dragging his boat onto bedrock, he walks for some distance down a narrow bay that used to be water, climbs a shallow bank, and reaches the mouth of the trail that winds through the shadowy, sun-pierced bush. On either side, the trunks of virgin white pine thrust up among the lesser trees. Here and there, one of the giants has fallen, its body ridged with fungi or buried in ferns, their filigreed leaves motionless in the heat.

Pausing on the trail, he hears again the clanking of treads – a sound so small and faraway it seems almost a memory. He begins to run toward it – he cannot help himself – over rock ledges, over roots, the pounding of his feet and rasping of his breath masking the sound he is running toward.

The fall after Ann Scott left, he and Matt made plans to go up to Silver Lake. Usually it was the most exciting time of the year for him: the launch of the trapping season, when supplies had to be bought and gear mended, and anticipation of a winter in the bush ran high. All over the Island, families were making their preparations and saying their goodbyes. It might be Christmas or longer before they met again. Every morning saw some new departure: another heavily loaded boat droning out across the placid lake, through the bright mists ignited by the frost, on the first stage of the journey that would take them to the lakes north of Nigushi.

But this year held no pleasure for him. He did not want to go north. Other than Ann Scott, he did not know what he wanted. He was sullen, distracted, and, two days before they were to leave, managed to drive Matt's canoe onto the rocks.

Matt being Matt, he said nothing. Billy found his uncle's silence torture – fresh evidence for his conviction that he was no good. Why else would she have left him? He was not strong enough to keep her, not good-looking enough or smart enough or educated enough. There was this thing in him – the expectation that he *would* screw up. It had been there as long as he could remember; it was there when he had to sit in the corner of the classroom with the dunce-cap on his head; it was there in Father McReavy's livid face that time the priest caught him drinking the communion wine. This dark, perverse belief in his own inevitable failure – a thing that could drift out of some backwater of his mind and choke him. Ann Scott had left. He had wrecked Matt's canoe. He had seen the rocks coming up and felt powerless to move the tiller of the outboard; then, running the hull over those jagged teeth, hearing the wood crunch and splinter, he had experienced, for a moment, a bitter satisfaction.

Over the next few days, as Matt repaired the big canoe, Billy's shame deepened. He stood silently, watching Matt work. He fetched tools. He was tempted to run away. But he sensed there were further depths of shame lurking in that direction, and he stayed.

They were the last boat to leave the Island. Droning at the flat stern, their little outboard pushed them up Nigushi, through the northern islands, down a long bay to the first portage. He set out with the canoe on his shoulders, glad of its weight, of the cut of a thwart into the back of his neck. Just ahead of him, visible under the sloping hull, Matt threaded the narrow trail with a big pack on his back, another balanced on top of that, in a silence that seemed aimed at him.

After two days, they reached the cabin on Silver. Immediately, there was wood to be cut, meat to be hunted, nets to be set – no end of work for which he was also grateful; for plying a bucksaw or digging a new trench for the latrine, he could expend some of his fury. He felt he had no right to this anger, but there it was: a pressure behind his face, a desire, at times, to shout at

Matt (he never did) or fling his axe through the trees (he did once).

Increasingly, the older man irritated him. The way he whistled softly and tunelessly through his front teeth. The way he would stand staring for twenty minutes at a time, lost in some thought he never cared to share, so that Billy was left with the impression that Matt would have preferred to be alone.

Emma was spending the winter in Black Falls to tend her sick sister. They were two men on their own: two mostly silent men, doing what needed to be done. They had no instinct for the extras that were second nature to Emma. There were no sweetcakes, no doughnuts, no bright cloth on the table. The little stove seemed to flicker less cheerfully.

After freeze-up, when Matt walked back to Pine Island to get the dogs, Billy stayed behind. At first, he experienced a loneliness that verged on panic. He lay on his bed, staring up at the gear hanging from the rafters. Eventually, he took his rifle and went out.

When he discovered the tracks of a moose, he followed them across the light snow – the deep, splayed prints, the wispy trail of a hoof, little craters filling with dusk, leading him into a grove where the animal had stopped to chew on a branch. With evening coming on, he gave up the chase. He was in a swampy area at one end of Silver Lake: a tiny lake in itself, where grasses had begun to blow dryly in a rising wind. On an impulse, he lay down, and after a while aimed his rifle at the sky. The echo of his shot seemed to split several ways at once, as if the ice beneath him, the whole bush, were tearing apart.

They woke each day in the dark to ice in the water bucket. Billy would make breakfast while Matt got the dogs ready. The men ran behind the sled, while ahead the dogs lunged under the cloud of their own breath: through spruce, their snow-sheathed spires motionless against the deep blue of dawn, or under the trunks of leaning pines that now and then let slip a glitter of snow. The lakes were dazzling: held in a silence so deep it lent to any sound – the snapping of a branch, a rifle shot – the significance of a spoken word.

They trapped mostly beaver. They would find a lodge – its mound of sticks frozen to the hardness of cement – and hack their way down through a foot or two of ice to the underwater entrances, where they set their traps. Often when they hauled them up several days later, they found them empty. Once, they found the beaver had escaped with all but two nails. "I guess we're toenail trappers now," Matt joked. But on those times when they found the heavy, sleek body of a drowned beaver, there was a quiet sense of celebration. They dried the beaver by rubbing snow on it. Then it was on to the next set of traps, the next lake.

After the long, cold day, they were glad to reach the cabin. Usually, they hung the by-now frozen animals in the rafters to thaw. They worked on the pelts in the evening, scraping the hides clean, lacing them onto home-made stretchers to dry them flat.

Matt opened up a little, telling anecdotes from the past,

often about Emma, set off by something she had made –
a bit of beadwork, a cake of dried blueberries. The older
man seemed to take more notice of him now. He might
grunt his approval over a pelt Billy was working on or tease
him about his cooking. One morning on the line, they
stopped to boil up some water for tea. As they hunkered
close to their little fire, raising and lowering their mugs of
steaming tea, Matt began to tell a story Billy had never
heard – the story of how when he got out of the army in '45
he had come back to Pine Island. "I was in pretty bad
shape. Nerves all in a tangle. I couldn't sit still for ten
seconds. Jumped when the door slammed. Emma didn't
know what to do with me." Matt chuckled at the memory.
He was sitting on a pack, with his ear-lugs sticking out, grinning as though having your nerves in a tangle was a bit of
a lark. He had come up to Silver Lake by himself, and except
for returning briefly to Pine Island at Christmas, he had
stayed up till spring. "I was a madman," he said. "Bad
dreams. Bad thoughts. They should have locked me up."

"You trapped up here?" Billy said.

"Trapped. Did the things you do up here. It put me
right. Not right away. I wouldn't listen at first to what it
was saying. But eventually."

In the little fire, the spruce sticks snapped. Deep in the
trees, a raven was crying, and for a moment Billy sensed
the deep bush all around them – bigger and deeper than
any man could think. He felt like weeping, but held it
back. He felt as if something were being offered. But he
did not know what.

One day, when they had stopped on an open lake, he saw a wolf trotting across the ice. It had its head down, and though it must surely have been aware of them, it did not bother to look in their direction.

The dogs, who had lain down, had not smelled it yet. But Matt had knelt to the sledge and was sliding out his rifle. And suddenly, Billy was in dread of him shooting the wolf. He could not have said why: only he felt connected to the wolf, and knew that it must live.

Matt raised his rifle: wolf pelts were getting a good price that year. But he did not fire; he turned his square face a little from the stock. Billy had never been able to meet Matt's eyes for long; in fact, it was a mark of respect not to stare at an elder, or at anyone, for that matter. But now he fixed on his uncle's dark, questioning eyes, which held him in return. All his self-consciousness was gone, as he pleaded in silence. Matt lowered his gun. Across the lake, the wolf trotted behind the next island.

They never spoke of the wolf they had let go. But a sense of release, of quiet gratitude, welled in him. Without knowing quite how it happened, his anger and shame began to fade.

Before him lies a dried-up slough. The hill on the other side has been half-stripped of trees – a vacancy of stumps and yellow dirt. Off to one side, a treaded machine is working. Wielding a mechanical arm, it grasps a big spruce at the base, cuts it off with a scream of its saw, then lifts the tree aloft where for a few seconds it seems to be dancing – its pliant boughs whipping and flowing like the hair of a crazed woman. But almost at once, the mechanical arm turns the tree on its side, runs it through its "fist" and, with a sound like a wooden box being crushed, strips off every branch. The tree – now a pole – is tossed aside.

Crossing the slough, he starts up the hill, struggling through a heap of debris as he makes his way toward the summit. He has no further interest in the machine: along with its driver, it seems an irrelevance, and he has soon climbed past it, arriving at a small plateau where two pickup trucks have been parked and several men lounge about eating lunch. He strides past them. One, as if readying himself for an attack, stands up. Billy walks quickly, his gaze locked straight ahead. "Hey, chief!" another of them calls after him. "Where's the fire?" Ignoring their laughter, he goes on past the last truck, past a splintered tree trunk, past a boulder sparkling with broken glass, up the deeply rutted road toward the sky. *Nothing left, Billy.* He had refused to believe her.

Before him, now, lies a desert. The trees are gone, or mostly gone. Here and there a solitary grove persists or an isolated poplar. But what dominates is an empty plain speckled with stumps, churned by the tracks of machines, stretching toward the horizon. He has seen clear-cuts before, but never here, on his home ground, and never on such a scale.

In the distance, windshields glint where machines chew at the remaining bush. Clanking treads float their music in the heat. A road has been cut down the centre of the clear-cut, and along this a truck is advancing toward him, dragging behind it a rising hill of dust.

The day is hot, still, overcast – a disappointment after weeks of blazing clarity. Richard only prays it won't rain. Stooping, he bounces a ball and regards the tanned, bald man crouched with his racket at the far end of the court. Reg Benoit is an intense competitor, but – as Richard has discovered – not a particularly skillful one. It's a problem: he can't go drubbing the man whose blessing he is counting on.

Across the net, Ann stands in her whites, tapping her racket idly against her bare leg, frowning at some private thought. He wishes she wouldn't make her lack of interest so obvious, her displeasure. The previous afternoon, Rowan had made such a fuss when Richard dropped him off at the Ducettes' that Richard had lost his temper; and though he'd tried to settle things down, he evidently hadn't done a very good job, because at Inverness, Ann, primed by a phone call from their son, was ready for him. "He says you yelled at him. Really, Richard, I don't see why you couldn't have brought him." "I don't yell," he'd responded grimly. He didn't dare admit the truth: that he'd left Rowan behind because he wanted a child-free weekend, though he hadn't framed it that way to Ann. Leaving Rowan had made him feel shabby. Driving away from the Ducettes' had been hard.

Again, he bounces the ball and takes another swipe at a moth. For the last half-hour, the little creatures have been fluttering out of the woods.

On Richard's side of the court, Marilyn Benoit faces her husband. A petite, shapely woman in a pleated tennis skirt that thrusts out at the rear, she's a good twenty years younger than Reg and given to outbursts of enthusiasm in a voice that seems not to have changed much since she was thirteen.

He serves.

"Out!" Reg calls, readying himself again.

Richard bounces his second ball, waves aside another moth, and delivers an easy serve that Reg slams straight at Marilyn. Raising her racket as much to protect herself as anything, she lets out a squeal and the ball deflects to Ann, who takes a half-hearted stab and misses.

"Marilyn, you genius!" Richard tells her.

"I just stood here!" she says with wide eyes. Beyond her,

Ann is ambling off the court as if she were on some solitary walk. Retrieving the ball, she strolls back toward the net and tosses it over, underhand.

Serving to his wife, Richard double faults. Facing Reg again, he is sweating profusely, and his suspicion that the afternoon is not going well has deepened. Behind Reg, another cloud of moths sails out of the woods. It blooms behind the backstop, and – and as Richard watches in irritation – makes its spinning way across the court.

In the end, the moths are so thick they have to call off the match. The air boils with them: they mat on their rackets, tangle in their hair, obscure the view of the baselines. "*You!*" Marilyn cries in disgust, spitting one out. She is slapping ineffectually at the moths as she hurries with the others toward shelter. "I'm amazed," Richard tells his guests. "It's never happened before. It's never happened before, has it, Ann –" His wife does not respond. Turning, he finds her gazing up like a child entranced by a snowstorm.

The two couples go off to change for a swim – Reg and Marilyn to the guest cabin, Ann and Richard to their bedroom in the cottage. Stripping off his damp tennis things, Richard flings them in a corner and pulls on his suit. "I know this isn't exactly your idea of fun," he says. She has turned her back to put on not the bikini she usually wears, but a one-piece, rather old-fashioned suit he considers unattractive. "I just wonder if you could try a little harder –"

Wriggling into her straps, she does not reply.

"Honey?"

"What." She turns back to him.

"Why aren't you wearing the bikini?"

"The way that man looks at me, I'd rather wear a bag."

"Oh, Reg's a bit of a rogue. But he's a good head."

On the path behind the cottage he waits for his guests to appear. Over the side-channel, a few moths go sparkling by – stragglers who soar among the branches or rest on the tree trunks like little bows, slowly fanning their tiny wings as if contemplating further outrages. The muggy air is oppressive, and in the cloudy light, Inverness seems to him seedy and depressing. He can hear the Benoits in their cabin – arguing, it seems. Two happy couples, Richard thinks, grabbing at a moth. He is wiping it off on his trunks when Marilyn appears in a minute bikini. She meets him with a smile that seems to say, Yes, I know I'm nice, you can look at me all you like! His spirits reviving, Richard stands talking with her until Reg arrives, looking gym-fit in his flowered trunks, if a bit grim. Richard leads the Benoits down the path, stopping to point out the carved brackets under the eaves of the old boathouse. "Ann's grandfather built it. He was a real old-country craftsman. We still have some of his tools from Scotland." Suddenly Richard is ambushed by a wearying sense of taking up a role, for he has spoken these exact words to guests many times. For a moment he is adrift, unable to find the chain of his thoughts while he smiles helplessly at Marilyn, who does her best to help him out with an enthusiastic "Fascinating!" Remembering, finally, he launches into the always popular anecdote of how Peter Scott first arrived on Lake Nigushi.

When Ann appears, she is still wearing the black swim-suit, but he senses she's making an effort now: laughing at Reg's joke about the moths; listening to him with an intentness that verges, Richard worries, on parody. But Reg seems charmed. When Ann swims out into the channel, Reg swims after her and soon their heads are bobbing together, under the far shore.

Later on the deck, over his gin and tonic, Reg compli-ments Inverness. He is a man who is used to being listened to, for as he continues, spinning out a tale of his own cottage on Random Lake, he takes his time, clearly enjoying himself. He speaks mainly to Ann, who listens with a kind of skeptical bemusement, not unfriendly, though after a few minutes Richard notices that her attention has strayed. "Rick tells me you paint," Reg says.

"Ann!" Richard says, laughing as she blinks from her reverie. "This is what painting does to a woman," he tells the others. "I give you exhibit A: my perpetually dis-tracted wife. Lost in her work still! Reg was asking about your painting –"

"Your husband tells me you're good," Reg says, clearly not put off in the least. "Are you good?"

"Yes, well, my husband is my number-one fan," she says a bit dryly.

"You must show us your work."

She shakes her head slightly but says nothing.

"I'm a bit of a collector, myself."

"*Are* you –"

"I've got a Robbins – one of his wolf paintings – fantastic. I think you'd like it."

"*Well*," Ann says, looking awkward for the first time. Richard knows that his wife does not like Robbins, whom she considers too photographic. *No surprises, no imagination, no soul* is her withering summary.

"So when can we have a look?"

"At?" Ann says.

"At your work!"

"I'm really not at that point," Ann says. She has spoken more quietly and more directly than at any time in the afternoon. "I am working on a piece, but I can't tell where it's going. I won't show it even to Richard. I lose focus when someone else looks too soon."

Saying she needs to see how Elaine's getting on with the dinner, Ann leaves. The minister's level gaze, emptied of its smile, follows her up the rock.

With her departure, a certain blankness falls. Richard turns the conversation to politics. They are well into a discussion of the new policy on hospital funding when the drone of a motor sounds from the channel. Richard goes on talking, but as Reg and Marilyn glance at the approaching boat, he looks too.

Billy. He is sitting in the stern, his arm crooked over the handle of his outboard, his gaze fixed straight ahead, as if he were so intent on the channel that he is unaware of them, as if he were going to drive right on by. But no sooner does Richard think this, *hope* this, than Billy thrusts away the tiller, sending his boat around the point and out of sight, clearly headed for their dock.

"Don't I know that guy?"

"Billy Johnson," Richard murmurs. He has risen to his feet and turned to follow the din of Billy's motor.

"Right, the land claim. Everybody in the area knew who he was. You guys had a pretty hard go with that case."

"Yes, well, ancient history now," Richard says, his face heating. "We haven't had much to do with each other for quite a while. Guess I better go see what he wants."

Richard hurries up the rock. Passing the cottage, he meets Ann, who has emerged onto the back step. "It's Billy," he tells her, in a slightly accusatory tone; somehow this ill-timed arrival seems her doing. They both look toward the dock, where Billy, having shut off his engine, is sitting placidly in the stern. "Why don't you go down and speak to him," Richard urges. "Try to get him to –" At the clatter of a pot lid in the kitchen, he remembers Elaine Shewaybick and lowers his voice. "Tell him now isn't a good time. He'll listen to you."

"There's plenty to eat –"

"*Ann, he can't stay.*"

She stares at him in apparent incomprehension until, exasperated, he goes down the path himself. The two men meet just as Billy steps from the boathouse and Richard sees for the first time his bruised cheek and swollen eye, the round, livid bump on his forehead, and for a moment he forgets everything else. "My God, man –"

"Ran into a bit of trouble," Billy murmurs. There is something drugged about his focus. Drunk, Richard thinks.

"Look, I've got something going on here – it's important. Now is not a good time." But Billy's attention has shifted to the cottage, where Ann is watching from the steps. "Billy, *listen* to me." The one good eye swings back to him. "The minister of natural resources is here. Political meeting. Goddammit, Billy, you can't just arrive here and expect –" The battered face seems to struggle toward clarity. But then, moving with shocking swiftness, Billy pushes past Richard and starts up the path.

"Billy, what's happened!" Ann cries as he approaches. Ignoring her, Billy disappears around the corner of the house.

"Drunk is what's happened," Richard seethes. Hurrying after him, they catch sight of his pale shirt flickering among the pines, descending to the deck where Reg, putting aside his drink, has stood to greet him. Billy ignores his outstretched hand.

"So you're the minister."

"Reg, I'm sorry," Richard says, arriving out of breath. "He's –"

"It's all right, Rick," Reg says, not taking his eyes from the other man. Ann is at Richard's side now – he can hear her breathing – and in her chair, Marilyn is transfixed.

"You're in charge of all this." Billy gestures sharply over the water, the islands.

"Well, 'in charge' is a bit steep," Reg says.

"The cuts north of Nigushi there, up toward Charlton Lake. How come you're taking everything?"

"Sorry, you'll have to explain."

"Look," Richard says to Billy. "Really, this isn't the time." But Billy, he realizes, is not listening to him; the minister is not listening to him.

"They've taken ninety, ninety-five per cent," Billy says.

"I don't think that's accurate," Reg says. "We have policies."

"We've a lot of experience with your policies. I was just up there. There's nothing left." Billy stands hunched forward a little, his fists hanging loosely at his sides, his eyes – still with that hint of misfocus – burning at the other man. Richard once saw him look exactly like this years before, when he had been threatened in a bar. Seconds later, avoiding a punch, he had smashed in his adversary's face.

"I'll have my people look into it," Reg says. "I'll get back to you. That's a promise."

Billy is grinning now, or rather grimacing, as if in pain. He is in such a state that for some seconds no one can speak or move, as if hypnotized by his intensity.

"Billy," Ann says softly, breaking the spell. But Billy seems not to hear.

"You people," he says, his voice catching. "A whole forest, gone like that."

"Billy, goddammit," Richard says. He grips Billy's shoulder, but Billy throws off his arm. Again, everyone stands motionless as Billy looks around, no longer so aware of them, it seems, but taken with some thought of his own. Then at once, he strides off the deck and up the path toward the cottage, with Ann hurrying after him. The others watch as he stumbles, flounders for a moment in the arms of a pine, then disappears.

Richard turns to his guests. "Reg, Marilyn, I'm so sorry. The man is beside himself and, of course, under the influence. Marilyn, are you okay?"

Soon they hear the roar of Billy's engine, then his boat sweeps around the point and into the channel. He sits as before, looking neither to the left or right as he goes by. Even after the boat can no longer be seen, Richard finds himself listening to the receding drone of his motor, the peaceful sloshing of his wake as it breaks up along the shore.

In the candle-lit cave of the porch, they eat the steamed ginger pickerel Elaine Shewaybick carries in on the good plates Richard brought from their house in Black Falls. At first, after Billy's departure, everyone had been subdued as they absorbed what had happened. Now over dinner, with the help of the wine, conversation flows again, almost hectically, as the tension is released. To Richard's dismay, Reg wants to talk about Billy, clearly fascinated by the man and even, it seems, impressed. "I remember him during the land claim. I was still running my outfitting business then and we had a TV in the office. Billy came on one day, on that old political program with – oh what's her name, the interviewer with the grating voice? The premier used to call her the Piranha."

"Iris Kirby," Richard says, reluctantly helping out.

"Iris Kirby!" Reg cries, jabbing the air with his fork. "Talk about your dragon lady. She tried to do her usual job on Billy, but he wasn't having any of it. He handled her so brilliantly – just stayed calm and said what he wanted to – not what *she* wanted him to say. A natural, really. The guy could go into politics, though, frankly he might not have the necessary knack for compromise."

"Indeed," Richard says, thinking that Reg has not yet brought up the subject of his own prospective candidacy. He's been waiting for the right moment to mention it himself.

"Seeing him come down the rock today. I hadn't felt like that since I saw Hammer Jackson come at me with the football. The man has a definite power –"

"Somewhat reinforced today," Richard offers.

"Didn't seem drunk to me. Banged up, certainly, but not drunk."

"I didn't think so either," Ann says. "He's had an accident."

"Or a fight," Richard says.

"He's a brawler then?" the minister says.

"He's seen his share," Richard says. He does not want to be critical of Billy, not in front of Ann, who will almost certainly defend him. He has seen her bring a dinner party to a stop with her passions. "He's been away since the claim – only just got back. We've only seen him once. He was down in the States, just drifting really. Working at odd jobs. It tells after a while, that sort of life."

"How does it *tell*," Ann says, putting down her fork.

Richard reaches abruptly for the wine bottle. "Marilyn," he says, turning to her. "Your glass is entirely too empty."

As he refills her glass, Elaine Shewaybick comes in to clear their plates. Everyone falls silent as she moves around the table – a big-hipped, solemn woman whose bare arm, wrist bound in a wide, beaded bracelet, reaches past their shoulders. "That was lovely," Marilyn murmurs. As Elaine takes up his plate, Richard thanks her warmly.

After Elaine goes back to the kitchen, Ann turns to Reg: "Will you really have your people look into the clear-cuts?"

"Certainly I will."

"Because I flew over them once. Billy's right. There's whole areas where there's hardly anything left."

"Well, the cuts aren't *pretty*," the minister allows.

"It's a lot worse than that. It's completely wrong. I knew *here* it was wrong," Ann says, tapping herself on the chest. "All anybody has to do is *see* them to know." Richard listens closely, ready to jump in if she goes too far. Yet Reg seems to be enjoying himself. He and Ann spar back and forth, the minister unflaggingly genial while Ann persists with unsmiling earnestness. Eventually Richard joins the fray on Reg's side, explaining to his wife that, as minister, Reg is involved in a complicated balancing act as he tries not only to protect the resource but to make sure the timber companies get what they need. *Resource extraction. The economic needs of the community. Needs of hunters and sports fishermen.* The ready-made phrases come easily. He breaks off, suddenly recalling that, years ago, he and Billy used to mock such officialese as the worst form of hypocrisy.

Reg, too, talks mainly to Ann; she has become the stubborn centre of the room, the person the men need to convince. "You know, I'm sympathetic to the man's position. That's their hunting and trapping grounds up there. But very few of them are trapping any more, it's a way of life that's passing. A lot of them work for the forestry companies now. Where you see a disaster, they see jobs."

"Trees do get replanted," Richard says, chiming in again. "And even if they didn't replant, the forest would soon grow back." He describes a piece of abandoned highway near the Falls. "After one year, there were weeds coming through it. After two, saplings. It's a small forest now. The trees are going to win in the long run!"

Dessert is lemon tart and coffee, which Ann helps Elaine carry in. Ann's silence – she has retreated entirely – seems to affect the others, and the conversation fails as their forks click on their plates. A few minutes later, while Reg is describing their February holiday in Saint Martin, she gets up abruptly. Richard watches as her shoulders under their thin straps disappear in the dimness of the hall.

The first time Richard saw Billy Johnson, he and Ann had been married all of six months and were on their way home to Black Falls in Richard's Volvo when they saw a young man in jeans and a red nylon shell, hitchhiking. He had put out his arm with an air of lazy indifference, almost contempt, as if he could care less whether they stopped. There was a pathos about the figure, Richard thought. The sight of Billy Johnson had moved him even before he knew who he was.

"Oh, my God," Ann said, looking through the back window, for they had already flown past. "Remember that Indian boy I told you about?"

"You want me to stop?"

"No! Yes! Richard, stop!"

He pulled onto the shoulder. In the rear-view, the young man was hurrying toward their car.

"Oh, my God," Ann said again, clutching at Richard's hand. He was half-laughing at her now, but he could not read her at all. She seemed to be reassuring him. Perhaps she was trying to reassure herself.

They had met a year earlier. Richard was twenty-nine, Ann twenty-six. She was living the artist's life in downtown Toronto. He was working with two other newly minted lawyers out of a storefront in the east end of the city. They were introduced by a mutual friend at a gallery where she was part of a group show. Talking to her that night, he had judged her out of his league. Her full, wide mouth suggested a sensuousness that lay beyond his own experience. Her casually confident manner and the understated tastefulness of her clothes marked her as a girl from a different social stratum; and this was quite apart from the fact she

was beautiful. Secretly, beauty terrified him. Beauty promised peace and delivered war. Stooping over her in the
corner by the cheese table, at the edge of the crowd's din,
he kept expecting her to move on; but she stayed talking
for half an hour, laughing at his story of his first appear-
ance in court, telling him of her own adventures with
unpaid traffic tickets, touching him frequently on the
arm. Much later she would confess, "I knew right away
you were solid. That I could depend on you." He did not
like to think of solidity as his primary attraction, but
when he objected, she added, "Do you have any idea what
the men are like out there, most of them? Ask me. I'm
the expert." He bought her most expensive painting: of a
narrowing V of mirror-like water held between dark
banks, with the tiny silhouette of a heron poised over its
own reflection.

A week later, he took her to a restaurant off Bloor Street –
a low-roofed place with a patio, boxed cedars, French doors
and waiters whose elaborate show of expertise left her
quietly amused. She wore a dark mauve shirt, its top
buttons open. He scarcely dared to glance there, to the
rounding of a breast glowing in the candlelight – for in his
nervousness, any acknowledgement of his desire, even to
himself, was disorienting. When she asked about his back-
ground, he told her, "Solid working class" with the bravado
he put on in such moments, for he was defensive about
where he had come from: ill at ease, for all his show of
sophistication, among menus written in French and offi-
cious waiters in white aprons.

When she asked him about his parents, he spoke of his mother, who was living still in his boyhood home. "She's got this great spirit," he told Ann. "A real light in her eye. Nothing gets her down for long." Immediately, he wondered if he'd gone too far, if he'd begged the question about what there might be to get her down. Sully was already haunting their table, his presence as charged as ever with unforeseen consequences. It was with some misgivings, then, that he told her about his father's love of nature: the camping trips, the midnight awakening to see an eclipse of the moon. It was all true, and yet he could sense the darker depths of his life with his father looming, like a sheer drop glimpsed from a mountain road, and to bring his discomfort to an end, he told her his father had died when he was eighteen, eliciting a cry of sympathy.

She spoke of her own mother, who had been ill for much of Ann's childhood. "I never understood exactly what it was. Nerves. Headaches. She spent a good deal of time in bed. I wanted her so much to be like other mothers. I was ashamed to bring my friends home. I think I was awfully cruel some times: I didn't like being with her. It makes me sick to think of it now. But I'd identified completely with my father. He was so full of life. There were times when I wanted to *be* a boy!" Lifting her wineglass, she added, "It sounds like it was better in your house."

"I was glad to grow up."

"I don't know if I was or not."

"Not that we have a choice."

"No, not that we have a choice!" Their gazes met then.

It was not clear to him why the hackneyed phrase "not that we have a choice" should move him nearly to tears. But across the candle-lit table a connection seemed to form.

He never got over his amazement that she wanted him. He had never considered himself attractive. At six-four, he loomed above most other people; holding her, he worried there was too much of him, and that she must inevitably find the weight of him, the awkward fitting of their bodies, distasteful. He was intimidated by her sensuality. She would pull apart an orange, slowly, and feed him bits with a playful curiosity, as if half-expecting him to transform. The first time they went to bed, he was so in awe of her beauty – so eager not to fail her – that, unusual for him, he could not perform. In the end she curled up against him, telling him in a child's voice that it didn't matter. That night when she bustled out in her raincoat, her head bowed, he feared she might not come back. Two days later, she reappeared with flowers and a red velvet bag stuffed with marijuana. Once he found love possible, everything seemed possible. He glimpsed a kind of happiness he had rarely let himself imagine: one that simply went on, day by ordinary day.

He was living in a low-rise building near the corner of Bloor Street and Bedford. His furniture consisted of a waterbed, a kitchen table, three chairs, a coffee table, and a leather couch, with nothing on the walls but a framed, signed photo of Arthur Ashe and Ann's heron painting, with his history and law books stacked along the base-boards: a poverty of taste and comfort he hadn't noticed until he'd brought her there. One night, undulating gently on their little sea, she asked him about his first time: "Come on. Don't tell me it's me."

Patsy Dinsmore had been a fellow law student. He had not loved her, with her lank hair, her skin smelling of copper, her passion for the more recondite points of corporate law, but they had drifted together for mutual study sessions, and out of loneliness and boredom had drifted a little further, into each other's hesitant embraces. He recalled a cold April afternoon on Toronto Island: a few fumbled, urgent minutes in a hollow screened by bracken, the aerials of boats going by. He made his interest in Patsy sound like more than it was, its consequences more troubling than they actually were. "And there were other *grapplings*. How about your first?"

He was not particularly eager to hear about Ann's love life, for he guessed she had far outpaced him in that department. But he was eager to deflect her scrutiny.

For a few seconds, she was silent. Her face slowly changed, seemed to grow smoother as it emptied. She was somewhere else: something in him hung suspended; a deeper level of attention, of seriousness, had been evoked. "It was a local boy," she said finally, and her voice, too, had changed. "He was from the reserve at the other end of Nigushi. I first met him when I was a young girl, actually. My father knew his uncle. The uncle did work at our cottage one summer and he'd come along with him." She sighed; Richard had fallen very still. "But then I didn't see him for a long time. Then one day he just showed up and we – we were both grown up. Well, we were nineteen. We had a summer together, on the lake."

Sitting up, she turned briskly cheerful. "Anyway, a familiar-enough story: two kids with nothing in common, no future at all. As my father kept telling me. I ended it. It was awful. *I* was awful. I went away after that – England. Art school. When I came back, I lived in Montreal with my mom. She and Dad were divorced. After that, I didn't get to our cottage much, and I never saw him again." She slipped out of bed. He listened to her filling the kettle in the kitchen. *We had a summer together.* Her words, spoken with such delicacy of feeling, had conjured something at once complete, pure, and unrepeatable. The local boy, whoever he was, had touched her, he suspected, in a way he never would.

He never forgot this exchange and never referred to it again. Yet the topic came up once more. They were married, and had moved up to Black Falls, where Richard had been offered a position in Doug Parson's law office. They had bought the stucco house near her father's. One night when another couple was visiting and the liqueur glasses had been filled and refilled, the women started to talk of old relationships. Giselle mentioned a Billy Johnson. "Ancient history!" Ann laughed, making a dismissive motion. But Richard was alert. Was Billy Johnson the "local boy" she'd told him about? Giselle leaned to Richard, slyly confidential. "Don't let her fool you. She was quite gone on the guy. Of course, they were mere children –"

"Just nineteen," Richard said.

"Well, you know all about it then!" Giselle turned to her husband. "I wonder what's happened to him? I haven't seen him for years." Her husband said he thought he'd gone to B.C. "Somebody told me he'd been in jail."

"That isn't possible," Ann said. "I mean, he had a stubborn streak, but nothing that would . . ." She was subdued for the rest of the evening.

That night, undressing, she was still pensive. Richard was getting used to Ann's moodiness; despite her high-energy competence, she had a tendency to melancholy abstraction. He often had the sense she was not entirely present, as if she carried an alternate life inside her whose currents at any time were liable to tug her away. "Still thinking about your old boyfriend?"

She was gazing toward the window. "I just can't believe he'd do something that would –"

"You know, it would be an easy thing to find out."

"What would?"

"Whether he's been to jail."

"I don't want to know," she told him.

And there he was, the Indian boy, the local boy, Billy Johnson, his jacket billowing as he ran down the shoulder toward their car. Opening a rear door, he slid in behind Ann.

Richard turned to him. "Black Falls okay?"

There was something eager in the broad face – a boyish openness concentrated in the widely set dark eyes. Of course, he had no idea what he'd just stepped into: Richard felt for him.

Ann did not turn, not at first, but remained facing straight ahead. Richard, perplexed by her silence, put the car in gear and drove back onto the highway. In the mirror, he could see their guest staring intently at the back of Ann's head.

A few moments later, she finally turned around. "Hello, Billy," she said quietly. Immediately, she burst into nervous laughter.

For the hour it took them to drive to Black Falls, Ann and Richard carried the conversation, for Billy didn't say much, and though they tried hard to draw him out (discovering that yes, he had just come back from out west, where he'd spent several years working for a lodge in B.C., and more recently in the Alberta oil fields), he passed most of the trip staring at the passing bush.

They let him out downtown, near the war memorial. Silent themselves now, they drove up River Street, past the paper mill, and across the Old Woman River into Cartier Point.

"Well, he seems pleasant enough," Richard said finally, as they pulled into their drive. "A bit quiet, maybe."

"He was nervous," Ann said defensively. "A shock like that."

That night, lying beside him in the dark bedroom, she spoke into the silence. "You know, when I ended it –" He realized she was talking about Billy Johnson, and from the way she simply started in on the subject, he knew she'd been brooding on it. "It was worse than I told you."

"Yes?"

"I was pregnant," she said at last. "Terrified. It wasn't in my plans at all, but then neither was –" Again she broke off, and he could sense her wandering a hidden landscape. "My parents took care of everything. I had it in London –"

"You *had* the baby," he said. In an instant, her past had become much more complicated; her present too, for where was the child?

She took in a shuddering breath. Was she weeping?

"Love?" he said, reaching for her hand.

"It wasn't a baby I had."

It took him a moment to understand. "Ah. I'm sorry. That must have been hard."

For a long time they said nothing. Through the open window he could hear the Old Woman River, hushing over its stones; the hoot of a horn from the mill, far upstream. He could sense her thinking beside him in the dark. "I'm here if you want to talk about it," Richard said. Her revelation had changed the mood between them, changed, in some way, who she was.

"He never knew I was pregnant," she said finally. "I mean, I couldn't have had a baby, and he – he would have wanted me to have it. He'd have been so upset, furious really, if he knew I was going to have an abortion. I wrote him later, from England, but I just didn't have the courage to tell him. What good would it have done? I was a mess."

A little later, she spoke more calmly. "Now that he's come home, we'll see him probably. He'll be around. He must never know what I've just told you, Richard. Promise me you understand." She had reared up on one elbow, and he could sense her determination as the pale, indistinct moon of her face hovered. He promised gladly, with a grateful realization that he could give her something valuable. He promised, hoping to bring this difficult pass to an end.

Ann walks toward the boathouse, the sounds of the dinner party receding behind her. The sun has set and in the silvering channel the inverted reflections of pines tremble in a deepening obscurity. She is thinking of the last time she went down the path, a few hours before, following Billy to the dock, wrapped in the queer sense they were leaving together, like a husband and wife called away by an emergency. On the dock, he had untied his bow rope and swung his boat around, the hull making a hollow, trickling sound as it slid lightly over the water.

Instinctively, to calm him, she had placed her hand on his back and was shocked at the heat radiating from him. "You're not well," she said, and pleaded with him to rest, to lie down, to let her get Dr. Clemens at his cottage. But he paid no attention. "Billy, what happened to you?" He did pause to regard her then, finally: paused with the rope in his hand, above his gently chafing boat. But whatever solace the contact brought her was instantly swept away, for his look held her with a terrible clarity.

He got into his boat then. She hovered as he ripped his motor to life, too stunned to say anything, and as he drove away, she turned and walked back to the cottage.

In the darkened studio, she sits on the small cot by the wall. From the house drifts the sound of laughter, and she thinks of Elaine Shewaybick, dignified, silent Elaine, whose grandson had hanged himself, moving around the porch as she served them. The taste of shame.

Drawing up her feet, she lies curled on her side. When a loon calls, its plunging, liquid cry seems to sound inside her. She is merely a point of consciousness now, an ear, an eye, alert in a corner of the dark studio – waiting for the loon to cry again. As if *it* might have the answer to the question in Billy's face: *What was she doing with her life?*

Some time later, she hears her husband call her name softly from the dimness beyond the screens. She can hear his feet scuff on the path. A flashlight beam flicks over her windows like a passing ghost. Now comes the creak and slap of the boathouse door, and her name spoken again. His heavy tread on the stairs, preceded by the probing light.

As its glare finds her, she shuts her eyes – not just the light but being seen is unbearable. His rubber soles squeak as he approaches the cot.

"Ann?"

"Don't shine that on me, please."

The light falls away: a white transparent blanket drooping from his hand. "What's going on? Reg and Marilyn are concerned. *I'm* concerned. Are you ill?" An impatient note: *Ill again?* She thinks of her mother. Was it like this for her? Feeling that to do anything but stay in bed was an impossibility.

All at once, she swings from the cot, an action that leaves her dizzy as she stands. He catches at her arm. "I'm all right," she tells him sharply and starts toward the stairs.

Single file they go up the path. Richard is trying to be helpful, shining the light over her shoulder. Rocks and steps appear momentarily, vanishing to be replaced by more rocks, more steps, the black bole of a tree. They pass the side of the cottage and go along the screens and up the porch steps into quavering candlelight, where two faces, scarcely known to her, look up expectantly.

She dreams she is lying in a hospital bed, so encumbered with tubes and pulleys and covers that she cannot move. She is having a dangerous operation – some kind of machine is drilling away at the back of her skull. She wakes to sunshine behind curtains. The machine is still drilling though; as she listens it grows fainter and she understands it is Elaine Shewaybick, setting off in her boat for Pine Island.

Beside her, Richard lies asleep on his stomach, a bit of drool shining at the corner of his mouth. He has thrown off the sheet and at the base of his back, just above the elastic waistband of his shorts, is the little tuft of hair that always intrigued and repelled her – like a small furry animal settled on his back. For a long time she studies him. Fourteen years together. She knows everything about him. And she knows nothing.

During breakfast, Reg Benoit slips off to make a call; returning, he announces that he and Marilyn must leave. The premier wants some revisions, *pronto*, to a statement to be released the next day. "'Twas ever thus." Reg shrugs while Marilyn confides a wan smile to her coffee mug.

The trip to the Harbour feels endless. Ann sits with Marilyn in the rear seat, excused from being sociable by the racket of the outboard. Ahead, Richard leans toward the minister and shouts over the din about his desire to run in Nigushi. *Confident I can beat Ferrero. Would like to really work the north side there. The new policies should help.* The fragments she can pick up seem propelled by boyish eagerness: she feels sad for him, protective.

At the Harbour, they tie up and walk the Benoits to their car. Richard and Marilyn make exuberant noises about the visit; everyone kisses like old friends. Reg says to Richard: "These things are a matter of strategy. I'm optimistic something will work out. But I've got a lot to consider – just not ready to commit at this point." Their guests get into their car, and Marilyn continues to shower them with goodbyes through a rolled-down window. As soon as they are out of sight, Richard stalks back to the boat without waiting for Ann.

That afternoon, she thinks she will paint, but when she stands before her canvas, not a single idea emerges. Going outside, she takes a chair overlooking the water. In the shadow of the next island, a duck is floating, motionless as a decoy.

Richard comes down the rock. He goes past her and stands for a few seconds facing the water, hands on hips. "Well, if I get the nomination, it'll be a bloody miracle –"

"We don't know," she says. "I thought he was encouraging."

"My God, Ann. It was a disaster. Your friend showing up didn't help." He says no more, but from the fierceness of his glance, she understands he is far from calm.

Above the BMW, a loose wall of logs slides past as Richard accelerates. Huge butts leaking sap. Scored trunks. The cab's assortment of mirrors, with the driver's face held in each of them. In a few seconds the transport is a toy in the rear-view, while before them, the flat highway divides the bush like a runway.

"Awfully fast," Ann says. Ignoring her, Richard speeds over a rise. And there's a jam – a chain of vehicles curving away toward the flutter of emergency lights.

Swearing, he touches the brake.

They join the slow parade. They're still an hour away from Black Falls. Beside him, Ann rustles in her bag. She has been mostly silent since they left. He feels that, this weekend, she has let him down. Badly.

"Want an almond," she says, holding out a small plastic bag.

He shakes his head. In the next car, a kid has raised a sign that reads, *Honk if you Believe in Jesus*. Richard heaves an impatient sigh; he leans back in his seat, his arms stretching to the wheel.

They are nearing the accident. A police officer directs cars along the side of the road. The remains of a compact sit on the opposite shoulder, its front half utterly crushed, the twisted steering wheel visible through the shattered back window. Beside it, on the ground, a blanket-covered stretcher lies, and from the shape beneath the blanket, and from the absence of any visible face or limb, they know what it hides.

They creep past, and even when the highway opens again, drive no faster than the other cars, which are all obeying the speed limit now. Everyone, it seems, has been affected, subdued. But as the miles pass, and the other cars gradually speed up, Richard, too, presses the accelerator.

After the night Ann told Richard about her time with Billy, neither of them brought up the subject of their affair again, though Richard thought of him often: his lonely figure standing beside the highway, his silence as they drove him to the Falls. He was intrigued by Billy and when, some weeks later, he saw him in Carton Harbour, he reintroduced himself. Billy was carrying several fishing poles and had just come back, he said, from taking out some clients for the Blue Osprey. They stood in the midday sun, among the tinkling masts of the boats, making awkward small talk. Billy would not keep his side of the conversation up, not in the way Richard was used to, so that Richard wondered if he had offended him in some way – offended him perhaps by marrying the woman he had once loved, and perhaps loved still. But he did not in the least hold Billy's past against him; he thought of himself as a generous person, and as a result tended to act that way. Standing with Billy on the quay, he was flooded with good-will, felt a rather sentimental affection for the shy, younger man who had known Ann as a girl and who smiled so dis-armingly and took such time with his answers. Without thinking, he asked Billy to dinner for the next evening at six, an invitation Billy accepted with a murmur.

"You *didn't!*" Ann cried when he told her. Outside the kitchen window, the top of a ladder went jouncing by. Her father was at Inverness for the weekend. Ever since Charles had arrived, he'd been on a mad fixing campaign, hammering on top of the cottage and under it, broadcast-ing (to Richard's way of thinking) his disappointment with how he, Ann's husband, was letting things slide. Richard was a bit wary of Charles Scott – a hardness in the man, and under his bluff, democratic friendliness, an impa-tience that seemed a cloak to disapproval. Richard had never felt accepted by him.

"I really wish you'd checked with me first, Richard."

"Actually, I wonder if he'll even come. He seemed rather vague about it."

"He'll come," she said with an odd certainty, and when Richard asked her how she could be so sure, she simply shook her head.

She began to move around the kitchen, taking items from the fridge, setting out bowls with brusque efficiency, while he watched with rising agitation.

"I've obviously botched this. Why don't we cancel?"

She looked at him as if not understanding. "Why?" she said, almost defiantly. "Why shouldn't he come to dinner?"

For the rest of the afternoon and into the following day, Ann seemed distracted. He saw her bustling in and out of her studio, as if she couldn't concentrate. A couple of hours before Billy was expected, he noticed her trying on dresses in front of their bedroom mirror. At six o'clock, she came out of the cottage in an off-white sundress with a low neck and joined Richard and her father at a table they had set up under the pines.

When Billy finally appeared in his boat, Richard rose from his chair, but Ann said, "I'll go," and started down the path toward the dock. Charles had lowered his newspaper and was following the boat's progress, his face expressionless. Recently, Ann had told Richard about how hard it had been to bear her father's excessive anger over what had happened. Hadn't he known Billy since he was a boy? "For years, he couldn't stand for me to mention Billy's name." But Charles had eventually softened, she'd insisted – to the point where, when she told him Billy was coming to supper, he had accepted the situation readily enough. Billy had reached the dock now, and as he climbed from the boat, Charles sent Richard an odd, questioning look, as if to say, *And you're all right with this?* Then he buried himself again behind his paper.

Ann and Billy stood talking together for some minutes on the dock. When they climbed the path together, Ann seemed ill at ease, while Billy could scarcely meet their eyes. "Billy," Ann's father said, in a grave, level voice as they shook hands: formal but not unfriendly. Ann had already moved into hostess role with a nervous energy Richard had rarely seen in her, offering Billy a chair, making a lame joke about her culinary skills, telling them in detail, for some reason, about the ingredients of a marinade she was using for the lamb chops. Richard felt for her, for Billy too: he looked overwhelmed.

Yet with the help of the wine, the little party gradually moved into a mellow phase. When Billy, finally, began to talk at length, his contribution was so unexpected that a deep, listening stillness prevailed around the table. He spoke in his quiet, rather droll way of a camping misadventure with some of his Blue Osprey clients, a saga involving a leaky tent, torrential rain, and a midnight visit by a bear. They all laughed. Charles especially seemed to come alive. He began to tell his own stories of life in the bush, directing them mainly to Billy, and before long they were trading anecdotes, Charles pausing to light a cigarette now and then, going on in his rough, warm voice that seemed to have been weathered in the remote camps and shooting blinds he was describing. Beside him, Ann turned the cork of a wine bottle in her fingers and seemed to be listening. Richard was content to let Charles and Billy do most of the talking: the world they evoked was new to him. He had drunk quite a bit and as the sun settled, sending shadows across the glowing rock, he felt a deepening sense of well-being. When Charles chided him about never having hunted, he wasn't in the least offended, but shook his head in dismayed acknowledgement. "A man's not quite a man until he's hunted," Charles went on. "Isn't that right, Billy. You people know that if anyone does."

Billy shifted uncomfortably in his chair, but Charles persisted. "How old were you when you killed your first moose? Twelve? Eleven?"

"Something around there."

"I was eighteen myself, an old man by your standards. But look, Rick," Charles said, turning with a glint in his eye. "We're going to go out one day. Induct you into the brotherhood. I predict you'll like it." And he went on to tell the story of how, hunting the previous fall – "black powder, one shot's all you get" – he had waited at the edge of a field where a wild apple tree had dropped its fruit. "The buck just appeared. You know how they are, so quiet. I couldn't have missed, but you know, I thought I had. I look up from the gun, the shot's still ringing in my head, and he just walks off.

"I followed him – found his body in the next field. I discovered later that I'd severed a big vein. Right beside the heart."

Ann stood up abruptly and began to clear plates. "I don't understand killing."

"But you do love your lamb chops," Charles said, sending a wink to Billy.

Somehow, the talk of hunting excited Richard. He thought he might like to try it some day, though it was Billy he wanted to go out with, not Charles.

That night, alone with Ann in their room, he struggled to express his feelings about Billy Johnson. "There's something about him. He feels so self-contained, so – I don't know – *trustworthy*. I'd put my life in his hands, I mean, if it ever came to that."

"Maybe the two of you should get together some time," Ann said. She was sitting propped against some pillows and had not looked up from her book.

"I wonder if he'd like to. Would you mind?" She didn't respond. "Ann, would you mind?"

"No, not at all," she said in her small voice – the one that sometimes emerged as if from some obscure corner of her childhood.

Three weeks later, Richard drove to Pine Island. He had never been on the reserve and he walked up the dusty, narrow lanes with some trepidation, aware of himself as an outsider. The place seemed deserted, though at the same time he had a feeling that somehow behind its screens and in the stillness of its shadows, it was conscious of him.

An old woman, her head wrapped in a checkered cloth, directed him up a lane to a small blue house. When he got there, he found a man working on a large, flat-sterned canoe overturned on trestles. He had bent over to sight along the hull, and when Richard spoke, he seemed not to hear but started to feel along the planks with a careful, listening alertness. Richard wondered if this was Matt, Billy's uncle, and was about to introduce himself when the man looked up. There was something sharp, almost hostile in his glance. Taken aback, Richard explained he was looking for Billy Johnson.

"Down along the shore there," the man told him in a flat, muffled voice before going back to work.

He found Billy sitting on the smooth rock of the shore with his legs out, intently examining a fishing reel. Loath to interrupt, Richard stopped a few feet off.

Billy looked up just then, but if he took in the fact of Richard's presence, he gave no sign of it and peered again at his reel.

"Hope this isn't a bad time." No response. In an inlet fifty yards or so away, some kids were swimming around a large inner tube. "Was wondering if you'd like to go fishing. If you've got the time. I'm no expert, but –"

Drawing up his knees, Billy gazed over the water.

They went in Billy's boat. Time and again Richard, sitting amidships, thought they were headed into a dead end, but the rock always parted and let them through. There were no cottages in this part of Nigushi, though occasionally a small cabin went by, or a mysterious clearing in the trees where a few boards nailed up between trunks were the only sign of human presence. Passing under a leaning pine, they swept into another gut on whose walls, close enough to touch, lichens bloomed like rust-coloured suns.

They emerged into a basin between islands: a wide, natural pool overhung by a cliff of shattered rock. Here, in the shade, in the hush of a small stream filtering among boulders, they dropped their anchor and began to fish. A flick of their wrists, and their lures snaked out, fell with a *plop* into the water, then moments later, to the clicking of their lures, came swimming back – spindling up through the tea-coloured water like tiny silver fish. Tugging gently on its line, the boat swung slowly, this way and that, caught in the subtle play of currents. Richard scarcely cared whether he caught anything. It was enough to be here, held, as he felt, by Billy's knowledge, a guest in a world that few outsiders knew about. As they continued to fish, they began to talk a little and their silences grew more companionable.

They had fished for about an hour when the sound of an engine – low, stertorous, dark – intruded on their reverie. Seconds later, a prow of startling whiteness appeared at the edge of the pool. It grew steadily – a two-tiered cruiser, steered by a man in a captain's hat standing under a canopy of royal blue. Behind him, on the low afterdeck, two other men, both shirtless, were fishing: one peered into the screen of a fish finder, the other leaned over the side, following the motions of his line in the water.

"There, fuck, I saw one! Stop there!"

"Pete, fuck, stop!"

"The damn thing isn't a car. Hang on."

With a clunking of gears the big boat reversed its course, churned back to a spot where, with much shouting and waving, the engines were turned off. As his two passengers fished, the captain drank beer and gazed around the pool. Discovering Billy's boat in the shadow of the cliff, he raised his bottle in salute.

Richard waved back but Billy did not respond, continuing to watch the other boat intently. The shift into action was astonishing. One moment, Billy seemed carved from stone; and the next, he was on his feet, hauling up the anchor, ripping the motor into life with a single tug. They roared off, across the pool. Richard assumed they were leaving, but Billy turned them in a wide arc and, still accelerating, drove them directly at the big boat.

Later, telling the story to Ann, he would laugh about it. "I mean, I really thought he was going to ram them." For the white wall of the cruiser had come up awfully fast. At the last moment Billy cut power and swung them alongside. "Hold us," he told Richard, and, climbing over the side of the larger boat, he dropped to its deck.

Richard stood up and seized a cleat. He had no idea what was happening, but whatever it was – and it seemed clear this was no friendly visit – he was part of it.

Ignoring the men, Billy strode over to a large Styrofoam cooler and threw off the top. Evidently finding nothing of interest, he ducked into the doorway of the cabin and disappeared.

"What the fuck is he doing?" the captain yelled from above.

"I think it might be an Indian thing, Pete," one of the other men said. They were all watching the cabin door; after half a minute Billy re-emerged.

"Okay," he said, addressing the men together. "You're trespassing here. You can't fish here. You can't be here. This place belongs to the people of Pine Island."

"You listen here," the captain said. "There's nothing about that on the charts." When Billy looked up at him, the man gestured in violent dismissal and turned away.

One of the others spoke now, with his hands out, placatory. "We didn't know, okay? It didn't say so on the map. Indian territory, right? We're cool with that, okay? No offence."

Billy climbed back into the boat and drove off a little ways, turning so their bow was pointed at the cruiser; and there they idled until the cruiser – a loose rope trailing behind it – trundled out of sight.

Billy had acted with more directness and physical daring than Richard had personally ever witnessed outside of a sports field. Richard was impressed. In fact, he was shaken. The blood continued to pound in his head for minutes afterwards. As they sat on shore eating the lunch

Richard had brought, he asked, "I was wondering – what you told them about these islands belonging to Pine Island – is that written in law, or –"

"It's not written anywhere," Billy said sharply. The menace in him had not entirely abated. He seemed ready to turn on Richard too, if necessary.

"So these lands –"

"Always been ours. These lands and waters, hundred miles north, hundred miles east and west, all around Nigushi. We've been here thousands of years. From the beginning."

Richard saw the seriousness of this issue for Billy. This was not casual opinion; he had run into the hard rock of belief.

"We never signed the treaty," Billy said. Prodding at the ground with a stick, he told Richard that in the last century, when the government called the bands of the region to sign a treaty at Sault Ste. Marie, Pine Island had not sent a delegation. They had not wanted to participate because a widely travelled elder had come back to the Island and told the people that a treaty was meaningless. "The government tells you it's just a friendship treaty. Next thing you know, your new friends are digging a mine under your house."

"But they took your land anyway."

"A hundred and twenty years ago," Billy said, throwing the stick away. "Yesterday."

———

That summer Richard began to read the great chroniclers of Ojibway life. Densmore. Schoolcraft. Warren. A new vocabulary entered his lexicon. Anishnabe. Nanabush. Totem. Babiche. He read of pictographs and pipe stems and tree burials, of the construction of birchbark canoes, of treaties and snakeroot and cradleboards. He learned, to his delight, that the name of the lake, Nigushi, meant "my mother." At first, he gleaned this information in secret, with a kind of guilty pleasure, as if he were walking around Billy's house, taking note of things behind his back. For the history of the Ojibway was Billy's history. After reading how the Ojibway had defeated the Iroquois in a great battle on Lake Superior, Richard seemed to see a trace of this long-ago event still living in Billy's eyes.

They were becoming friends. They went out fishing again, several times, and often talked over coffee in the Harbour. Billy had opened up, at least to a degree. There was still an air of reserve around him, a sense that he did not always speak what he was thinking, which Richard attributed to shyness. He noticed that Billy never mentioned Ann, and when Richard mentioned her himself, Billy seemed uninterested in following the subject very far. Yet he accepted their invitations to Inverness. By the end of the summer it seemed natural to find him on the big porch, regaling them with stories of his time out west or answering Richard's questions about the families of Pine Island. The place fascinated Richard. He and Ann went there often, to visit Billy or to buy crafts at the co-op, and he never tired of hearing about the family rivalries, the love affairs, the tales of living on the land. *That winter,* Billy would say, or *That time we walked up the Vermillion,* and there was a tone in his voice, a particular gleam in his look, at once amused and far-seeing, that told Richard, as he settled comfortably in his chair, that he was about to hear another story. "They flew this big floatplane, eh? Catalina – used them in the war to bomb submarines. They'd fly in at night across the border, sneak into a lake, toss in a few sticks of dynamite, kill every fish in the lake, throw what they wanted into the bomb bays, off they go. We saw it take off once, me and Matt. The thing was so loaded it barely made it over the trees."

At times, he is dizzy, and at night he is often woken by the twitching and churning of his legs as they pedal in the blankets in their futile attempts to carry him out of the quagmires and threats of his dreams. Plastic tubes burrow their needles into his arms, held by patches of clear, blood-stained tape, and down the tubes creep the liquids that hang in plastic bags by his bed, which he is convinced are making him weaker. He is in the Black Falls hospital – this fact keeps registering with the dull pulse of a labouring engine, for there, out his tinted window, the murk of the city spreads toward the citadel of the paper mill, toward the titanium glint of the Old Woman River. Each time he opens his eyes, he searches for the river; but even its sight does nothing to still the nauseating sense of placelessness, of being adrift beyond the borders of his own body.

His day nurse, Carmine, bustles in, the treads of her runners squeaking on the polished tiles. She speaks as if to a child not bright enough to understand. "How we doin' now? Would you like me to fix your pillows?"

He accepts her ministrations with indifference. A sense of exhausted aftermath has enclosed him, as if he has survived some great blast and now must lie with ringing senses. He had been looking at the clear-cuts; and then – the time between annihilated – he was sitting at a table in the Rendezvous. Around him, as always, the golden cylinders rose and fell, while on a stage no bigger than the roof of a semi, a woman in buckskin breathed some hard-luck song over the steel phallus held delicately between her fingertips. And then: the world slowly capsizing, and the jostling in the parking lot – the cool darkness of the parking lot filled with the moon-scrubbed roofs of cars – and a hard hat careening hollowly on the asphalt. The first blow came like a soft push against the side of his head – hardly any pain at all – and then he was curled on his side feeling the toes of their boots drumming into his back, his head, while he went far inside himself searching for the deep hinterlands where he might wait out their attack. *Hey, Injun, you like that? That'll teach you to talk back. Want another one? Hey, warrior!* And somewhere in there, in the far redoubt of himself, he had curled around a singular and shameful knowledge, which was the core of his resistance and of his shame: a kind of dance – manic, perversely joyful, triumphant. In some way, he *had* liked that. For a little while he had found a punishment equal to what he had seen – capable for a little while of obliterating it – though at the same time, it seemed to flow from the same place. Whatever power had felled the trees had felled him.

Then, later: hitchhiking back to the Harbour, finding his boat, driving off in a fog of pain, slipping in and out of coherence: there was something wrong with his head. His memory of the facts – the clear-cut, the Rendezvous, the hard hat spinning through the parking lot – cannot explain the total dislocation of the world. Everything is in pieces now, each existing on its own little island of time. He sees his tube-pierced hand lying on the sheet beside him. Then he discovers it in the air, waving vaguely, and does not know how it got from one point to the other. By old instinct, he had driven the boat to Inverness. He needed their help.

People come and go. The slabs of darkness and of light come and go, and though the darkness is not really dark (the glow of the night light) and the light is not really day-light (the tinted window), he feels he is being carried through these repetitions without choice. Everything now happens without choice: his day nurse; his night nurse; the orderly in blue who takes him shuffling with his portable bag to the bathroom; the doctor who writes on his clipboard without looking at him; the minister who tells the joke about the Irishman and then stands praying in a voice trembling and insincere; the groaning from behind the curtain where a man he has seen only once – a pinched

snout hooked by the transparent line of an oxygen tube –
performs the relentless ceremony of breathing.

Yvonne sits in the reddish-brown armchair under the
window. She, too, has come and gone. She has told him
that on Sunday morning (what Sunday, what morning?),
they found him passed out in his boat, among the new
shoals at the mouth of Pine Island bay.

"Ann Scott called. I guess she'd been worried, been
trying to get hold of us. When I told her what happened,
she said you were at their place – it must have been the
night before we found you."

He turns his head away on the pillow, away from her
prodding. He has not told her anything about that night,
or about the clear-cuts; he has not even told her what happened to him in the parking lot, though about that part
she has guessed. *Were you in a fight?* Her old refrain,
repeated throughout his boyhood. *What – another one?*

"Can you remember what happened after you left the
Scotts?"

"I remember enough," he says. "Did you tell her I
was here?"

His sister nods. "I told her they were keeping you for a
few days. She says she's coming over."

"What good will that do?" he says and struggles to
his elbows.

"You lie there. They have to make sure you don't have
brain damage. You don't want to end up like Knobby
Carriere with a plate in your head." Yvonne goes on
talking, her mouth moving so that he can see the gap in

her teeth where Nelson Longbranch hit her many years before. He is no longer listening to her. His mind is being carried sideways into a place where even the thought of Ann Scott disappears, like a stick dragged under by a current. "What I don't understand is if you were injured when you got to the Scotts', why they didn't *do* something."

"Do what," he says.

Sometime later – the same day? the next? – he wakes and Ann is there. She is sitting in the chair, absorbed in a small book. He watches her turn the brightly coloured pages.

"There you are," she says, looking up, as if she has been searching for him.

Raising his hand, he gives a little wave.

For some moments they go on looking at each other, but he can only bear it for so long. There is something shameful about being found here, with his piss hanging in a bag by his bed, in a backless gown. He gestures at her book.

"Matisse," she says.

Perching on the edge of the bed, she turns the pages. A scarlet carpet. A blue room. Four oranges in a turquoise cabinet. The colours are too much; and anyway he cannot concentrate on the pictures with her so close, her arm brushing his shoulder. He would like to touch her, there, on the back of her hand. She turns another page. Five naked figures, their skin an orangey colour, sit or stand on a green hillside, against a blue sky. Some are playing flutes, the rest singing with open mouths. The figures are simple, as if drawn by a child, yet he cannot stop looking at them. Above him, Ann's voice goes on, stops, goes on.

She is talking about the painting. Just let him lie here, with his eyes closed, her arm pressed against his shoulder, not listening now to her words but to her voice. Some time later, he opens his eyes and her voice is still going on, but no longer about the pictures, he realizes. Now she is saying, "You think you know someone. You know him pretty well. I mean, you've lived with him for almost fifteen years. But you don't know him, not really: you don't know what he's like. Maybe he doesn't know himself. You think he's solid in such and such a way. *He* thinks he is – but what is solid?"

He knows that what she is saying is terribly important to her; it should be important to him. But he keeps drifting off.

A little later, she says she has to leave. She has to pick up Rowan. But she doesn't move.

Then all at once she bends to him. Her damp cheek slides past his. "Love you," she whispers. Over her shoulder, at the foot of the bed, his nurse is shaking her thermometer.

Ann and Rowan drive through Black Falls in her Honda.

"Why are we going home this way?"

"Thought we might like a change," she says mildly.

"It's longer," Rowan says critically. He is flushed after his scrimmage and cradling a bottle of water that despite her urging he is refusing to drink. Normally their best times are in the car, the two of them talking easily, but today he is stubbornly uncommunicative.

And the hospital is already on top of them: her hands weak on the wheel. A vast grid of windows – which is his? – a flock of pigeons beating out, and they are past.

At home, as she makes supper, the current of her thoughts keeps tugging her away from the rounds of meat, the slivers of potato. *Fuck*, she says, as her knife slips and a berry of blood swells on her finger. Sucking at the cut, she goes into the bathroom. As she rummages in the medicine cabinet for the bandages, boxes and tubes tumble out. "Just stop right now," she tells herself, gripping the edge of the sink. "It's madness and you know it."

At seven, Richard calls to say he'll be another hour. She feeds Rowan, who soon runs off outside – too soon for her, for she feels a need to keep him close this evening. Upstairs, she goes to the bedroom closet and decides to change into a dress. Back in the kitchen, she pours herself some wine. When Richard finally arrives, she greets him warmly, but he is weary and dismissive, as he has been all week. It is past eight-thirty by the time they sit down to their meal. His dishevelled hair, falling over his forehead, trembles a little as he cuts his steak.

"I saw a bit of Rowan's scrimmage today," she says, trying once more to connect. "He seems to be doing well."

"Good," Richard says, not looking at her.

"One of the other parents – that big fellow with the cane – he said Rowan had good hands. Soft hands. I wasn't sure what he meant."

Richard brings another piece of meat to his mouth. Ever since the Benoits left, she has felt this remoteness in him, this hard air of disapproval. Does he blame her for the foreshortened weekend with the Benoits? Is he still grinding an axe over Billy, as if it's her fault that he showed up that night? "Richard, please, *tell* me what's wrong."

"Nothing. I told you."

They go on eating in silence. A pall descends, and her sense of danger deepens. "For God's sake, Richard, we can't keep doing this!"

Picking up his wineglass, he takes a sip, sets it down, and goes back to his steak. Her anger is boiling up now, and for several seconds it leaves her speechless. "Billy's in the hospital," she says suddenly. She *will* make him talk. "I called Yvonne the day after we got back. That night he came to us, he *had* been in a fight. Yvonne said he didn't make it home after he left Inverness. They found him the next morning in his boat. He'd blacked out, run up onto a reef. They're watching him. Doing tests."

Briefly Richard's blue eyes, hollowed with fatigue, find hers. "And you went to see him."

"Why wouldn't I go to see him?"

"Well, if you have to ask –"

"I *am* asking! Tell me, Richard. I really want to know." He is shaking his head. "Stop patronizing me."

"Well," he says, speaking with exaggerated gravity. "He came to my house and insulted my guest. He undermined a critical situation. *Critical,* Ann. I don't know why you persist with this. I'm sorry for his troubles, but the man is no friend to us. I don't trust him. In fact –" Richard puts down his fork, frowning as he considers his words. "I don't want you to see him again."

"I really don't think you can tell me that."

He is silent.

"My God." Pivoting on her chair, Ann sits, grinning in disbelief. A moment later she picks up her plate and, hands trembling, carries it out to the kitchen.

That night, unable to sleep, she goes down the hall to the studio they built in the new addition. All week, since they've returned to Black Falls, she has tried, without much success, to work here: sketching the view from the balcony, trying her hand at a watercolour. Going directly to a shelf, she pulls down the artist's sketchbook where, a few years ago, at her therapist's suggestion, she had begun to write down her thoughts, her dreams.

Leafing through the journal, she pauses to read lines and passages at random.

No ideas, no feeling. Why do I try? Am I trying to please somebody else? I think sometimes of my father. He's usually enthusiastic about my work, though I don't think he gets it at all. "How did it go today? Any breakthroughs?" Already moving on to something else . . . Yet it matters terribly to me what he thinks – even more than Richard. If Dad frowns at a painting, my heart sinks – and can stay sunk for days.

Erica thinks I should get over London. She doesn't know how hard I've tried. A woman's body is her own, men shouldn't decide for us, it's not a child at that stage – I believe all that. For months at a time, I'm convinced. Then one day, rain falling, or I'm alone in the car, waiting for Rowan to come out of school, and it hits me . . .

– the little girl in the park. Red hat. The seagull.

. . . this guilt sometimes – a stone in my chest

Sometimes I get this crazy fear Rowan will be taken away from me – to pay for her. She's always been a girl to me. A boy for a girl. Crazy, but the thought persists. If we stay stuck on a thought, even one that's not true, can we make it true? Can thinking something, fearing something, draw it toward you?

That nature program. The biologist said the lions could tell when another animal feared them too much. Was paralyzed by fear, already giving up.

Dr. Break (what a name for a doctor!) gave me the test results in his office. I was so upset I phoned my mother in Montreal. Please don't tell Dad. She wanted me to come to Montreal. But she was as confused as I was . . .

everything in me trembling . . .

The flowers in the market today. Little joy-bursts. I saw but couldn't feel.

The flower-seller's wife – a cheerful woman with a black eye. Did he give it to her? We have no idea of other people's lives. Dark caves, with secret entrances . . .

Richard came home today with tickets for New York. He means well – a surprise intended to cheer me. I feel sorry for him, putting up with me. Me with my uncombed hair and not even dressed yet,

pretending to be delighted. I can't imagine going to New York –
the effort! Even the thought of MOMA leaves me cold.

I suppose we'll go. I see Richard smiling, out of love for
me – at least I think it's love – and all I feel is a kind of pres-
sure. I've always felt it around him. He knows what's best for
everyone and insists on it, for their own good, of course. It's a
kind of blind willfulness. The first time I met him I felt it. At
our wedding too –

Idea for a painting. A man asleep with his mouth open. His
mouth frowning. His whole face, body, slack, unconscious. While
sunlight floods in from the window, making a glory of sheets,
yellow wall, a child's toy on the floor. What he doesn't, can't see.

We haven't made love for three months. He doesn't insist. I
don't know whether he minds or not. I mind: not not making
love, but not wanting to. At twenty it was different. Sex: part of
my love for the world. Indistinguishable from it. Who next?
What next?

Thought of Billy today. That glimpse of Mad Jack's as we went
up to the Harbour (I often look there). A year since his last
card from Florida.

Made the mistake of telling the above to Erica. I hate the way
she talks about Billy, like a typical therapist. You can hear her
brain turning him into the "love object." The fantasy object.
The locus of immaturity, she calls it.

I'm drawn to him so much these days, or at least the thought
of him. His absence seems part of this ache in me, the emptiness.

Sometimes I feel if I could reconnect with him, if I could talk with him about – anything – a lot of this would come clear. As if with him I could go back and reclaim my life. As if with him my mistakes might be dissolved somehow. Resolved? As if, as if. Erica's probably right: I'm immature. Yet is maturity always the answer?

London. There was a moment going into that house that was actually a hospital. My father brisk and cheerful – everything was going to be fine. We were both scared. He had climbed the steps, but I lingered on the sidewalk, looking off toward the railings of a little park. A grove of trees. I knew that what I was doing was wrong for me. I also knew it was right.

The light in the prep room like a flying saucer . . .

So much of the last ten years gone up in unhappiness. Years of not being there for her family, not really. Years of not painting, or not painting very well. Years of not being there for life. She wishes she had never opened the journal, for the sense of waste is overpowering. She can feel again the flattened, identical days. Often she wouldn't get dressed until late afternoon when Rowan came home. She would try to paint – struggling to find an opening. And small openings *would* occur. But they would last for only a few minutes – a few days, at best – before the darkness descended again. Sometimes, she'd decide to give up painting altogether – and for a week she would feel a burden had lifted. But her malaise always returned. It came back despite everything, even the antidepressants, their joyless levelling worse than her sickness. And so, not knowing which way to turn, she would go back to her studio.

Turning to the last entry, she draws a sharp line below it and on the next empty page writes: *What does it mean to love somebody?* For some time she sits, thinking. Then she adds, *I suppose that I have to ask tells me something – but enough?* Some minutes later she scrawls furiously, in block letters: *I HAVE TO LIVE.*

At five-thirty on Friday afternoon, Richard phones to say they won't be able to go up to the cottage until Saturday morning – he has a late meeting tonight with a client. He speaks with a show of cheerful nonchalance, as if their quarrel were behind them, as if *of course* she and Rowan will comply – all of which has the effect of putting her back up. "Well, I'm taking Rowan with me tonight," she announces. "I have to get back to work." He says nothing, and in the silence she can sense their hostility, like two obdurate forces set against each other in darkness.

She and Rowan stop for ice cream on the road, and as they drive into piney uplands, they seem to achieve their old, easy intimacy. But that night the boy comes down with a fever, and it is not until late the next afternoon that he's himself again and she can climb, exhausted, to her studio. On the huge canvas, shiny with oils, her giantess rises. The face is unfinished – it resembles a mask of melted flesh – but the force of her, the force and freshness, stop Ann in her tracks.

Some hours later, the low sun flooding through her western screens, the dabbing of her brush is interrupted by the sound of a boat arriving. Moving to a window, she watches the water taxi pull up to the dock with her husband aboard. She hears him go through the boathouse and on up to the cottage. Some minutes later, he returns, the trudge of his feet on the stairs.

"You want me to make supper or what?" he says. His head, thrusting out of the stairwell, seems disembodied, as if it had been cut off and set there.

"Sorry," she says, piqued by his tone. "I forgot the time." She cleans up and goes to the kitchen, where she finds him with an apron over his suit pants, hacking at a carrot.

For the rest of the weekend, they are civil but restrained. It makes it hard to paint, this covert war. It has become its own raison d'etre, an atmosphere they can't seem to escape. She fights to see her work clearly. She stands before her giantess, while arguments with Richard run through her head. On Sunday evening she announces she won't be going home with them to the city.

She expects Richard's disapproval, at the very least. But he accepts with a shrug and the next morning, waving goodbye to them in the Harbour, she is surprised by how upset she is as they draw away – a sense of mortal parting, as if she might not see them again.

The following morning, she calls Yvonne and asks after Billy. Yvonne tells her the hospital is releasing him the next day. "They told me to pick him up at eleven, but I don't know how I'm going to do it. Eddie needs the car for work and my cousin's is getting fixed." Ann offers to do it for her. "Just bring him to the Harbour," Yvonne says, quickly taking up her offer. "We can leave his boat there for him." As soon as Ann hangs up, she experiences resentment – she is entirely wedded to her canvas again. The next day, it is close to noon when she arrives in Black Falls. In the distance, the roof of the ice-hockey arena hovers like a black umbrella in the haze. To come so close to her family and not be with them – there is something deeply unsettling about it, and as she rounds the corner and sees the high, brown facade of the hospital, she is tempted to drive past.

In the lobby, Billy is waiting in a wheelchair.

"My rescuer," he says, rising. He insists on walking to the parking lot. His grin irritates her, his slowness.

In a few minutes, they pass out of the old neighbour-hoods into the spreading frontier of plazas and parking lots; then just as they are about to break free onto the open highway, they must slow for a detour. Huge machines are levelling a mountain of solid rock. Through clouds of drift-ing dust, she glimpses a blasting mat, lying by the road like a huge rubber mattress; the dust-browned bumper of the next car. Beside her, Billy has braced himself on the dash. Pulling over, she helps him out. He stoops, gagging, but nothing comes up; finally he gets down on all fours, bending over so that his forehead touches the ground.

"Not used to so much movement," he says. Around them, awkward as film dinosaurs, the machines fill the air with their congested roaring. She gets him back into the car, but when she suggests they return to the hospital, he insists they go on.

At last they climb into pristine country. The road winds among pink outcrops, under groves of old pine. He has closed his eyes.

"There's a park. You can rest for a while."

She runs the Honda into the grove where picnic tables sit in the shade. Again, he wants to get right down on the ground. He lies on his back with his knees up, one arm flung over his face, while she sits beside him.

After a while, he drops his arm and looks wearily above him. They hear the muted swish of a speeding car and, moments later, the dropped gears of a transport tackling the grade.

"Don't you think a doctor –"

"Never," he says to the high treetops where a squirrel chitters.

"I know you don't like the hospital."

"A place of death," he says.

She snorts, disdainful of his melodrama.

For a long time she is silent. This place with its patches of sun and shade, its dry piney heat, has begun to oppress her. She feels spacey, a little unreal. She picks at a needle that has got onto her jeans and is about to say, "Well, shall we get going?" But she continues to sit, stunned by the heat.

They seem to be waiting for something that must inevitably arrive, like a train that is barrelling across the drought-stricken land. But where they are, boredom and stillness reign.

A needle has fallen on Billy's shirt. Plucking it off, she tosses it away.

Abruptly he moves his arm and looks at her. Then he reaches up and touches her cheek, lightly strokes her cheek with the back of his finger.

The Nap-A-While Motel sits by itself in a slot carved out between the highway and the bush. It is covered in pink clapboard, the flat roof protruding over the office to make a 1950s-style carport. She leaves Billy in the car and enters the office, where she finds the usual high counter and a curtained doorway leading, she presumes, to living quarters – sights that bring back travelling with her family: the sun-slaked hours in the car, Rowan's cries of "Can we have a pool?" She strikes the little bell. Behind the flowered curtain, a radio proclaims the worst summer for forest fires in half a century. *In Ontario alone, over a hundred fires are burning, including ten that –*

At the rear of the building, hidden from the highway, picture windows, each curtained, look blankly toward the turquoise of a pool, sparkling behind chain-link. A floating toy – it looks like a small red whale adrift under the diving board – seems to her impossibly lonely. No one else is around.

The room is dim. The air conditioner over the door failed some time ago; the only light leaks from the Venetian blinds, slightly parted, so that tiger stripes of sun fall across the carpet where their clothes lie strewn. They lie on damp sheets; above, a missing tile reveals a wood beam, a bit of electric wire.

"Are you okay?"

"Oh, yes," she says, nestling into him. "How about you? That wasn't too much for you?"

"Nope. Like coming home."

"It was good," she says, though some sound – the clatter perhaps of the maid going by with her cart – had broken in upon her too soon.

Her head on his chest – so flat and hard after Richard – she listens idly to a tap dribbling in the washroom, not wanting to move, to disturb their closeness.

"Did you think of me when you were away?"

"Constantly," he says.

"Don't tell me you didn't have other girls!" She is pleased to be calling herself a girl. As if when she goes out that door, she might go anywhere.

"This one time," he says and tells her how, one night in Georgia, he was camping on a sandbar – his fire burning by a river whose name he cannot remember. "I'm sitting there, stirring my beans – and all of a sudden I sense there's someone behind me." He pauses for a moment. "You," he says. "Just at my shoulder. You touched the top of my head."

"And did I stay for supper? I mean, *really* –"

"I looked around, you were gone."

She is silent for a while. He is deadly serious, she realizes: Was it a dream? Had he been drinking?

"You were ill," he says. "I could tell from your touch – something wrong inside you."

Her heart begins to pound and she asks when it happened.

About a year ago, he tells her, at the end of August. He had been pruning Christmas trees for a farmer and camping near the plantation.

She tells him how she and Richard had driven to southern Ontario at that time, to see some plays at Stratford. One afternoon in their motel room she had found a lump in her breast. In the end, after several tests, it had been declared benign; but she had been as frightened as ever in her life.

She pads to the toilet and a few minutes later peers at her face in the mirror. A river in Georgia.

In the car they are mostly silent. Billy puts the seat back and is soon snoring in a way that reminds her of Richard. The sun of late afternoon throws tree shadows across the road and floods the interior of the car. Ahead, a cliff opens. High on the rockface, people have painted messages. MIKE WAS HERE. KILL SIRHAN SIRHAN. DON'T FORGET ME JENNIE. And her favourite: A.M. LOVES P.M. FOREVER.

In the Harbour, they sit with the crowd on Lola's deck. Everything – the masts in the Harbour, the cup in her hand, all subtly different – as if a grain of weight had been added. Or taken away. Across the table, he smiles at her – his haggard face lit briefly with a look that melts in her chest.

The Gotliebs are here, surveying the deck from the entrance. She looks away, but already they are approaching. Their tanned, grinning faces. Their heartiness. She hears herself answer them, cheerfully, in a voice from another life. "You remember Billy –" "Yes, we met at Inverness." No one mentions the bruises on his face, his arms, though she sees Pamela looking. They chat about an idea Ted has for a documentary. About a line of clothing Pam's bought for her boutique. They laugh over nothing, loudly and self-consciously, while Billy's neutral gaze wanders the quay. I'm going to go mad, Ann thinks. Suddenly Billy says he has to go and pushes back his chair. Ann is bereft. She cannot find words, cannot reach out and touch him, though he is standing beside her.

They watch him step from the deck and go across the road to the docks, where he soon disappears among the mass of boats.

"He looks in pretty rough shape," Pamela says, turning back to Ann.

"Yes, well, he had an accident with his boat. It's a concussion, apparently. I just drove him back from the hospital. Looks like he'll be all right."

"Good," Pamela says. "Still an attractive guy, in spite of all –"

"I suppose," Ann says dryly, reaching for her bill.

An hour later she ties up her boat and starts up the path toward the cottage. A beautiful evening – the pines across the channel wavering in deep reflection. Nearing the back steps, she turns aside, and for some time sits on the rock with her arms wrapped around her knees. Her sadness has deepened: a floating expansive emptiness that seems to bear her back into girlhood. She has *always* sat just here, among the still, shadowy pines, by the bright water.

Bestirring herself, she gets up and continues toward the cottage, but a few steps shy of it she turns and goes back along the path and into the boathouse. Even before she reaches the top of the stairs, she feels the presence of her painting. She does not look at it, however, but walks the length of her studio and back in a state of suspense, only turning to it when she is directly in front of it. The giant woman still marches through the mob of her tormentors. Her mouth is still open. But there is expression in her face now, which meets the incoming light with surprise – an instant of understanding poised on the near side of horror. In her right hand, she carries a large pine cone, which she holds just under her breasts; in her left, she grips a staff, whose top is twined with leaves. Around her, below knee level (below the tide of flooding light), the horde of much smaller figures moil in shadow. Some of them have managed to loop a cable around the woman's wrist and are pulling as if to bring her down. A man is hacking at her calf with an axe. Most of the men and women in the crowd seem curiously zombie-like, unaware of what they are doing. But one of their number, who is being crushed by her descending foot, has come awake, and his face is contorted with recognition.

Ann has given the giantess very pale skin, tinged a faint gold by the incoming light. But she sees now that this is wrong. The woman needs to be red, a real red, to indicate simultaneously her power and her agony. Ann paws through her heap of tubes. Cadmium Red. Rose Madder. Vermillion –

Sitting with his old golfing partner Bob Feydeau on the dining deck of the Wolf Lake Club, Richard catches the drone of a familiar voice riding the murmur of the lunchtime crowd. Among the umbrellas, it takes him a moment to pick out Reg Benoit, but yes, it's him, vivid in tennis whites as he stands at a table, bald, fit, bronzed, holding forth while a circle of diners looks up at him with smiling and half-smiling faces. Waiting beside Reg is a dark-haired, well-built young man, also in whites, whom Richard does not recognize. As the two men make their way along the rail against the glittering field of Wolf Lake, he continues to watch intently.

Reg and his companion take a table and immediately a

waitress is there with a sheaf of menus. Laughing at some remark of Reg's, she rises like a young girl on her toes. The minister's own rich laugh drifts over the crowd, and when the waitress moves away, he leans to the young man and speaks close to his ear. The young man grins. There's something familiar in his face, but Richard can't place him.

"You know?" Bob is saying across the table. "They're still mired in the 1930s – the whole organization. If you wanted to change the Leafs, you'd have to fire everybody, from the top down. But why should they change? Damned fools like me buy tickets anyway. One of the worst teams in the league and the place is packed, game in, game out. So blame us suckers."

Reg is now scanning the crowd, checking to see who's lunching with whom – the college president with the visiting paper executive, the socialist MP with the union leader, the doctor with the woman not his wife. Richard has conducted a similar inventory himself, and observing Reg do it charges him with reassuring fellow-feeling, a sense they are connoisseurs of the same intelligence, insiders really. Now Reg seems to be looking his way. But the minister does not, apparently, see him – does not, at least, acknowledge Richard's upraised hand.

Richard experiences a despondency that only increases as the lunch goes on. He throws himself into the conversation with Bob. He jokes with the golfers at the next table. But his attention keeps straying across the deck, where there's a steady trickle of people stopping to talk with the minister. The MP. A man in a yellow shirt who laughs with exaggerated jollity at something Reg says. Beside Reg, the young man picks at his food and says little. Richard is beside himself with the sense he knows the man or at least *should*: that party last year at Reg's place?

It's almost 1:45, and Richard remembers he has an appointment at two and a mountain of work that's been growing all week. But when the waitress who served Reg goes by, Richard calls her over and begins chatting with her about the unusual brands of beer they have on tap. A great crowd, he suggests. "I see you've got the minister of natural resources over there." The waitress seems uninterested. But Bob says, "Where?" and turns around to look. "That guy's a fool," Bob says, in a voice Richard is sure is carrying over half the deck. "With all due respect, I know you're thick with that bunch, but that new tax –"

"Well, it's pretty complicated . . ." Each time Richard tries to change the subject, Bob continues his attack on the new tax, which he claims will ruin his business. Richard excuses himself and goes into the bar, where he calls Marg and cancels his two o'clock. He is at loose ends, not knowing whether he should go or stay, whether he should approach the minister or leave it to a better time: you don't want to be seen lining up with all the rest. He starts away, then stops.

Marilyn Benoit is passing through the bar and onto the deck, where Reg stands to pull out a chair for her. Already Richard is making his way among the empty tables of the bar, out onto the deck where he moves toward the Benoits' table, carried on a tide of desperate bonhomie that feels more expansive and genuine with each step. Marilyn sees him first, her face lighting. She whispers to Reg, who, turning from their companion, says, "Rick, good to see you": warmly enough, Richard thinks. He stands at their table talking.

Marilyn introduces him to the dark-haired young man: her brother, Peter.

"Of course!" Richard cries, relieved. "I've met you at Random Lake!"

"Rick and his wife have the most beautiful place out on Nigushi," she tells Ron. "A tennis court in the woods – really divine!"

"When it's not under siege by moths," Richard says, and Marilyn launches into the story of the moths. The minister has gone back to scanning the crowd.

That night, Rowan in bed, Richard carries his second Scotch into his study and calls Inverness. He had called Ann the previous night, three times in all, and got no answer. He had not slept well. This time he lets the phone ring a dozen times before he gives up. It is only on his fourth attempt, close to midnight, that Ann answers.

"Where were you? I've been trying to reach you."

"I was painting – not actually painting, staring at it. I think it's good. I'll show it to you when you come up. You'll see."

"I just wanted to say." He stops to swallow. "All this business between us – well, I was wrong, what I told you. To tell you what you couldn't do – not my business."

"I appreciate that," she says, in a small voice.

"Good. Good. That's all right then."

After a while they hang up and he sits for a long time without moving. Over his desk hangs a framed historical map of North America, drawn in the early years of European discovery. Absently, his gaze lingers at a name, drifts farther west, where the names grow sparse and the continent fades into mystery.

They had been friends for more than a year when Billy asked Richard to go hunting that fall up at Silver Lake, where he had a cabin. Billy had been elected a band counsellor and was also working as a regular guide at the Blue Osprey, as well as running a trapline in the winter months. He was doing well enough, financially, to drive a second-hand Chrysler – a big golden boat with a dream catcher swinging below the rear-view, fender skirts, and an insatiable appetite for gas. Richard had joked to Ann about the car: "Taste was never his forte." "Actually," she came back, "in certain ways, he has perfect taste. The taste of modesty, you know? He never pushes himself on you. He wouldn't think of it." "Except with his car," Richard insisted with a smile; somehow, he'd felt criticized.

He borrowed a rifle from Ann's father, who was more than pleased to give him some shooting lessons. Being athletic and a quick study, Richard picked up the basics soon enough. But there was a world of difference, Charles told him, between shooting at bottles in a quarry and hitting an animal at a distance of a hundred or more yards. "The heart," Charles said, sketching the outline of a moose with a stick. "The best shot is here. A lung shot is good too. If you lung him, he'll drown in his own blood." The weight of the gun in his hands, the cool, snug perfection of its parts, the pleasing richness of its chestnut stock, the pale wafer of light with its crossed hairs through which he sighted at the bottles, the teasing tension of the trigger – the gun was not just a novelty but called up in him a keen sense of anticipation.

When the day came, he helped load up the floatplane they had hired for the trip north. Richard sat beside the pilot. It was his first time in a bushplane, and he peered out the windows the whole way. Below, the Vermillion River crawled past, banded with the small, quivering threads of rapids, between flatwater stretches as still and dark as a bog. Seeing such planes cross the sky, he never imagined how rough, how deafening, their ride actually was. Everywhere he looked, the hazy bush spread to the horizons. Here and there, water flashed where immense lakes caught the sun, their shapes like pieces of jigsaw flung across the carpet of trees. In the distance, the bush seemed to retreat even as it came forward, into the unassailable keep of the horizons. He felt that no matter how far on they flew, they would never come to the end of it.

Directly below, the tiny shadow of the Beaver raced with them – fleeing like a spirit over yellow poplars, skimming a marsh, darting up a bluff to flicker through the crowns of pines. He kept looking down at it, entranced and oddly moved by its companionship, its tenacious demonstration of loyalty and good faith.

Now and then Billy leaned forward from his rear seat, shouting over the engine to answer Richard's questions or point something out. Richard had travelled, but walking for the first time into Chartres or glimpsing beyond sun-baked hills the historic blue of the Mediterranean had not moved him like this. And it wasn't just the bush, flooding below in its incalculable immensity, or the prospect of hunting: Billy's invitation had spawned a sense of possibility, of a new spaciousness as immeasurable and beckoning as the forest unfurling below them.

And now – Silver Lake – its long jagged shape broken here and there by islands, joined by deep bays that sent up sparkles of light. Just before the pilot brought them in, Richard found the roof of the cabin. The smoke took him aback: he had not expected others.

A native man in a tweed cap emerged from the trees and stood waiting as they taxied toward shore. Catching the rope Billy flung to him from the pontoon, the young man turned with it to a tree and tied them snug. Immediately – there were no introductions – Billy and the man began to unload the plane. Richard helped pile up the packs and boxes, and as the plane drummed away across the lake, he took up a load and began to climb the path toward the cabin, feeling queasy from the ride. The steep path wavering under him, the box cutting into his back, sharpened his sense of disappointment. Perhaps the man was only helping temporarily – perhaps he had just dropped in to get the place ready – to help them stash the supplies Billy had brought in for the winter season. But others were here as well. Across the clearing, two women were working at a table, one of them Matt's wife, Emma. Her hand pausing over the fish she was gutting, she acknowledged him with a nod. Beside her, the other, younger woman kept her head down.

Dumping his load, Richard paused in the bright sun. A small triangle of pain had lodged behind his eyes.

Near the women, smoke filtered from a teepee of poles wrapped in a plastic tarp. Fresh kindling littered the dirt, a rifle stood against a stump. He only wanted to lie down.

Matt appeared from behind the cabin, tucking in his shirt.

"This is how he gets out of the work," Billy told Richard as he slung down his load. "Spends all day on the thunderbox."

"Can't resist the view," Matt said. Since their first wary meeting on Pine Island, Richard had got to know Billy's uncle a little better. But he could not completely relax around the older man. His silences conjured a world where Richard did not feel welcome.

Nearby, the young man who had met their plane stood quietly, his pocked, grinning face fixed on the ground. George. He took Richard's offered hand. Richard felt overbearing – large and out of place. No one spoke. Across the clearing, the knives went on clicking.

George, he learned, was Billy's cousin. He and Hattie, his wife of only a year, were helping to get the cabin ready for Matt and Emma, who would spend the winter on their trapline. That morning they had hauled in the mess of lake trout the women were now cleaning and hanging in the smoke to cure. They would need dry meat too: moose meat. Richard and Billy would be hunting for necessary food.

Over the next couple of days, Richard tried to make himself useful. He and Billy cut evergreen boughs for the bivouac they would share outside the cabin. He carried buckets from the lake, and in the bush worked with a bucksaw to fell standing deadwood for the stove.

His sense of his own awkwardness never entirely went away. His size seemed an impediment, as he stooped into the crowded cabin for a meal. Billy's family was cheerful and friendly around him, far more so than the people on Pine Island, who could be withdrawn to the point of sullenness. There was a feeling of celebration at Silver, which Billy clearly shared, as if their time here signified a release from the constrictions of the reserve. But all the same, Richard could not forget that he was out of place – a guest eager to earn his keep, but who for all his goodwill could not enter the complex current of their lives. He felt this most around Hattie, a Cree from James Bay. He had never seen such shyness in an adult person. With others – with her husband, with Emma – she could be quite chatty. But when he approached, she immediately fell quiet. And this quietness, this sense of stillness into which she withdrew, bothered him: it seemed a rejection. He would watch her covertly, admiringly, as she worked, her head bowed over her sewing, or heaved her bad leg (she had been crippled at birth, Billy told him) up and down the banks of the lake. He sensed an innocence about her that he felt could not survive the assaults of the larger world. He wanted to protect her – though from what, exactly, he could not have said.

As dark fell, they'd sit in the warmth of the stove, in the fluttering light of the Coleman lamps. Often they worked – mending equipment, fashioning new parts from wood or leather, or sewing clothes and blankets. Now and then a few stories might be told. Richard heard of near-drownings, of hungry times, of a man who had walked three days and night without sleep to get help for his sick wife. They spoke with a drollery that belied the hardships they had endured.

Occasionally, Billy and George referred to the upcoming hunt, casually dropping the name of a locale where moose might be found, recalling a past success or failure, making random comments about browse, about the weather. Over at Crown Lake? Maybe not: there was a logging road in there now and Harry Jansen said there was lots of trucks on it. At these times, Matt contributed little, though Richard had the impression that the younger men were waiting for his comments.

Turning the thin pages of his bible, Matt sat smoking his pipe with an absorbed air, seeming to ignore the others until, one night, under a drifting island of smoke, he remarked that two cows should be enough for their purposes: "Two nice fat ones." Billy and George glanced up, as if expecting more. But the old man went back to his reading.

Richard was tired of cutting wood and found these endless deliberations frustrating. Why didn't they just *go?* When they were alone, he asked Billy what they were waiting for.

"Have to figure where they are," Billy said at last.

"The moose –"

"Takes time," Billy said. Richard was in his sleeping bag, which was covered by the tarp Billy had also drawn over his own blankets. A small fire flickered at their feet. "You can't rush the animals, they don't like it. They don't come to you."

"What do you mean, come to you?"

"Same thing you mean, I guess." But it was not the same thing. The moose came twice, Billy explained. They came in a dream, or in a sudden thought. You would see them by a certain lake, in a certain grove. Later, they would turn up in exactly that place.

At least, this was Richard's understanding. Privately, he was skeptical. Was this just another irrational holdover from the old days, like a belief in thunderbirds? Remaining silent, he settled more deeply into his bag. Overhead, stars pulsed.

Then Billy was rousing him. It was still dark, and very cold. There was already a light in the cabin. The men ate an enormous breakfast of bannock and fried fish, bent in silence to their plates as if to some crucial job.

Matt and George left first, setting off in Matt's canoe. Long after the mist had enveloped them, Richard could hear the steady drone of their motor, and then, as it faded, the tentative knocking of a woodpecker across the lake.

He and Billy followed the shore path. Billy walked quickly with short, unvarying steps. Richard's jeans were soon soaked from the dewy bushes. They turned inland, climbing through pines. There was little undergrowth, and the going was easy over the duff where the shadows of the great trees striped the hillside, among slabs of sun.

Richard found it hard to get used to the weight of his gun, the lethal power it held. He kept shifting it from one hand to the other and checking the safety, conscious of Billy on the path ahead.

They descended the far slope, in shadow now, and came to a marsh, its borders rimmed with ice. Down an avenue of reeds, the open water of a lake gleamed. But it was not Branch Lake, the lake they were heading for. It was only a small lake, Billy said, scarcely more than a swamp – just the first of several they would have to pass that morning.

It took them three hours to reach Branch. Richard was hungry and tired; his soaked pants chafed his legs. Along the frozen mud of the shore, Billy searched for tracks. Squatting, he picked up a ball of dung and crumbled it.

They reached a burned-over area where the charred trunks of trees streaked the brown air. Billy made a gesture with a crooked finger: there was something over the hill. Straining, Richard could hear only the shivering of a few dry leaves.

Creeping up the incline, they crouched behind a granite ridge. On the other side, perhaps twenty-five yards away, a bull moose was whipping his antlers at a bush. Then he paused and lifted his head, sniffing at the air. A scrap of something, like a rag, was dangling from his rack.

Now the animal began to walk away; picking up speed, he rode the stately carriage of his own bulk up a slope. Richard could see all of him now, the freakishly long legs, the powerful hump of the shoulders, the muscles working under hide, the great, absurd rack riding above him, with the scrap swinging to and fro.

Richard felt the kick and seemed only later to hear his shot, though perhaps it was only his shot's echo. By then he had discovered Billy's hand on his gun, and the moose was trotting up the hillside, his rump jigging over his flashing hocks as he climbed among the burned trees and out of sight.

"What!" Richard shouted. He knew something had gone terribly wrong. "I had a clear shot! What did you do that for?"

Billy had knocked down his gun. Richard had never met the anger of those eyes before, and it was like a physical assault.

"It was a bull," Billy said, through gritted teeth.

"Yes, a big one." Richard was tired of Billy's indirectness. Tired of tiptoeing around his sensitivities. "I want to know why you did that!"

"Just forget it." Billy wheeled away. He said nothing further, not immediately. Down by the lake, he took some food from their pack. Richard sat with his slab of bannock, unable to eat.

"Bulls this time of year," Billy said finally as he tossed a bit of bannock on the water, "don't have much meat on them. Don't smell too good either. Got their minds on other things." Puzzled, Richard looked at him. "Women?" Billy said.

They did not get a moose that day, though they hunted a wide area around the lake. Richard wondered if his shot had scared them off. But he did not ask Billy, because Billy had withdrawn and in any case by now he had remembered what Matt had said about wanting cows.

They did not go home by the same way. Billy worked them farther south, and eventually they came out on a bluff with a view of a valley where several graders and bulldozers sat abandoned, vivid spots of yellow against the dull bush, along a road of raw earth.

There was a sadness about the valley, Richard thought. The violence of the roadway, the sleeping violence of the machines, and over the bush, the shadows of clouds lying like a dark lake on the trees. It seemed to him that his failure was connected with what he saw. He was not used to thinking of himself as a representative of his culture, of his race. But he glimpsed this now – the new road was in some way his creation, his fault. In the view of his Ojibway friends, it was a destructive force aimed blindly at their way of life. It was not what the road-builders intended. *They* believed they were bringing a better future: raw materials, jobs, prosperity. They meant well. But he had meant well too, shooting at the moose, and now the hunt was ruined.

The incursion of logging roads into their traditional hunting and trapping grounds brought considerable anxiety to the people of Pine Island. Some had begun to talk of launching a claim to defend those lands, and later that fall, Billy asked Richard what he thought of their chances in the courts. Richard said he'd look into the matter and found the names of some lawyers to call in Quebec and British Columbia. In a few days, he reported that the situation looked promising. "The federal government's started giving research money to any band who wants to initiate a claim. Really, since the Calder case out in B.C., there's a feeling that it's only a matter of time before native title to the land gets recognized as a right."

But Billy was concerned that there still wasn't enough support on Pine Island for a claim. Many, he explained, were wary of rousing the sleeping dog of white alarm. After generations of quietly surviving on the edge of things, they thought it foolhardy to draw attention to themselves by taking up the white man's instrument, the law, and turning it against him. Some feared for their jobs in the lumber industry, or for their relationship with cottagers around the lake. Others felt that Pine Island should not be squandering its meagre resources on the long shot of winning a claim.

On the other hand, most acknowledged that something had to be done. Nearly every family on Pine Island depended partly on hunting and fishing for their food; a good many derived part of their income from trapping. Yet the bush wasn't just their larder. It was also their pharmacy, their church, their home. "It's who we are," Billy told Richard. "Lose that and we might as well call it a day."

Yet the community remained divided. At least half his fellow band councillors were opposed to a claim, Billy estimated, including the current chief. "Old Dan – you might as well ask him to plant a bomb in the legislature. The man's tiptoed around trouble his whole life, he's not about to change now."

"So become chief yourself," Richard suggested. They were sitting in front of the fireplace at Inverness.

"It's occurred to me."

"Look at Billy Diamond up on James Bay – got elected at twenty-one. There's younger chiefs everywhere now. You said yourself Dan's not very popular. People feel they made a mistake. Run against him next election. Make the land claim an issue."

Ann had just come in from a paddle and, face glowing, thrown herself onto the couch.

"So, you want Billy to run for chief." Without waiting for a response, she turned to Billy. "I mean, I think you'd make a great chief, but – I've heard it's pretty onerous, that job. I remember when Marvin Maclean was chief. He once told my father that all he did was phone up government offices. If somebody's cheque didn't come in, he'd lose half the day tracking it down."

"We're talking about starting a land claim," Richard said, sorry she was discouraging him. "The thing is, *somebody* has to take the lead. And if not Billy –"

They both looked at Billy. "So you think the gun's pointed at me?" he said, with the hint of a smile.

"I'd be there too, if you wanted," Richard said quietly. Billy looked at him. He seemed surprised.

"You two would be good together," Ann said.

Billy turned his head toward the window, where a late sun was streaking through the pines. Richard suddenly felt exhilarated, as if his life was about to take an important turn. He not only felt that the band could be successful with a claim, he had already sketched out, in his head, a possible legal approach. But everything depended on Billy. And Billy, lost in his own thoughts, had remained silent.

Slipping from his house, he hurries away from the settlement, anxious to avoid others. He can't bear the clatter of their words. The small knives of their eyes. Under pines, he lies on his stomach, his cheek turned to the ground, desperate to still the surging restlessness – it is close to panic – that has gripped him since the clear-cut. In the lap of water he senses peace. In the green shadows mantling a boulder, where a single fern quivers in the sun – peace. But he can't get hold of it. Lying as still as he can, he closes his fist on a stone.

He keeps thinking of Silver Lake, the cabin in the clearing. *I'll go up tomorrow.* The thought is an instinct, too quick to suppress, and as comforting, momentarily, as cool water. But it is also a mockery. The cabin might be there, a few trees left around the lake. But *his* Silver is surely gone.

Sometimes he feels that all he has is Ann. Rocking with her in the striped light of their room, he had forgotten for a while. All he needed was what he had – the hunger with which they devoured each other.

From Yvonne's empty kitchen, he phones Inverness. "I'd really like to see you," he says.

"I want to see you too." But he senses reluctance in her voice, a withdrawal.

"When do you think . . . ?"

"Soon, soon. But there's so much I have to do. Richard and Rowan are coming up tomorrow."

He visits Martin Clearsky. A spark of triumph in Martin's mournful eyes, as if Martin were saying, *I knew you would come to it in the end. Because really, you're no better than the rest of us.* As chief, Billy managed to shut the bootlegger down for a while, but here he is like any Simpson or Mackay, counting out his bills and fretting, dry-mouthed, as Martin disappears behind a shower of clicking beads.

That night, he drinks at his own kitchen table. Before him is the whisky bottle, and a tumbler where a painted fisherman's rod bends and a big red fish leaps in the foreground. He fills the glass until its tail is under whisky (ha!), raises the glass, drains half of it off, puts down the glass, and sits motionless until he feels moved to drink again. From somewhere on the Island come the shouts of those who are drinking more openly, or whose drunkenness has reached a deeper pass. A baby is crying. He closes his eyes. *Wah! Wah!* He picks up the glass. The liquid burns down his throat. *Wah!* Will no one tend to it? He goes to a window, and the baby squalls across the darkness. The moon is there, blunted on one side.

Stumbling outside, he makes his way to the lake, drinking straight from the bottle. A figure is making its way along the shore. It falls down with a groan, gets up, disappears, is reborn in another place, staggers on, stops, puts back its head, tilts up its bottle of sloshing moonlight.

"You," it says when it comes close, reassembling itself from shadow. It sits on the log beside him.

Chilled suddenly, he dares not look.

Wah! Wah!

Legs stretched out: the white rims of running shoes.

A ripple gleams like a snake moving sideways, to collapse along the shore.

So where you been?

He huggers up with his bottle, ignoring the question.

Hey, you.

Here, everywhere! Down in the States.

What you do down there?

His time away – the blink of an eye.

Pruned Christmas trees.

The other is silent.

Worked on a boat. Fed the dolphins!

Silent.

He remembers the intelligent eyes of the dolphins. The ripples laving their grey heads, the smiling of their lipless mouths. The dolphins knew something people did not. He had wanted to go away with them.

And.

Lived in the streets, in Orlando. Sat cross-legged with a can in front of me. Because I had fallen into the black place I used to fall into when I was a boy. You drink because nothing matters and because you drink it matters less. Your face goes numb. Your heart. You might cut your arm or pick a fight, just to get some feeling.

Where?

There!

Where?

There! He slaps his chest.

Where?

There! He slaps his own face. One morning I was sick of it. I walked away and got a job making wooden pallets.

And?

And? And? Won't you ever shut up? I lived with a woman, Moira Simms. Had a son with Down's syndrome. I never saw a woman so tender with a boy, or a boy with so much love in him. But I left. I always left.

Why did you leave?

Restless. Too many thoughts. And – I didn't love them, the women.

Did you love anybody?

Johnny Simms. A little girl in Atlanta. She used to bring me a book and say, "Story!" Rebecca Jane. I'd stay longer than I wanted, because of the kids. They'd get attached, and I wouldn't want to hurt them by leaving. I learned to find out first if a woman had any kids. If she did I wouldn't go with her.

A ripple collapses.

Loved no one else? Only them you left?

He knows the answer to that one, the feeling of her would come to him sometimes. He finds it pathetic – and a wonder – that in his whole life he has loved, really, only one woman.

What she feel for you?

Not even now does he know.

One running shoe rises and falls, digging into sand.

I was chief here.

Yes?

I started a land claim, tried to get all this back.

Yes?

I staked everything on the claim. I thought because of the fire in me, we would succeed. Such fire I had! I could have slept in the snow!

Why did it fail?

Why don't you go away! Discovering the bottle in his hand, he tilts it back. Empty. He throws it aside.

Richard Galuta, he – didn't execute. We agreed on a plan, but he'd go off on his own. He was always convinced he knew best. But the other lawyers were better.

You hired him.

Again he digs his heel in the sand. He can't get around that one. He had hired Richard. And not fired him.

So why did you launch it?

Why do we do anything! Because you look at your people and you see what's been done to them. Because one time she said I would make a great chief. Because –

So you did it for her.

Dammit, no!

For the people –

Shut up, why don't you!

And for the land.

Remembering the clear-cut, he laughs bitterly. Those trees there. He gestures to their dim shapes. Behind them –

Yes?

He clutches his face.

Is that what you wanted then?

What?

Nothing?

He raises his head. The clear-cuts, the land claim, Ann Scott, his life, just so much glitter in the moon's net.

He stands knee-deep in water. The baby is crying again. The moon is sinking over the islands. He takes another step, bumps his foot, stops, moves forward. The water covers his thighs now. The surface sucks at his fingertips.

When Richard pulls into the Harbour with Rowan, he sees Ann, waiting on a bench along the quay. "There's Mom!" Rowan cries as they swing into the parking lot. As she crosses the road, she waves to them but goes directly to Rowan as he gets out, fussing over him with an enthusiasm that to Richard seems exaggerated. He has convinced himself that when he first lays eyes on his wife, he will know, in that instant, whether he has anything to fear. But as they walk to the boat, he finds himself as uncertain as ever.

And something else has cropped up: her sudden, unsettling attractiveness. He wants her with a feeling close to hate. And this feeling persists – an almost rancorous desire that increases through the afternoon.

Stealing up behind her in the kitchen, he wraps her in his arms – lodging the sides of his hand under her breasts. "You look ravishing," he breathes and feels awkward saying it. Laughing – a false note there? – she pauses with her paring knife. "My nose is peeling and my hair is filthy. But thank you. Now let me finish."

Determined, he kisses her neck and she leans away.

"So later then?"

She falls still. "We'll have to see," she says quietly. When she pats his arm, he retreats.

Later, after supper, Ann goes off to her studio and Richard sits down at his worktable on the porch. But his concentration is in tatters. All he wants to do is rush after her. But there are papers to read, arguments to prepare, and just outside the porch screens Rowan keeps drumming on the steps with a stick. Manic, Richard thinks angrily, shoving back his chair.

"Rowan!" He has to speak twice before Rowan looks up. "Give it a rest, will you?"

Rowan stands sullenly, averting his eyes, his hair plastered in sweaty points on his forehead.

"Did you have your afternoon pill?"

"It's summer holidays."

"Yes, but you know what the doctor said. Going without your medicine wasn't working. Didn't Mrs. Paisley give you one?"

"I don't want one."

Richard goes off and comes back with a pill and a glass of water.

"I don't *want* it," Rowan says. "I don't feel like me."

"What's this?"

"When I take it, I don't feel like me."

"Well, who else could you feel like, eh? Rowan?" When Richard holds the pill near Rowan's mouth, the boy twists his head away. "Come on, take it."

Rowan puts the pill in his mouth. Richard hands him the glass of water and he takes a sip.

"Go ahead. Swallow. *Rowan, swallow.*" The boy swallows. He is crying silently now, staring in fury at Richard's shoulder.

Some time later, at work again in the porch, Richard hears Ann and Rowan in the living room. By leaning forward a little, he can see his wife as she squats before a bookcase, exposing a strip of skin where her T-shirt has slid up. But it is another two hours before he can be sure she is alone: before the light is out in Rowan's tent, and she is back in her studio. Richard leaves the cottage and hurries to the boathouse, where, pausing to run his fingers through his hair, he mounts the stairs.

The woman stops him. A large, naked, completely red woman, striding through the scalding light of the lamps.

Ann is approaching from the other end of the studio, looking none too pleased. It's a rule he's not to come up here unless asked.

"It's not finished," she says.

The woman is as tall as he – huge, with stocky limbs and a strong primitive face in which her open mouth suggests a cry of rage or anguish. And she is red, red, the paint slapped up with an almost careless freedom. He lingers, fascinated, over her long hair billowing behind her, which on closer inspection reveals an interweaving of tiny trees and animals, a river like a flowing ribbon. Her force is tremendous: she seems about to burst from the canvas.

"My God, Ann –"

Now he finds the crowd of diminutive figures surging around her legs. Some tug on cables attached to her thighs, her wrists. Several men in hard hats, suspended by cables, are attacking her thigh. Using chainsaws, they have cut away a huge block of flesh, which now hangs by a shred of skin. The wound beneath is as cleanly defined as a swimming pool. In its depths, the pallor of bone.

The longer Richard studies the woman's expression, the more tragic, the more knowing, it appears. She understands she is being dissected alive.

"I can't see it any more. Do you think it's done?"

"It's incredible. Hugely powerful." They stand together, looking at the painting. New aspects keep revealing themselves to him: it is as if the painting is growing, actively changing, before his eyes. "Her face." He points, indicating the ridge of the woman's cheekbone. "There's a bit of *you* there."

"It's not me," Ann says sharply; and a few moments later, more reflectively, "I've come to think of her as a

sort of Mother Earth figure. You know, Lilith, Eve, the
first woman –"

"I don't know," Richard says. He has slid his arm over
her shoulders. "Looks more to me like the last."

Later, in bed, he moves on top of her. For all their efforts,
she cannot come, and when she urges him to come
himself, his sense she is lying in passive acceptance brings
him off with a bellow.

She is soon asleep, while he sits with his back to the
headboard, unable to settle. In the moonlight, the blotchy
shadows of pines move against a wall.

The next day, he wakes to an empty bed. Ann is in her
studio, as he discovers when he peers from the kitchen
window. He feels obscurely distracted, as though he has
forgotten something important. Through the windows of
her studio, he can just make her out in the vicinity of her
painting wall. He hopes she's not going at the red woman
again: he has seen her spoil more than one painting by
not knowing when to stop.

Rowan is eager to start for the Gotliebs', where he's to
spend the next two nights with the twins. Ann comes
down to see them off. Before he climbs into the boat,
Richard stoops to embrace her.

"That was good," he says, while she makes a vague
murmur of assent. "Good, good," he repeats, hugging her

closer, as if he could plant the notion of good deep in her body, quell his doubts.

At the Gotliebs', he sits on the deck with Ted and Pamela while the three boys play nearby. He does not feel entirely present – his thoughts still with Ann. He had not wanted to leave her, even for this short trip.

"I tell you, I can smell it," Pamela says. She has lifted her head alertly. "You can't smell that?"

"Bambina," Ted drawls. "The breeze – such as it is – is from the other direction. That's not the forest fire you're smelling, it's Sudbury. Or Toronto." His rangy form draped in his chair, Ted smiles wanly, emanating, as always, quiet self-satisfaction.

"I just wish it would *rain*," Pamela says, and for some seconds no one speaks. "Where's Ann? You should have brought her with you."

"Well, she's got a big painting going," Richard says.

"You know, she hasn't showed me one of her paintings for years."

"Well, she'll show you this one, if I have anything to do with it. It's good."

Ted is moving his head in time to the Bob Marley pulsing from the cottage and seems to have dropped out of the conversation.

"We saw her last week in the Harbour," Pamela says. "She was bringing Billy Johnson home from the hospital. He didn't look good."

"No. Well," Richard manages: he plucks at the leg of his shorts. "He's run into a lot of bad luck lately. Can't seem to stay away from it."

"I hadn't realized he'd come back. I gather he had an accident."

"Well, if you can call a fight an accident."

"Oh, I thought he was found in his boat."

"That too. One thing after another. It seems to be his way these days. A sad case, actually." Richard offers a bland smile and falls silent.

At supper that evening in the porch, every remark he and Ann make settles on barren ground. In truth, he has little to say; nor has he much appetite. Pushing his plate away, he gets up abruptly with his wine. Beyond the screen, late sun has found a mossy rock, and for some seconds he fixes on it, uncertain whether he will speak his mind or not. His words, when they come, float out of him with a sense of unreality, as if drawn against his will. "I hear you brought Billy home from the hospital."

At her silence, he turns to find her sitting absolutely still, staring straight in front of her. The sight, for some reason, chills him.

"The Gotliebs told me. It wasn't pleasant finding out that way –

"I can't do this," she says, as if to herself.

"Can't do what, Ann? Have a civilized discussion?"

"I can't *breathe*, Richard." She looks at him, her face filled with terrible candour. His first instinct is to grin. "I have to have space."

"Space! You've got nothing *but* space up here! When did I ever deny you space?" Stunned, he watches a tear slip down her cheek and disappear under her jaw. "Ann," he murmurs, as if he is stroking her poor head. While somewhere inside him, the walls of a city are crashing down.

"Did something happen between you and Billy?" His voice breaks, scarcely sounding like his own.

Her eyes roam the table, as if searching for something she has misplaced, and for a moment it seems to him that this thing will stop what is happening. They have lost some precious object, some tool, some clue, some memory, some good intention, some plan, and if they can just lay their hands on it. . . . So his eyes, too, dart among the plates, the unlit candle, the turned-over novel.

"Ann, I'm asking you."

She shakes her head and after a moment says, in a quiet voice, "I was with him. It's something old between us. But, Richard, that's not what this is about –"

He has to put down his glass; and the impossibility of this – the glass seems welded to his hand – floods him with such rage he flings its contents at her. He flings the glass too. It pops on the wall behind her head and its fragments shower to the floor.

The weekend passes in a heavy tread of confusion and pain. They cannot be together constantly, but after bouts of "discussion" – of argument and recrimination and silences – they take refuge apart. They might embrace before they go their separate ways; there is something both real and formulaic in their tenderness, fighters leaning on each other briefly before retiring to their corners.

From the kitchen window, he sees her lying on her back on the dock. She brings a hand to her forehead. She crooks a knee. It is maddening, and in some way incredible, to have her so close, looking as she has always looked, doing simple, ordinary things, as she has always done; to have her so close he can, if he chooses, touch her; and to know at the same time that she is drawing away. If he can just think of the right plan, speak the right words. Yet no matter what he says to her, he runs into something fixed in her, stubbornly fixed, a thing immune to reason, it seems to him, even to the appeals of love.

And here, she's coming up the path. Richard turns in the kitchen, unsure whether to go or stay. He feels unseemly, out of place.

Pushing through the screen door, she seems surprised to find him, though her face quickly closes as she passes on.

Later, hearing a bump from the dock, he glances out to see her setting off in the canoe. Leaving the cottage, he hurries along the path to the marsh. Beyond, the light burns orange on a cliff; but where she is, among the rushes, a blue transparency holds her motionless canoe.

Picking up a stone, he lobs it toward her. It splashes near the stern. For some time they simply look at each other across the oil-blue water, and for those few seconds, before she paddles away, it seems to him that anything is possible.

That night, at his insistence, they make love. At one point she pulls away, her heavily lidded eyes regarding him with mineral neutrality, then they are at it again, pounding away as if they could break through to a place where contradictions did not exist: some simple exhaustion.

The days of the land claim, what were they? The best of his life, Richard had thought at the time. He had a wife he adored. A friend with whom he could share those particular satisfactions men kindle only in each other. And he had a cause he could believe in.

Running for chief that November proved more of a trial for Billy than Richard would ever have expected. Hostile messages were spray-painted on the walls of his house; threats were uttered. It was rumoured that an old woman had cast a spell. "If you find me face down in the lake," Billy said to Richard once, "You'll know old Betty got me."

Winning by a mere twenty-two votes, Billy moved swiftly to bring Richard on as the band's lawyer. They registered a claim to a huge area around Nigushi – five thousand square miles of bush and water – and set to work developing their case. They met mostly at Inverness or in Ann and Richard's house in Black Falls: late-night sessions conducted among a litter of books and maps and sheets of canary notepaper, among cooling mugs and the crumbs of sandwiches and pizzas. Richard was astonished by Billy's intensity. He would show up with articles he had clipped from newspapers, books he had borrowed from the library or bought himself, bursting with ideas about how to proceed. And he rapidly learned the law, or such parts of it as pertained. "I told him when this is over, he should go to law school," Richard said to Ann. At times, Billy's passion worried him: it seemed a potential source of error, and even seemed to set Richard's own judgment precariously on edge. He tried to be the cooler head, and in return had to bear Billy's impatience with his caution.

In Black Falls, Billy often spent the night. After Richard went to bed, he could hear him downstairs – the knock of his coffee mug, the gush of a tap, the long silences when he imagined him brooding over the map of the Nigushi region – that wilderness scattered with a thousand lakes and scores of rivers where Billy seemed to know every portage, every camp, touching at the spots with thick middle finger, as if he could somehow feel the very stones. He usually slept late, and in the morning when Ann and Richard came down to breakfast, he was nowhere to be seen. During the day, Ann painted, while Billy – so Ann reported – went off downtown, where he "saw people" or visited the library. Arriving home for supper, Richard might find Billy and his wife talking at the kitchen table. Ann became someone else with Billy, in the way a person is said to be when he changes languages. She was more talkative, he thought, she laughed with more abandon. She was quicker to anger too. More than once, Richard heard her chew Billy out for one thing or another. He expected an explosion, but Billy bore her criticisms with a grinning, half-pleased sheepishness as if they were a kind of compliment.

That Billy was clearly in some way still in love with Ann was obvious. Richard accepted this with amused tolerance. He chided Ann affectionately about Billy's devotion. She laughed his comments off, though she never seriously denied them. It never occurred to him to mistrust her. The three of them were close: that was the point. Richard thought they balanced one another rather well. Passion needed reason, he once quipped, when Ann teased him in front of Billy about his habitual prudence. But her remark stung.

Those days, the cottage was often full. Ann's father might drop by with his girlfriend. Bea, a middle-aged, sporty type who drank strong gin and tonics and claimed to have met, in her youth, the Prince of Wales on an Alberta ranch. There were scholars too, whom Richard and Billy were consulting about the claim: snorting at recondite jokes, their shirt-tails loosely anchored, they droned on about kinship systems among the Indians of British Columbia; about the crushing indifference of university administrations to their important work. And then there was Glyn Thomas. Billy found Glyn on one of his jaunts around the Falls, a young grad school dropout, down on his luck and waiting booths in a Chinese restaurant. Richard was skeptical – shouldn't they advertise in Toronto for a researcher? But Billy insisted on Glyn, and he turned out to be right, for the young man proved as dedicated, in his way, as Billy. In several cities, he turned archives upside down and came back with gold. On Pine Island, he and Billy lugged an old tape recorder from house to house, collecting people's inherited memories of the treaty signing. Glyn also compiled a genealogical chart of all the families on the Island. "The official version," Billy liked to call it, in deference to the fact that on Pine Island, not a few people could point to more than one father.

For convenience's sake, and to save Glyn money, Ann and Richard lent him a room in their Black Falls house. When they moved to Inverness for the summer, he and his cartons of papers moved with them. Tall, fiercely intelligent, with a kind of lingering teenage shyness, he doted on Ann, whom he followed around with not-so-idle questions about her painting. Richard scarcely minded. All their guests loved Ann; later, he would think she was never more attractive, more bountiful, than at that time. People rushed to help her. They brought her gifts and stared at her during meals; he felt himself truly fortunate.

Her painting was going well in those days. She had found a Toronto dealer and her first show all but sold out. It was the period of her cottage paintings. Her bright colours, put down with apparent carelessness, were balanced by passages of darkness in which something uncanny and threatening lurked. "In a lesser painter, these subjects might have been sentimental," the *Globe and Mail* enthused. Richard's favourite canvas showed a family picnicking by the water. Standing off by herself, unobserved in a cave of shadow, a small girl watched the others with an air of otherworldly detachment, as if she did not understand what she was seeing or why the others did not ask her in.

Later, Ann would turn to such waifs as her main subject. They usually appeared in distant windows and doorways, or were glimpsed in passing cars, always with the empty faces of those removed from life. Richard was fascinated; in some way he identified with these children, for he was one of those, he secretly felt, who had never entirely engaged.

After two years of preparations, the case of *Pine Island versus the Crown* was heard in a windowless Toronto courtroom, under the provincial crest with its rampant bear and stag. The walls were panelled, the floors carpeted in moss-green broadloom, the benches and tables of solid, lacquered oak. Richard had never appeared in so high a court, and put on his robes with anxious pride, eager to be a success in what he hoped would be the defining moment of his nascent career. Self-conscious about his lack of experience, he tried to speak in a slower, more considered manner than usual, standing behind his table or, when he was questioning witnesses, moving up and down before the bench, his dark skirts swishing in a pleasant way around his legs. Judge Wannamaker proved difficult to impress. He would wince as he rubbed the top of his huge, bald head in what seemed to Richard barely concealed impatience; or he would gruffly interrupt to demand clarifications. Richard felt he showed the Crown's lawyers an easier hand.

Yet Judge Wannamaker did say yes to the traditional clothing. When the Crown, as expected, tried to argue that the Pine Island people were mere wanderers who had drifted about the north country for generations – and that therefore the present-day inhabitants were not likely descended from the people who had lived on the Island in the treaty period – Billy said to Richard, "Let's bring in the ladies' work." For the same distinctive style of beaded decoration had been made on Pine Island for time out of mind – proof of the established customs of an established people. A score of old Pine Island garments, made during the last hundred and fifty years, were imported from the Royal Ontario Museum. These were hung around the walls of the courtroom, alongside more recent creations by living members of the community. Tunics, moccasins, leggings, gloves, vests: all bore the same patterns of beaded curlicues, geometric shapes and flowers, while some were fringed with the fur of beaver or wolf, and the newest gave off the pleasant, smoky scent of tanned hide.

Billy was exhilarated by the arrival of the clothing. It was as if he had found the key to victory, as if the garments themselves would somehow sway the court, conveying the influence of the ancestors into the judge's mind.

Apart from the lawyers, the judge, and the court recorder, tapping away on his machine, the courtroom was nearly empty. Occasionally a reporter from one of the dailies drifted in, or one of those mysterious people who make it their business to follow trials. Richard would remember a small, wrinkled woman in a soiled raincoat and an old native man from the city, who always entered with two plastic bags stuffed with other bags and sometimes giving off the odour of food. He would sit breathing heavily through his mouth, and from time to time Judge Wannamaker would frown at him in irritation.

Now and then a few individuals from Pine Island appeared. Sitting nearly motionless, they watched the proceedings intently, their faces rarely betraying their reactions. Sometimes during a break, they would wander over to the display of clothing, running their fingers over a pattern, peering inside a vest, studying the craftsmanship of their ancestors.

In the rows of spectator benches, the one constant presence was Billy. Upright, as still as stone, he usually sat at the very back. Richard could never forget him for long. He felt that every word he uttered was being scrutinized by that silent figure. The other side was clearly aware of him as well, for when someone made a telling point, one or two of the Crown lawyers might glance around to see how it played with Billy.

When the judge struck his gavel to signal a break, Billy would rush to their chambers at the side of the courtroom with some new suggestion he thought Richard should take up. Richard found the relentless pressure distracting. At times, words were exchanged. Silences burned. The figure at the back of the court began to seem like a second judge.

Yet when it came Billy's turn to take the witness stand, he performed superbly, Richard thought. Under close cross-examination by the Crown's lawyer, he deftly picked his way through the traps laid out for him.

"So let me understand, Chief Johnson, for a hundred and twenty-six years your band accepted an annual treaty payment."

"That's right."

"Yet it's the whole basis of your claim that Pine Island never signed the treaty. All the evidence you've mustered here is in support of that argument."

"That's right."

"So why did Pine Island, over all that time, accept the payments that were intended for those who had signed the treaty?"

"We no longer accept them."

"Yes, but my point is, if there's an oral tradition on the Island that you never signed, how, if that's true, could the community have accepted, for well over a century, the payments in good conscience?"

Billy paused for a moment before looking at the other man, waiting in his robes. "What would you do if the government sent *you* a cheque?"

"Order!" Judge Wannamaker said as a ripple of laughter rose from the few spectators who had wandered in that day. "Answer the question, please."

"It was understood as a gift to all the bands of the region, with no strings attached," Billy said. "We are a poor people. We could not afford to turn it down, and thought that it in no way compromised our independence. If the government bureaucracy had made a mistake, then it was their responsibility to correct it."

"Do you think, now, that it compromised your independence?"

"No. It didn't compromise it in law. But perceptions are important, so now we send back the payments."

"All right, let's turn to another matter. You claim not to have signed the treaty, but there's a signature on it, or rather a mark, attributed by the treaty commissioners to one Peter Bluelake. And it says on the treaty itself that he is from Pine Island. Was not Peter Bluelake a member of your band?"

"Yes, but he was not a chief. Not a person of authority. He was only eighteen years old at the time, as our genealogical charts show. He had no permission to sign."

"Well, why would he sign, if he didn't have permission?"

Billy flashed a look at Richard: they had been expecting this. "There was a lot of drinking at the treaty signings. Perhaps someone liquored him up, flattered him, coaxed him to sign."

"That is speculation, isn't it? Do you have proof?"

"Do you think an eighteen-year-old boy would be delegated to do something so important?"

The days turned to weeks, the weeks to months, the arguments went round and round. Endlessly, the court recorder's machine made its pattering-rain sound, the judge scratched at his notepad, the lawyers murmured and paced – a team of four on the Crown's side, Richard on the other – and in the witness stand a steady stream of historians and ethnologists cleared their throats and offered their long-considered opinions. There was the respected and well-known historian who could not read French (though many of the relative documents were in that language) and there was Glyn Thomas, who could (though his testimony was later discounted by the judge because he did not have a Ph.D.). There was the outdoorsman who had made detailed maps of the Nigushi district, painstakingly noting the native names for every river, stream, lake, slough, portage, camp, and island, and there was the author of ten books who, despite never having been in the area, proclaimed that their accuracy was "dubious." There were native elders, men and women of such dignity that even that quiet courtroom attained a deeper hush. Some spoke in Ojibway, and for a moment in the spell cast by those clicking consonants, the plaintive drone of vowels that seemed to emerge from under the earth, the rampant bear and stag and the beautiful garments made perfect sense – for how could anyone imagine that these people had not, in a deep historical sense, carried the whole province on their shoulders? And the court recorder tapped on, and the thickly padded doors at the rear opened and shut, and someone coughed, and at times, in that windowless hall under its shadowless fluorescent lights on its scuffed moss-green carpet, Richard would momentarily lose track of what time it was, what season.

To conserve funds, he and Billy shared a room in an old Toronto hotel where the pipes clanged in the walls and in the alley across the road the girls from a strip club smoked in their heels and tiny skirts. Billy, who had taken up cigarettes, would sit at the open window exhaling as he watched them. "She's back," he'd say of a tall blonde he professed to admire.

While Richard tossed, sleepless, Billy snored in the other twin. While Richard waged a steady guerilla campaign for order, Billy left his clothes and papers all over the room. The room took on the particular odour of two men living together, of deodorant and sour sweat and smoke laid over the deeper fug endemic to the ancient furniture and walls. They padded about in their underwear. They talked endlessly of the claim. They quarrelled in voices tense with restrained anger. Richard insisted the trial was going well. Billy was skeptical and, at times, almost despairing. He thought Richard was missing some important opportunities; he wondered if he was trying to do too much on his own. After all, there were four lawyers on the other side. Couldn't Richard use some help? Richard felt insulted, but he brushed aside the proposal with a show of breezy indifference: they were doing just fine.

One night, after a particularly strained disagreement, Richard went for a walk and found himself in a bar where a member of the government team had also washed up. He was the junior counsel, not long out of law school, a prematurely stooped young man who grinned narrowly to himself and seemed consumed by some private resentment. At first, they conscientiously avoided any talk of the trial. But then, after a drunken pause, the young man said,

"I'm afraid your Indians are going to get screwed again."

"Oh yes?" Richard said. Nervous at being seen to linger with his opponent, he was on the verge of leaving.

"Got screwed once. How much land did the bands in the region give up – an area the size of France? For what, five bucks a year – and a flag for the chief? I think that lady said it all."

"You're persuaded by the diary then –" For Glyn Thomas had come across a diary written by the wife of one of the treaty officials, and Richard had entered it as evidence. In it, she had confided she did not believe the various bands assembled at Sault Ste. Marie fully understood what they were signing away at the treaty ceremonies. "Not enough has been explained to them," she wrote. "They smile and nod and seem to be under the impression this is a friend-ship treaty." Richard had entered the diary as part of his attack on the treaty process: a second line of defence in case their argument about not signing the treaty failed. Several Crown witnesses, all male, had questioned the woman's judgment and character.

"What we believe isn't the point. What anyone believes. The truth's not the point, is it? Not in there. Winning is the point." They went on drinking. The young man was shaking his head, as if he regretted the state of things. Richard pitied him – so cynical, so early. "Pine Island didn't properly sign the treaty," the lawyer went on. "We know it, you know it. But there's a name on the treaty over Pine Island and that's all that matters. A name on paper. This whole civilization is built on paper. My friend, you're screwed."

When Richard got back to the room, Billy was lying on his bed watching TV. He scarcely looked up when Richard came in. Richard was laughing. "Just had a conference with the enemy," he said, and he described his conversation in the bar. "The smug little bastard says we're in the right. He also says we're going to lose." Richard shook his head; he couldn't take any of it seriously.

Over on the bed, Billy had already turned back to his program.

After an eight-month run, the trial ended in June, and Judge Wannamaker retired to consider his decision, to be announced the following October. Billy went up to Silver Lake. Richard returned to full-time practice in Black Falls, a great relief to Doug Parsons and the firm's other junior lawyers, who had had to cover in his absence. After the drama of *Pine Island versus the Crown*, he found *Smith versus Smith* less than compelling. Dividing assets, handing out Kleenex, drawing up boilerplate wills, he recalled the panelled courtroom, the beaded garments, the energizing awareness he was fighting for a good cause, in the public eye.

He began to miss Billy; for all they had been at loggerheads, their "trial by fire" had deepened their friendship, he felt. When he thought of Billy, alone up at Silver, a pleasant, nostalgic pang went through him. He was grateful to his friend for introducing him to the mysteries of another culture. At dinner parties, he would regale people with stories of Pine Island; his pièce de résistance was the tale of hunting with Billy. He didn't hide the fact that he had spoiled the hunt that day; his faux pas became part of his tribute to "those wonderful people" who had seen fit to show the blundering white man their ways.

Then October arrived. Two days before the decision was to be announced, Billy came to dinner at their house in Black Falls. If he seemed less stressed, he was still taciturn, picking at his food and taking less part than usual in the conversation. When Richard finally went off to bed, he left his wife and their friend at the table. The next morning, Ann had come down with a heavy cold. Richard and Billy drove south without her.

The courtroom was nearly full. There were reporters, curious members of the public, some senior civil servants, three lawyers representing the federal government, and a sizable contingent from Pine Island. Seated once again behind the familiar oak table, wearing freshly laundered robes, Richard waited anxiously for the arrival of the judge. Billy was sitting just behind him, and from time to time Richard would turn to pass on some information about who was here, or a comment one of the other lawyers had made to him. Finding Billy unresponsive, however, he soon gave this up.

When Judge Wannamaker appeared, the court rose together. Then the judge climbed the steps to his seat and spoke a few introductory words, raising a little laughter when, referring to the traditional clothing, he remarked with mock sternness that he hoped that never again would his courtroom resemble a Hudson's Bay store. Then he put on his glasses and began to read his judgment. Richard listened carefully, but although he heard the words well enough, something in his understanding was blocked, and he was slow to grasp what was happening. In any case, it was not immediately clear that they had lost. At first the words seemed neutral, capable of leading to any number of conclusions. But then certain phrases began to fall, and an overall tendency began to assert itself. *Failed to prove. The preponderance of the evidence. A distinct and characteristic lack of authority. Evident in the poor quality of certain expert witnesses.*

As the voice droned on, Richard found himself staring bleakly at the crest mounted behind the judge's head.

After the court was dismissed, Richard turned to see Billy pushing through the crowd toward a side door, leaving Richard to face the reporters on his own. It was nearly an hour and a half before he could escape the courthouse, and when he got back to the hotel room, Billy was not there. Richard called Ann to give her the news of the verdict, and he was still talking to her when Billy arrived, looking dishevelled. She asked him to put Billy on and for a few minutes as they talked, Richard went on studying the judgment. "Listen," he told Billy, after he'd hung up, "Listen to this tripe." Pacing, Richard read out a particularly egregious passage. "Complete rubbish!" he cried. "Wannamaker's made three mistakes in law right there. This has got appeal written all over it."

Pacing up and down, he continued his evisceration of the judgment. Wannamaker had ignored what had been established in the Calder case, he said. He'd dismissed their entire genealogical argument in one sentence, though it had taken a week to present and had been backed by one of the finest historians in the country. Richard was in full flight now. Not even in court had he spoken so passionately, with such conviction and clear sense of the truth. Billy made no comment but continued to sit on the edge of the bed, his gaze locked in space. "Hey, cheer up," Richard said, swatting him on the shoulder with the binder.

When Billy did eventually speak, it was as if to himself. "I should have fired you months ago."

"What? Oh fuck off – we're just getting started."

"You lost," Billy said. His glance brought Richard up short. "They ran circles around you out there. Every strategy we agreed on – how to question a witness, where to lay the emphasis, what to bring forward next – you'd ignore it."

"I was thinking on my feet, you have to out there." Richard held up the binder. "Believe me, in the long run this is going to be good for us –"

"Do you really think you know what's good for us? It's all a big game to you of win or lose. Either way you're still cock of the walk – look at you, going on like we've *won*. No one can tell you anything. Nothing can get you down." Billy shook his head. "You're not serious –"

Blood pounded in Richard's head. Planting himself before Billy, he made his defence in a voice he could no

longer control. It kept rising in pitch, an odd, angry, pleading thing he seemed to hear from a distance. "I haven't had
a penny for this. I've given months and months to it.
Because I believed in it. And I'm not *serious?*"

Billy just stared at him with contempt. Richard found
his suitcase, fumbled the last of his clothes into it, caught
up his briefcase, and left the room.

Over the decade that followed, Richard came to the conclusion that he had been lured off track by the case, by his
assumption of Billy's friendship, by his naive ideas about
helping the country's native people – drawn into something that was *not really him*. He returned to his practice
with renewed dedication. He got involved in politics. With
Ann's encouragement, he changed his way of dressing,
giving up his cheap off-the-racks in favour of tailored suits
he bought in Toronto. He replaced Monday-night pickup
hockey and joined the best club in Black Falls, cultivating
connections with the wealthy and powerful. His manner
became more weighted, his speech more considered and
precise, and in the end, for the most part, he was satisfied
he had claimed his place among the serious men.

Billy sits in his outhouse, intent on a fading newspaper photo Matt had tacked to the wall years ago. Like a great grey tube of steel, the body of a monstrous sturgeon has washed up on the shores of a lake. Its eyes have been pecked out, giving it a spectral look, but its long, plated body remains intact. A girl of fifteen or sixteen, wearing baggy shorts and a plaid shirt, poses beside it. She looks happy – happy to be having her picture taken, happy to be young. Billy is entranced by this young woman, and envious of her. She probably doesn't care about the great fish, doesn't care that sturgeon of this size will probably never be seen again; but she holds the future as effortlessly as she holds the sunshine falling on her pretty face.

Voices float from the direction of his house. The query-
ing twang of his screened door. "Don't think he's here," a
boy says. The scuff of shoes. More talk. Then silence. He
waits several minutes before emerging.

He rounds the corner of his house to find Jimmy and
Dwayne sitting on his front steps. They see him immediately, so he has no choice but to approach them. Since his
binge of three days ago, he's continued to avoid people; it's
as if his old skin has been stripped and he hasn't grown a
new one yet, hasn't the means to deflect their curiosity, to
defend the weak shoots of healing inside him. As he stands
talking to the boys, he keeps eyeing the object in Jimmy's
hands. "Mom found it," Jimmy says, holding it out – Billy's
old ball mitt. Black leather laced with yellowish thong, the
maker's name fading on the heel. He slides his hand into
the cool interior and pounds his fist in the deep pocket,
sensing, for a moment, the sweetness of certain evenings
on the old diamond. The crack of the bat and him already
ranging left, into the path of the skipping grounder –

He thrusts the glove at Jimmy.

"Here. It's yours."

Looking puzzled, the boy takes the glove.

"Jimmy was thinking we could play catch," Dwayne says,
his voice seeming to come from somewhere outside him.

"Sure," Billy says. But he goes up the steps and into his
house, shutting the door behind him.

Some time later, peering out a window, he sees them
sitting on the ground, in the shade. Dwayne has the glove
now and is tossing a ball into it with his free hand. Clearly,

they are waiting for him to come out. He pulls back. Minutes go by. The pump in the sink lets another drop fall, into the brimming basin. Outside (he looks again), the white ball flies up, falls, disappears into the mitt. He is trapped.

He is not aware of deciding anything. He simply turns to the door with a sense of surrender, of yielding to an action that is not entirely his own, and walks out of the house and down the steps, toward the boys, who, in the shade of the cedars, have the stillness, now, of stones.

They make a triangle, Billy near the house, Dwayne by the woodpile, Jimmy with his back to the lake. Dwayne cocks his arm and throws hard at Billy, who watches the ball spinning, growing larger, coming straight at his head, yet he cannot move. He can sense the old ballplayer stirring, the old instincts, but there is a heavy weight in him, a sense of unreality. Then, with a life of their own, his hands fly up and the ball stings into his palms.

The next day, he roots in the shed until he finds Matt's weed-whacker – one of the old-fashioned, manual kind with a rippled blade attached to a metal shaft topped by a wooden handle. He spends an hour trying to raise an edge, without much success, then carries it down the road to the ball diamond. Beyond the rusted, leaning backstop, the entire field is overrun with weeds: chicory, plantain, fireweed, monstrous mulleins sticking up like spears. Ten years before, grass had spread toward a white-washed fence. Now sections of the fence have gone down before the wave of vegetation, under the somnolent, forbidding gaze of the bush.

He turns to the waist-high goldenrod beside the road. At his first blow, a single stalk droops. At his second, it droops a little farther. The tool is next to useless, but he goes on hacking, first with one hand, then with two, until after an hour he has cleared an area around home plate.

That night he dreams of the field as it used to be: the smoothly gravelled infield, the baselines running white toward distant trees. He is standing at the plate with a bat in his hands. Facing him on the pitcher's mound is an unusually tall man with a cap pulled down over his eyes. The giant wears a grey uniform, but his exposed hands and forearms, and the lower part of his face, are red. Taking a ball from his mouth, he begins his windup – throws one leg over his shoulder, peeks out between his own knees, takes another ball from his ear –

Billy wakes laughing.

The next day, it is early afternoon by the time he starts off with his weed-whacker. Fifty yards from the diamond, he hears voices and sees, in the centre of the outfield, three men swinging scythes, laying down weeds with rhythmic, hushing strokes. In the shade near third base, Eileen Masse, sitting in a lawn chair, tilts a pitcher over the cups held out by a group of children.

He steps out of sight, and is about to walk off, when his sister appears pushing a lawn mower down the road. "Didn't want you to have *all* the fun," she says as she rattles past. He follows her along the edge of the diamond and stands talking with her and Eileen, aware the whole time of the men working in the outfield. "We thought you could use some help," Eileen says, nodding at his weed-whacker. "*That* puny thing." Her big face beams at him, slit-eyed. He had thought the Masse family was set against him, because they had opposed his pursuit of the land claim. But it seems they've got past that. Roy Masse is coming in from the field. He has to leave for the Harbour, he says. Billy takes Roy's scythe and, putting it over his shoulder, walks out, into the sun.

When he gets back to the house, the sight of Ann Scott strolling across the rock surprises him: he hasn't thought of her for hours. She regards him without expression as she approaches, and he has the sense she is testing her idea of him against her experience: this sweating, shirtless man with a strange, orange-handled tool in his hand.

"Whatever have you been up to with that thing?"

There's an archness in her voice, as if he could only be doing something trivial, amusing. He shakes his head. He does not want to tell her.

They go into the house together, and after he sponges off, they undress on either side of his bed. There is a distance between them, and their love-making is fierce, impersonal, as if they had agreed to put aside who they are, who they *think* they are, and come together as strangers. Then they lie in a companionable torpor.

Reaching out, he lazily traces the curve where her back spreads into her hips: a place he loves.

Later, they walk to a cove near his house. She strips to her bra and panties and swims off, while he washes in the shallows. Gazing over the water, he watches her stroke briskly toward an island. So much strength and confidence in her; he feels his weakness in comparison. She is far off now, just a flashing of arms and legs. Regretting his neediness, he watches as she swims behind a rock, and goes on watching until, smaller now, she appears on the other side.

She swims back and strides from the water, looking happy and invigorated. They lie on towels on the warm rock. Directly overhead, the pines hold long, indented shards of sky.

He wants to go up to Silver Lake, he tells her.

"I thought you said it would be all clear-cut there now. Do you really want to see that again. Isn't it what started all this?"

"'Have to see what's happened to the cabin." He knows it's probably a ruin now. But he has to see it anyway. Because it is his.

She opens a can of beans, and they sit outside on two chairs, passing it back and forth.

"I told Richard I needed some space," she says after a while. "But I'm not sure how much he understands that. He's in pretty bad shape –

"I'm going to live at the cottage, at least for the time

being," she continues. "It feels good to be there, except for missing Rowan. He's coming tomorrow for a week. He hates the situation – well, he *should* hate it. He's not sleeping very well – wet his bed twice. Oh, God!" She gives him a look of exhausted candour. *See, this is what I am.*

Billy leans forward, elbows on knees, his head in his hands. So much pain, and he's helped make it.

"Don't worry," she says. "You're not going to have a madwoman on your hands. I'm not expecting you to do anything about this."

He looks up in surprise. It's not what he's been thinking. Not at all. She's gone back to the beans now, briskly scraping in the can with her spoon.

Late August. The Old Woman River has shrunk to a putrid trickle; on Ann and Richard's street the lawns have turned to straw. Richard sits on the edge of their bed, in the hum of the air conditioner. Across the dimming room, Ann's mirror glints above her dresser. Getting up, he begins to pace. It is never worse than when the boy is with Ann at Inverness and their big house expands around him. Evenings, loath to come home, he is tempted to eat downtown, but not wanting people to see him on his own – it is bad to fail, worse to be seen failing – he usually grazes from his own fridge and drinks a bottle of Merlot from his own cellar, and tries to work: surrendering eventually to the call of the TV in the den, and the buttons of

the remote that allow at least a modicum of control as he
dismisses in rapid sequence the preening talk-show host,
the weatherman scrawling on his transparent board, the
milling of a crowd in some distant city, stopping, finally,
(who knows why?) at a scuba diver swimming, dreamlike,
among spires of pink coral. He has thought of finding a
woman to go out with, to go to bed with – a statement of
his independence, proof that *he's* all right – but although
he has looked at women, he has not approached any. He
wants only Ann. He's confessed to her in a phone call that
he's not paid her the attention or respect she deserves –
sentiments of deep sincerity, born of loss. What hollows
him is her reluctance to respond at any length. He suspects she has already made up her mind about him and is
merely hearing him out for kindness' sake.

Doug Parsons has taken him out a couple of times for
drinks. But his easy optimism – "In a month you'll be over
it," "plenty more fish in the sea" – hides an instinctive
avoidance of anything "emotional." Despite his longing
to talk only about Ann, he is relieved to be carried off
into safer topics like the latest machinations in Ottawa or
Doug's search for the perfect boat. Yet while the distrac-
tion is welcome, he is beginning to realize he has reached
early middle age without a single close friend.

He paces in the room they once shared. Stopping
before her closet, he flicks a switch, illuminating the
hanging mass of her clothes. Seizing a dress, he pulls it
out and brings it to his nose but can smell only the lingering tartness of dry cleaner. They had bought it in Paris.

He remembered her modelling it for him, in an expensive shop on the Right Bank where he sat on a low hassock and the saleswoman swanned about in her snotty Parisian way – they both laughed afterwards. Ann, he thought, was happy. But he wonders now. How much of her "happiness" was something to make him feel his own gesture in taking her to Paris was not wasted? Yet wasn't this, still, a kind of love – wanting to protect him from her sadness? While he was trying to take care of her, wasn't she, in her way, taking care of him? For a moment, he holds the dress, then abruptly throws it aside.

He goes over to her dresser and begins to open drawers. Socks, bras, underwear – all in the usual tangle. A small sewing kit. A sleeping mask. A box of oil pastels. A smooth, perfectly round stone. A postcard picture of the Grand Canyon, its red depths seamed with a tiny river. It is the topmost of a packet of Billy's cards, saved all these years. An aerial view of Wheeling, WVA. A large fish held by a boy. A transport truck. A McDonald's restaurant. *Writing this in an abandoned house. Rain dripping on my feet. Wish I was there.*

He starts to rip up the card, thinks better of it, and shoves the whole pack into the drawer. Digging farther, he finds a black artist's notebook. It has been years since he has seen her writing in it. He opens it, tilting it toward the failing light from the window.

Erica says it might help if I write here. I hardly know what to write. So I'm doing this for my therapist. As I do other things for other people. Do I do anything for myself any more? My painting – but I'm not even sure of that. I lived for it once. Now I stand staring at the canvas. No ideas, no feeling. Why do I try? Am I trying to please somebody else? I think sometimes of my father. He's usually enthusiastic about my work, though I don't think he gets it at all. "How did it go today? Any break-throughs?" Already moving on to something else . . . Yet it matters terribly to me what he thinks – even more than Richard. If Dad frowns at a painting, my heart sinks – and can stay sunk for days. So I avoid showing him paintings, but tell him it's going fine. Which means these days that I'm lying to him. I lie to Richard too – pretend I'm making progress. And painting used to be like a bird singing.

Spied on Rowan today. I just got suddenly, awfully, worried about him. I was trying to paint, and I just knew he was in trouble. As if he had just stopped existing. I drove down to the school and sat across the road in the car. I thought, If he's in trouble in the school, people will know, an ambulance will come. But what if he's not there! Totally crazy. I knew it was crazy, but I couldn't stop.

So I went to the office and gave them an excuse about needing to see him. The principal went down the hall with me and knocked on the kindergarten door. When Rowan came out, I could see in an instant he was all right. I wanted to fall on him, weep with relief. When the principal left, I took him down the hall and told him I wanted him to have some money. "Just in case," I said, and I gave him a five-dollar bill. It was all I could think of.

I could see I had alarmed him. Maybe he lives over the same kind of abyss I do. Maybe I've put it in him – some huge unspoken fear. I'm always imagining the worst, which would be losing him. Erica said once: Be careful of thoughts. They have power.

It's London. I know. If I care to stop, really stop and feel what's there – it's there. All the time.

Erica thinks I should get over London. She doesn't know how hard I've tried. A woman's body is her own, men shouldn't decide for us, it's not a child at that stage – I believe all that. For months at a time, I'm convinced. Then one day, rain falling, or I'm alone in the car, waiting for Rowan to come out of school, and it hits me. Her. I always think of it as a girl. The life I ended. I see little girls going past with their mothers and I think, That might have been her. Us.

Erica believes I should think of her as myself – she's the self I haven't let live. This seems reasonable, and I've had some dreams that supported it – the little girl in the park. Red hat. The seagull.

But then, why this guilt sometimes – a stone in my chest. And the wondering about what she would be like. The sense of the life she might have lived – that I deprived her of.

The future is real too. We say it doesn't exist, but when someone dies, they are deprived of the future. I cut a piece of the future away.

Dr. Break (what a name for a doctor!) gave me the test results in his office. I was so upset I phoned my mother in Montreal.

Please don't tell Dad. *She wanted me to come to Montreal. But she was as confused as I was, I could tell. She did tell my father. One day he walked into my room and told me in no uncertain terms I wasn't to see Billy again. He'd already forbidden it once, after catching us that day coming down from my bedroom. I was terrified of his anger. I didn't see it often, but when he let it out – nuclear.*

I think I was always afraid of his rage even when I hadn't seen it. But I went up to Mad Jack's again, everything in me trembling. I didn't tell Billy I was pregnant. I didn't want to hear him say, Let's get married. I didn't want to see him happy about it – because he would have been. Women on Pine Island don't have abortions. They just don't. I couldn't have married him. I had no place for a baby.

Dad saw me coming back in the canoe – all hell to pay. Yelling through Inverness. Yelling about his brother, how he'd ruined his life by marrying the wrong woman, yelling about ancient history, about his own life gone wrong (I'd never heard that before). Yelling so hard he was weeping. Gripping me by the arm, making me promise I wouldn't see Billy again.

I locked the door of my room and took off all my clothes and lay down on my bed. I was amazingly calm. There was another life in me. I remember the window was open, I could see the pines through the screen. A soft breeze. It was all so simple, really. I had a baby in me. I loved the baby's father – why not have the baby? So simple – a calm, good place beyond all this insanity. The feeling lasted about an hour.

I saw Billy once more – went up to Pine Island. I almost told him, then I didn't. What was the use?

The flowers in the market today. Little joy-bursts. I saw but couldn't feel.

The flower seller's wife – a cheerful woman with a black eye. Did he give it to her? We have no idea of other people's lives. Dark caves, with secret entrances. If we could suddenly be transported into another person's body, another life, and just feel for a few seconds what it was like, we might come back to ourselves with amazement. Shouting in amazement, that such other feelings, thoughts, were possible. Or crying out in horror. Or maybe it wouldn't be so very different, maybe the old man whose face is covered in warts feels much like me – I hope not.

Richard came home today with tickets for New York. He means well – a surprise intended to cheer me. I feel sorry for him, putting up with me. Me with my uncombed hair and not even dressed yet, pretending to be delighted. I can't imagine going to New York – the effort! Even the thought of MOMA leaves me cold.

I suppose we'll go. I see Richard smiling, out of love for me – at least I think it's love – and all I feel is a kind of pressure. I've always felt it around him. He knows what's best for everyone and insists on it, for their own good, of course. It's a kind of blind willfulness. The first time I met him I felt it. At our wedding too. There was a moment at the banquet – people striking their forks on glasses, that horrible custom, to make us kiss. Richard seized me, bending me right back in an elaborate show, making a real production of it. The complete ignorance, or at least sweeping aside, of what I am.

Richard can suck oxygen from a room. It was different with Billy. He creates a space I can expand into. With him, talking, I used to go on holiday; I made discoveries.

Idea for a painting. A man asleep with his mouth open. His mouth frowning. His whole face, body, slack, unconscious. While sunlight floods in from the window, making a glory of sheets, yellow wall, a child's toy on the floor. What he doesn't, can't see.

We haven't made love for three months. He doesn't insist. I don't know whether he minds or not. I mind: not not making love, but not wanting to. At twenty it was different. Sex: part of my love for the world. Indistinguishable from it. Who next? What next?

Thought of Billy today. That glimpse of Mad Jack's as we went up to the Harbour (I often look there). A year since his last card from Florida.

I'm drawn to him so much these days, or at least the thought of him. His absence seems part of his ache in me, the emptiness. Sometimes I feel if I could reconnect with him, if I could talk with him about – anything – a lot of this would come clear. As if with him I could go back and reclaim my life. As if with him my mistakes might be dissolved somehow. Resolved? As if, as if. Erica's probably right: I'm immature. Yet is maturity always the answer?

Can we ever really escape the things of our childhoods?

Read an article today about parents losing a child. Sometimes it drives them apart – sometimes brings them together more strongly. It's been like that with Billy a bit – except, of course, that Billy isn't here and doesn't know. All the years since that summer, it's been a bond he's not aware of. It's there in my attraction to him, like a painful little hook – the loss we've endured together, though of course he doesn't know about it. I used to imagine telling him one day, when the moment was right, but somehow it never was.

I remember once, sitting up late with him in the Black Falls house, after Richard had gone to bed. He started to talk about having children one day. How he wanted to. How he wanted his son or daughter to have a different kind of experience from the one he had growing up.

I keep thinking of the land claim years. We had something then, the three of us. Something was in balance, or as near to balance as it was likely to get. Erica wanted to explore this today. Did I think of myself as loving Billy? As a friend, I said, as an old, dear friend. But I used to catch myself watching his hands, his mouth. Also, I had a sense around him of permanence, as if he'd been there from the beginning, like a twin.

And Richard? Erica said. Well, he's my number-one guy, I said. My rock.

And how is it, living with a rock? Erica said.

I laughed while she waited, as she does.

I love him, I said. And this felt absolutely true. I was moved. But there was something sentimental in this, just a touch of maternal pity. What do I pity Richard for? For having to endure my moods? That, partly. But also because in some way he seems innocent. I know I'm in some way older than he.

I remember one time when the three of us were together. We had driven over to Maiden Falls for a picnic. Billy's girlfriend was supposed to be there, but she'd had to go somewhere else. We sat at a picnic table overlooking the Falls. We were drinking wine. Richard started to tell a story about a paper route he had when he was a kid. He was doing imitations of his customers, or trying to. It wasn't at all funny, but he kept pushing it, laughing hard at his own caricatures, as if he could compel a reaction from Billy and me. Anyone else would have sensed the failure and quietly given up. But he just kept pushing. I think Billy was as chagrined as I was, though we tried to laugh a little – to spare Richard.

Later, he and Billy explored the gorge while I sat and sketched. They were like two boys leaping over a gap in the rocks, one after the other, peering into a pool. I remember that very clearly. I loved them both.

Richard flips to the final entries. They are made in pencil, not ink like the others. And they are brief.

What does it mean to love somebody?

I suppose that I have to ask tells me something – but enough?

I HAVE TO LIVE.

In the mirror's pool, his own face is pouched with shadow. Unable to sustain its stare, he turns from the dresser. He has thought of his life as being a certain way. Childhood, law school, meeting Ann – a comprehensible story, both like and unlike other stories – a basis of fact he could count on, that he could recite to others: here is my life. Now in the dusk-lit room he sees that for all these years, unknown to him, another story has been unfolding in front of him, under his own roof, in the bed beside him. It is possible that his own story, the one he has been telling himself about himself and Ann and Rowan, is only a subplot to this other. It is entirely possible, in fact likely, that it is false.

Shoving the journal back where he found it, he shuts the drawer.

In the morning, he drives up to Carton Harbour. Parking beside Whitbread's, he walks to the water taxi depot and within a few minutes is sitting beside the driver of a fast launch, on his way to Pine Island. He hasn't been on the reserve since the days of the claim, and when they swing around the last point, the familiar huddle of rooftops appears above the bay where the same dock still floats, surrounded by the same mob of steel boats, stirring in their bow-wave.

Leaving the dock, he crosses the beach and climbs among the small houses where, through a screened window, the sounds of Saturday-afternoon opera drift from a radio. In another minute, he spies the blue house amid its cloud of cedars. Billy is sitting outside, at small table in the shade. At the sight of him, heat floods Richard's face and chest, and he has the sense his arms have been drained of their strength; but he keeps on, aware now that others are here. Behind Billy, a boy with long hair stands swinging a bat; a second boy, a little fellow who wears his oversized ball cap backwards, stands beside the table, watching Billy thread a rawhide lace into a catcher's mitt. Noticing Richard approach, the boy at first stares unselfconsciously, then at once, as if confused, his gaze dissolves into blankness. Billy looks up then, just as Richard stops before the table, and begins to rise slowly to his feet. Richard's breathing is shaky, and he feels an urge to throw himself at the other man. But he manages to say, "Don't worry. I'm not going to kill you. Not yet anyway. Look, can a guy get a glass of water around here?"

Billy hesitates, then, gently turning the little boy by the shoulders, he sends him off toward the other, who has fallen motionless with his bat. "You guys go on to Mike's now," he says, as he walks toward the house. The boys trail off, the little one casting backward glances until they disappear.

As Richard waits for Billy, he fixes blankly on the lake. He can no longer remember why he has come; he is not sure, any more, what he will say. He feels he is waiting for understanding to arrive – from out there, maybe, where a herd of tiny islands has paused in the sun.

Ahead of their canoe, islands detach themselves from the wooded shores – advance, loom, and fall behind to the steady bite of their paddles. Small sandy beaches drift by, solitary rocks surrounded by water, cliffs where ferns stand motionless in the shade, hillsides deep in pines. On a low point, a tent has been pitched. A striped towel drapes an overturned canoe. The little camp passes with an air of pre-occupied stillness – perhaps its occupants are having sex or simply sleeping off the heat of midday. Ann watches the meshed doorway float by like a last outpost of civilization. She is bound for more extreme places. Sweat trickles from under her wide-brimmed hat, stings in her eyes. She would love a swim but judges her chances slim just now.

In the bow seat, Billy is at war with the water, stroking as if bent on shovelling the whole lake behind them – a pace he has kept up all morning. Several times she's asked him to slow down, and though he does for a while, whatever it is that's driving him soon takes over again. They are heading north, to the cabin on Silver. She sympathizes – Silver is so important to him – and apparently he thinks that going up there will help, will even heal, though really she is guessing, for on the subject of Silver Lake he has remained stubbornly uncommunicative.

And she could bear his silence, his attack on the water, were it not for her sense that his behaviour is in some way directed at her. Driving up that morning to Pine Island, her canoe in tow, she found him in a dark mood. She asked if he'd changed his mind, if he'd rather go alone. When he ignored her questions, she demanded, bluntly, to know what was wrong. Nothing was wrong, he told her. She did not believe him. And so she dropped the matter, thinking his ill humour would pass once they got out on the water. But presented, hour after hour, with his feverish paddling, she finds herself dreading the days to come.

Yet they had been getting on so well. The previous week they had driven to Perry Rapids Lodge, on the Armand River, for a few days of fishing and sketching among the pinkish cliffs around the rapids. He'd been out of the hospital for three weeks, and she felt he was much improved – more relaxed and readily affectionate. No one had ever come as easily inside her guard, or been as welcome there. And there was something else: a subtle confidence, a sense of deeper reserves. He told her he had lined up some jobs at the Blue Osprey and was even thinking of getting back into band politics. He'd told her, too, about how he and a couple of his old ball cronies were hoping to get a boy's baseball team together on the Island. Apparently his nephew Jimmy and a friend of his had brought him back to the sport again. But there had been trouble. The friend, Dwayne, had overdosed on something and had to be taken to the hospital. Billy had clearly been shaken. "It never stops," he said, speaking with a tone of inevitability, as if this was something he had always understood.

After being with her for much of August, Rowan had gone back to Black Falls to get ready for the start of the school year. Ann was planning to stay on at Inverness until the end of September, to get as much painting done as possible before she moved into a rented place in town. But even with Rowan at the cottage, she'd been able to work three or four hours a day, the only time when she was tolerably free of anxiety about the pain she was causing. She was still not sure whether *The Last Woman* needed more work, and in the meantime, she had started in on a series of three smaller paintings. Rowan, for the most part, seemed to be adjusting to the new rhythm in his life, though it sometimes broke her heart to see the brave face he put on. When he asked when she and Richard would be living together again, she told him, "Honey, I don't know. But you're always going to have two people who love you more than anything." He answered with terrific fierceness:

"But I *want* you to." And he had gripped her arm so tightly, it hurt.

Three or four times a week, she and Richard talked on the phone. Dialling his number, she would find herself looking forward to hearing his voice – *needing* to hear it, really, for their life together still had its place in her. And often it was good for a few minutes, but then his anger would begin to seep through. At times, she felt, his vulnerability was palpable. Once, awkwardly confessional, he admitted he had been doing "a lot of hard thinking" about himself. "I haven't been there for you, Ann, not really – always working. And I haven't been the best listener. I want to change that – want to mend things with you. We can do it, I feel that very strongly. We've already come through the worst – I know we're on better ground already." She was moved by his sincerity, yet like a forcefield coming down the wire, she could sense his old willfulness. She wanted to tell him that people don't change, at least not very much, only circumstances changed, but it would have been unfeeling to say so. She said something vaguely encouraging, instead, aware that she had not thought hard enough about what their separation meant, or where it was leading – the subject was simply too painful. She only wanted to cling to the ledge she had hauled herself onto, it was all she could manage.

Steeling herself, she'd told Richard that when she moved back to Black Falls for the winter, she was intending to rent an apartment of her own. After a long silence, his voice came, thick with rage: "This isn't what you led me to expect." It took several calls before they settled back into smoother relations. *Would* she ever live with him again? One day, she came across a book he'd given her years ago. Barbara Tuchman's *A Distant Mirror: The Calamitous Fourteenth Century* was not something she would ever have bought herself, and indeed she hadn't been able to read more than a few pages. So much goodwill, on both sides; and yet, in some fundamental way, they had always missed each other. And it was her fault, primarily, wasn't it? For she had wanted stability and goodness and a certain kind of maturity; and she had found them. But even at the time, she knew she was pushing against the grain of her own instincts. She had been, in her way, as willful as he.

One time, after a particularly stressful call, she went outside and made her way toward the water. She was in a state – her face hot, her breathing constricted. She reached the deck almost without noticing, and stood for some minutes before the evening began to make an impression on her. The shadowed water held a green limpidity and the air was scented with pine. It was as if the place itself had enfolded her in its balm, and she began to weep – knowing she had given herself, her whole family, over to consequences that could not be foreseen, and that many things, already, were unrecoverable.

Over the weeks, she and Billy had drawn closer, in the way that two people, who were once close, find a version of themselves in each other that is both familiar and open to new possibility. She could not imagine their living together in any conventional, ongoing sense; though his absence, if it went on too long, would begin to hurt.

The sun is terribly hot. She asks him to stop, and as they drift for a while, she takes out a kerchief and drapes it from the back of her hat. Then they set off again. Ahead of her, under the skin of his back, his muscles churn as if looking for a way out.

The change, when it comes, comes silently and with little warning. At one moment they are in forest, paddling down a deep defile, in the welcome shade of trees. Then they ease round a bend into the next lake, and at once there is more light behind the trees. Then the trees themselves peter out and a dazzling expansiveness radiates from the hills. It seems to her – her paddle arrested in mid-stroke – that something in her rushes to meet this new reality, exploding into a vacuum. The bush that has all along accompanied them, the bush of shadow and unimaginable depth, has simply stopped, and in its place is another world, sunstruck, stark, pullulating with heat. On either hand, thousands of stumps – stumps and rejected logs and piles of debris and slabs of exposed rock – cover the ruined slopes.

They have both stopped paddling. There has been an assault here, an act of such violence it seems to evoke some other order of reality. The sun seems more ferocious; it bites at her face, her arms. It bakes the yellow hills where little dust devils rise up, twirl, and vanish – the only movement visible.

Conscious of Billy, what this must be for *him*, she keeps still. He has placed his paddle across the thwarts and is leaning on it while he peers up at the devastation. They are drifting: past a great boulder like a turtle petrified before it can escape into the safety of the lake, past a rotting log. He is rocking a little now, forward and back, in some gesture of self-comfort, though what comfort he might find here she cannot imagine. She feels it was a mistake to have come.

She has an urge to move: to go back, or at least to go on, to let action absorb what contemplation cannot. But she waits, for him. She is exhausted, soaked with sweat, and it seems, as they sit – several minutes have gone by – that they *cannot* move. The negative power of the place holds them, and they can only wait for worse: as if some new idea, some creature, some image must rise to instruct them. He has stopped rocking now and is gazing into the water.

They go on. The first shock has passed, and now a hor-rified fascination sets in. She must see exactly what this thing is, this presence that has gripped the hills. A few miles back, in the untouched bush of their last portage, she had felt wrapped in a green fecundity, invited into its depths. But here, she is radically repelled, her very spirit repelled. Yet she cannot stop looking – up the slopes of dusty yellow earth covered with stumps whose raw, open surfaces shine with sap. At the top of a hill, a clutch of tall spruce persist, their crowns bristling against the blue. Why were those few trees left? Some token gesture of conservation? The surviving trees seem absurd to her – a quixotic flourish over a field of death.

Oddly, she feels she knows this place. She has a sense of bleakness at once familiar and obscure. She knows this place: in some way it belongs to her.

That night, they camp on an island where a few low, contorted pines twist up among several large flat rocks – a little Bonsai garden untouched by the loggers. The mood that wraps them deadens conversation. They talk only briefly, of practical things: what to have for supper, where to find firewood. They sit on opposite sides of their fire, prodding at it or shifting a pot, their small nest of light burning in the darkness that has hidden the devastation on the mainland – although the silhouette of a hill, teethed with stumps, humps against the faint glow of the western sky.

"How long will it take to grow back," she says, wanting to connect with him: the only comfort that seems possible now.

Across the fire, Billy shakes his head vaguely. He doesn't know. Or: it doesn't matter. Or: it's an ignorant question. She resents his dismissiveness, his continuing refusal to talk. Wrapping a rag around the handle of a pot, she pours out boiling water for tea and punctures a can of evaporated milk, holding it out to him.

"Billy? Do you want milk?"

"I said no."

She refrains from saying, No you didn't. She will give him a pass, for today. For the rest of the trip, if necessary. But something in her withdraws, and as they sit drinking their tea in silence, she understands how little she knows this man. She knows something essential. She has a certain *feel* for him. But there are rooms behind rooms, some of which he may scarcely know of himself.

They sleep outside – no need for the tent on such a clear, bug-free night – spreading their mats and sleeping bags on a patch of open ground. He is soon snoring softly while she lies on her back looking up at the stars: that forest no one will ever destroy.

On the afternoon of the third day, they reach Silver Lake. She has carried a hope that the bush in that area remains intact, for all along they have passed places where the clear-cutting has temporarily relented. But no: the devastation returns. Behind a thin screen of trees the empty, barren hills rise once more. They scrape ashore under a high bank. He starts up the slope immediately, while, knowing how important this moment is for him, she stays behind to unload the canoe. Struggling up the eroded trail with a couple of packs, she reaches the flat, open space at the top and sees the cabin. She has heard so much from him about "the cabin on Silver," about the life his family lived here, that she must stand for some time, simply taking the place in. It seems so small, so utterly forlorn, with its holed, sagging roof. She can just make out Billy in the little grove that survives near the cabin, holding up a chain from which some rusty-looking object swings. Dropping the packs, she approaches the door. Inside, in the shadowy depths pierced by sun from the broken roof, she discovers a small, overturned table, a section of fallen stovepipe, a half-destroyed mattress. There is a smell of rot, of animal excrement.

They pitch their tent on the edge of the bluff. Billy claims to be pleased with the view – a few trees, then the lake, then a few more trees on the opposite shore, with more of the scraped yellow hills beyond. His remark seems bitter – a blade turned against them both.

The next day, he sets to work repairing the cabin. She joins in, but wonders if they can ever do enough to make it habitable again. Using a small trenching tool, she scrapes away at the rotting floorboards, carrying out little piles of leaves, dirt, and shit, while he braces the roof and climbs onto to it to repair the hole. There is a pathos about their efforts, she thinks, as if they are trying, against all reason, to hold back a flood of ruin. Out of loyalty to him, she hides her sense of hopelessness, but it is a relief, finally, when he goes off to fish and she has some time to herself. Sitting under a kind of awning he has rigged up with a tarp, she tries to read her novel, but the words seem weak and irrelevant, unable to compete with the vast space around her, the brutal assault of sun and heat on the devastated hills.

That evening they eat the pickerel in silence. Forks scrape on their metal plates. The little fire crackles to itself, with a kind of dry merriness, as if it knew something humans did not.

"We've hardly made a dent," she says. "Do you still imagine you can stay for a month this winter? You said yourself the animals are gone."

"We just ate one, didn't we?"

"Well, *one fish.*"

"I didn't say they were gone," he says. "I said I couldn't see any tracks. They'll come back. There's still lots of bushes around. The moose will sniff them out sooner or later."

They are silent for a while.

"Tell me what's been on your mind," she says, pleading. "I understand that it's hard for you here –"

He shrugs and blows out through his lips.

For no reason she can grasp, they are estranged. They sleep side by side without touching. In the day, they are civil, even cheerful in a brittle way. She laments what they have lost – so good together only a short time ago. She wonders what can be recovered, what they have in them for each other. Has she always felt most intensely for him when they are at a distance? When she is with someone else? Has she made him up?

Out of sight of the camp, she sobs. She comes back determined to get on with *her* life, and when she finds him sitting on the ground, picking at a tangle of fishing line, his total absorption in the task, his apparent contentment, enrages her.

"We'll soon be out of food!" she announces, exulting. It means they will have to go back.

"I'll catch some fish."

"I'd really prefer not to eat fish for the next three days. I think we should start for home." He has fixed again on his reel: the stoicism of a man waiting out a storm. "Anyway, you haven't caught a fish for three days. I hardly think you're going to now."

"Whenever you like," he says.

The decision to go generates a brief satisfaction. But the bleakness of her melancholy, her sense of estrangement, does not shift. Things are still wrong between them. Will leaving change anything?

Later they sit again at their fire. A few high, stately cumulus have drifted in, pink against the darkening blue. "Look, clouds," she says, momentarily forgetting herself. "Maybe we'll finally get some rain."

He jabs at the fire with a stick, then tosses it in.

"All those years ago," he says. "Why didn't you tell me about the baby?"

"Oh God," she says. Her body feels insubstantial, as though it might blow away. He is looking at her, at last, though not in the way she wants: his eyes burning. "I couldn't have told you then, it would have hurt too much. It wouldn't have done any good. Billy, I could not have had a baby."

Desperate to be close to him, she scrambles around the fire. At once he stands up, and when she tries to embrace him, he moves away. Her heart is beating crazily, and she has a sense of them being tumbled about in some pocket of chaos, as if a wave had caught them. "Billy," she pleads.

"I was only nineteen. I was already enrolled in art school –"

"You do whatever you like, I guess."

"That isn't fair! It wasn't like that! You didn't have to go through it –"

"There would have been – someone else now!" It tears from him with a half-choked cry. Speaking rapidly, touching him on the arm, she tries to make him see how it was for her: the fights with her parents, the agonies of doubt, the *impossibility*. But his gaze remains locked in the region of the fire: there is something adamant in him, set against her. Breaking away, he begins to pace up and down the campsite, turning, coming back to the fire, going off again. Finally he stops. "Richard came to the Island . . ."

She is astonished.

It happened four days ago, he tells her. "I figured he was coming to kick my head in, but he wanted to talk. Talked a lot about you. He said he'd never realized how bad things had been for you sometimes – that's when he told me what happened. I acted like I already knew, but it *cut* me, Ann." He pauses, closing his eyes for a few seconds. "Ever since I was a kid, I've had this place in me. *Raw*. Nobody was allowed to touch it. It was like he'd reached in there and squeezed it good."

For a few seconds, he allows her to hold him. Then he breaks away.

"Where are you going? It's almost dark."

Not answering, he plunges down the bank, out of sight. A moment later, she sees him – his T-shirt moving rapidly along the shore path, then turning inland to climb like a white travelling spark among the shadowy stumps and heaps of debris. Just under the summit, it winks out.

She wraps herself in a blanket and sits down by the fire to wait. She assumes he won't go far, but really she doesn't know, doesn't know when he'll be back, doesn't know if they'll get past this. It is all but dark now. In the open doorway of the cabin, firelight quivers on the handle of an axe. Some time later, she crawls into the tent and curls up on her bag. She dozes, then wakes to a distant grumbling of thunder. She slips outside and calls his name, but nothing comes back. Around her, the night seems as dead and still as if every living thing, even the wind and water, has deserted it.

She climbs inland, floundering through debris. Her flashlight beam stops at a small evergreen, pitched nearly upside down, and seeming, in the pool of her light, to have been caught out in some shameful act. The stars have disappeared.

Back in the camp, she adds fresh wood to the fire and again sits down to wait. Poplar leaves rattle in the rising wind.

Shivering, she retreats into the tent and, sliding into her bag, falls into a shallow sleep. She dreams she is being hunted by a vast, low-flying machine – like a steel shutter being drawn down the sky. If its searchlights find her, she will be sucked upward into its liquid, quivering mouth. She hides under a hospital bed, where a seagull has been caught in a trap. When she tries to free it, it pecks at her; she escapes down a corridor.

And arrives on a hillside, where she stands looking out over a landscape of forests and rivers – rivers and forests, as far as she can see – livid in an ominous light that roils on them like the roiling glow of hot coals. The wind is gusting and the ground trembles underfoot. She wakes suddenly. A cold wind is blowing at the tent – the walls are billowing, a bit of metal shivers wildly. From a distance comes the slow monotone of thunder. Someone is tapping at the roof.

It comes more swiftly now – drumming on the tent, hissing in the coals of the dying fire. Peering out, she can just glimpse something white moving, but when she leaves the tent, it has disappeared. The darkness is nearly absolute, there is only a faint, striated glow from the fire near her feet. The rain is coming more heavily now, a torrent under which she turns, crying his name.

Then at once he is there –

Many years later, near the end of her life, she will recall their trip to Silver. Much will have altered by then, and she will think that the world she is leaving is not so fine a place as the one she was born into. Of course, the old are notoriously disapproving, and the young must have their truth. Still, she will continue to find her own – in certain faces, in the shifting moods of Inverness, in sudden, ecstatic couplings of idea and colour. As for the events at Silver Lake, she will hold them as her passage into the second half of her life, less materially stable than what came before but more open to the subtle flux – the deep current of ceaseless change – that sustains all things. And so one October afternoon, bundled up in her chair, she will receive for a last time the memories of their journey north: the long moment of their embrace in the rain, and the moment, two days later, when they paddled around a point and found themselves once more among the trees.

ACKNOWLEDGEMENTS

I would like to thank Cathleen Hoskins, Alix Bemrose, Aaron Lumley, Fred Bemrose, and Kathryn Bemrose. Also Jim Morrison, for his invaluable history lessons and social commentary; and my editor, Ellen Seligman, whose patience and skill continue to astonish me. To those many people, native and non-native, who over the years have communicated their love and knowledge of the wild places of this country – *Megwich*. Among authors, I am particularly indebted to Hugh Brody for his account of native hunting practices in his 1981 classic, *Maps and Dreams*, and to Rupert Ross for his penetrating 1992 study of cultural differences, *Dancing with a Ghost*. *The Last Woman* could not have been written without the contributions of these people. Its inevitable shortcomings are mine alone.

Thanks, as well, to the Canada Council for the Arts.

A NOTE ABOUT THE TYPE

The Last Woman has been set in Scala, a type family created in the late 1980s by Martin Majoor, a book typographer and type designer based in the Netherlands. The principal forms of Scala are derived from humanist faces such as Bembo and Fournier, yet feature lower contrasts and stronger serifs – ideal for modern electronic book design and typesetting. Of particular note is the rare balance and compatibility of the serif and sans serif. Originally designed to address the peculiar challenges of setting multiple levels and weights of information within a music concert program, Scala is named after the Teatro alla Scala in Milan.